I.A.M. PUBLISHING

Flight to Forever

Isabel A. M. Cole

6/16/2013

To my daughter Alex: Never settle for less than you deserve, especially in love.

Chapter 1

Watching a Boeing 747 take-off was like seeing a charging rhinoceros leap into the air and fly with the grace of a Great Blue Heron. It seemed to move so slowly. I was sure it was never going to make it right up until the time it clawed its way into the air. I got a little clutch in my belly every time it happened.

I reached for the button to activate the airfield lighting at SeaTac International Airport and turned for one last look at the huge airliner soaring through the twilight. The thrust of its giant engines turned all of the surrounding clouds into a swirling mass of vapor. I think it was the power that gave me a tingly, almost sexual feeling. *Ha! What didn't make me think about sex these days?*

"Hey Cassie, are you going to turn the lights on or what?"

Way to kill a daydream, Rob! I pasted a smile on as I turned toward him and made a great show of pressing the button to turn on the lights. He frowned at me. Yes, I knew I shouldn't be daydreaming while working in the control tower. I could hear my manager … "Yada, yada, yada, pay attention, yada, yada,

yada, maintain awareness". But this small amount of traffic was barely enough to keep the brain alive.

Frowning Rob was working Local Control at the Air Traffic Control Tower. He got to clear everybody for take-off or clear them to land. That was the cool job, the one that gave me a rush. Ground Control, where I was stuck, could be fun too, but only when it was really busy. I mean, how much brain-power did it take to taxi an airplane back and forth from the runways to the gates? Okay, at O'Hare where they had tons of taxiways it was hard work but here we only had one major taxiway. I felt like a glorified traffic cop, SeaTac Airport's finest, of course, but a traffic cop nevertheless.

Five jets in varying sizes were waiting at the runway for their chance to "slip the surly bonds of earth". Their super-heated engines were creating mini clouds in the cool evening air. From the approach end of the runway as far as I could see, more airborne buses lined up like a string of twinkling Christmas lights. I wondered how much trouble I would get in if I "accidentally" knocked Rob out of his chair and took over. *Probably a suspension at least.....I could use a vacation anyway.*

Watching Rob with his sloth-like speed was making me want to slam my hand in a door to distract me from the pain. He used ten words when two would have worked. He spoke with the slow pedantic tone of one who was more concerned about sounding important, than the clipped rapid rate of most controllers who were worried about getting the planes out on time. Ok, I was envious but, so what? Nothing compared to the rush of working heavy traffic.

The thin clouds framing Mt. Rainier glowed with the orange of the setting sun. The sky looked like it was on fire. The deepening colors should have been a clue that I had a few more buttons to push, but once again, I was caught up in the beauty. We here, at the Seattle Air Traffic Control tower, had a picture postcard right outside our windows. When there wasn't much else to do, the view was constantly clamoring for attention.

Glancing down at the clock, I realized it was three minutes past sunset. If I didn't want to have to kill Rob, because I would certainly kill him if he gave me that just-sucked-on-a-lemon look one more time, I'd better turn on the rest of the lights.

I watched all of the green, blue and yellow lights come to life on the airfield as I pushed more buttons. It reminded me of a game I played as a child. What was that called? Lite Brite or Brite Lite? Something like that. I would poke different colored pegs through a black piece of paper and then turn on the light behind them. I'd made some pretty cool pictures.

"Did you get the beacon?"

"I'm doing that now." I gritted my teeth because doing so was a great way to keep myself from 'going postal' on a co-worker. Of course the dentist who had to keep replacing my mouth guard told me I should come up with an alternative method of self-control. He'd recommended Enya.

Joe, another controller, came trudging up the tower stairs and plugged his headset in next to Rob's to get a briefing so he could relieve him from position. I flashed a smile at Joe. It was code for, 'Thank-you for saving me from a twenty-five year prison sentence for aggravated manslaughter.' It is certain that I would have murdered Rob if I had to watch his s-l-o-o-o-o-w methodical pace for one second longer. Joe smiled back. I correctly interpreted his smile as code for, 'No problem, I live to serve you.'

I was so busy watching Rob plod through his checklist of relief briefing items that I didn't even notice my relief had entered the tower cab until Chuck plugged his headset in next to mine just a moment later.

"I'm here for ya Cassie and it looks like it's not a moment too soon." Chuck smirked at me.

"Thank God!" I said, and despite my agnostic views I really meant it.

Rob paused in his briefing long enough to tempt fate one more time. "Ha, I'm the one who was doing all of the hard work, what do you need out so bad for?"

I could actually feel my face turning red as I contemplated the damage a pair of binoculars would do to the human skull. Chuck was trying not to laugh and wisely stepping out of the line of fire. I took a deep breath and let it out slowly, ignoring Rob, and pushed the button to record the relief briefing. It only took a minute to give Chuck a summary of all my traffic so he could take over the position.

Chuck glanced around to make sure that Rob was no longer in hearing distance and then said, "Better watch it! If you grit your teeth any harder you're going to need a mouth guard."
"Too late, I'm already on my third one."

Chuck laughed then nudged my arm, "Rob is driving you nuts isn't he?"

My father's voice echoed in my ear, "If you don't have anything nice to say don't say anything at all."

My upbringing was warring with my need to vent. I put my headset away without taking the bait. I didn't want to be one of those people who complained about everyone behind their backs. I congratulated myself on my control. It turned out, though, that the road to Hell may be paved with good intentions but it is sealed by a steamroller named Chuck who doesn't know when to shut up.

"Did you learn a lot from watching Rob work?" Chuck asked me and even though I knew he was goading me I just couldn't resist. *Sorry Dad.*

"I learned that aging doesn't always lead to perfection," I said with a sarcastic tone.   At first when everyone started laughing I thought they were laughing with me. Chuck said something about winning a bet and I realized that I was the butt end of the joke.

Great! They were betting on whether or not they could goad me into saying nasty things about my coworkers. I felt momentarily guilty; then realized I must do a pretty good job of keeping mum if they had to goad me into it. Still, I hated living down to someone's expectations. But, since their expectations were already lowered I gave in, once again, and stuck my tongue out at them.

Chuck laughed at me and said, "Better go take your break so you can come back and show Rob how it's done."

I grumbled a bit about all the good traffic being gone as I trotted down the stairs to the elevator. Apparently I didn't speak softly enough because I could hear all of them chortling as the door closed. It was time to get a little exercise to exorcise the demons of frustration.

As I exited the elevator I glanced into the darkened radar room. The Terminal Radar Approach Control, or TRACON, was housed in the same building as the tower but several floors beneath it. They were the controllers who spent all of their time just looking at little radar blips on a screen as they guided the planes that had just departed the airport onto their initial airways to their final destinations. I could barely make out a few TRACON controllers hunched over radar screens in the large room. They shared a break room with the tower controllers. They also shared our sick sense of humor. A few of them were in the break room playing Hearts.

They tried to get my goat as I walked through the room but my goat was firmly tethered. We controllers were an irreverent group. Nothing was sacred.

"Didn't have many departures during that arrival rush, huh?"

I smiled sweetly at them and mimed locking my lips together as I walked past. They laughed and tried a little harder but sometimes I actually learned from my mistakes. I quickly continued on toward the second set of elevators that would take me down to the terminal as they all started calling out insults about Tower Controllers. I was grinning and feeling a bit self-righteous by the time the elevator arrived.

I loved to get a quick walk of the terminal whenever I could. It seemed that exercise was the antidote for adrenaline….made sense to me since fight or flight were both forms of exercise. Since September eleventh it'd been difficult to walk the whole terminal. If my break was long enough and the lines were short enough I'd go through security so I could access the gate area. Neither was true tonight so I settled for a quick walk through the ticketing area.

Several of the employees of the airport shops waved as I walked by. Some even called out greetings. Sometimes I'd stop and chat but tonight was all about burning off excess energy. I waved but kept chugging along to keep my heart rate up. I loved how I felt after a brisk walk. I wasn't always this way. I used to be a complete schlub. Amazing what a divorce would do for your motivation. *Maybe it wasn't the divorce as much as the desire to have sex one more time before I died. Well, actually, I would like to have sex more than once but beggars can't be choosers.*

I stopped in the restroom on the way back to the tower. I was looking forward to my time on local and I didn't want to ruin it by feeling like I had to pee. While I washed my hands I looked in the mirror and discovered that my nicely coiffed auburn hair had turned from a topiary to a tumbleweed. I had forgotten to make an appointment with the stylist once again. I pondered for a moment that I always seemed to forget to take care of myself but I rarely failed the people around me. There was probably a lesson in there somewhere.

"Well what is a working single mother to do?" I asked my reflection with a southern drawl and a bat of my lashes. *Jeez, Cassie, smoke any crack lately?*

In a small burst of defiance I flicked the water on my hands at the mirror and then smirked as it ran down the glass. Of course, instantly, I felt bad and grabbed a paper towel to wipe it off. *I am such a rebel....not.*

When I climbed back up to the tower cab and plugged in next to Joe to wait for the briefing, I could feel my attention draw into a tight focus. Was it the adrenaline? I didn't know; I only knew that colors were brighter and sounds were sharper and I felt completely alive. I started ticking off information, waiting for Joe to start talking. *One aircraft on the runway, how far south is the last departure? Two aircraft are on final approach.* Some people called it being 'in the zone', in controller speak it was known as 'having the flick'. I built an image in my mind of where all of my traffic was while Joe ran down the relief checklist.

There were only two aircraft on final approach and three taxiing out for departure. I still loved it but it just wasn't as exciting as seeing the sky filled with airplanes.

I told him I had the position and started clearing planes for take-off. It was a clear dark night and I could see the lights of the inbound flights turning on final approach thirty to forty miles out but I could barely see the aircraft taxiing northbound, just a thousand feet from the tower. Only their lights shone through the pitch-black, moonless, night sky.

For the first twenty minutes I was on position the traffic was light. When I finally ran out of traffic my mind tuned into what was going on around me. I realized Ben, the ground controller, was talking a lot. When I looked at the console in front of him I saw he had eight aircraft pushing back from the gate and a few more waiting to push back.

"Don't say I never gave you anything," he said to me with a wink.

He gestured at all of the flight progress strips now lined up on the departure pad. Each strip represented an aircraft taxiing out to the runway and there were already six on the pad and more on the way.

I couldn't help the grin that spread across my face. "You are a prince among men."

I was almost trembling with the desire to be tested, the need to pit my abilities against anything that was thrown at me. The excitement made my heart feel too big for my chest and I couldn't help tapping my foot in time to a rhythm that only I could hear.

The first of the stream of taxiing aircraft reached the runway. I put planes in position on both runways and then cleared them for take-off. As they started forward I was putting two more in position.

"United Four thirty two, Runway one six left, position and hold. Be ready to go, traffic on a four mile final for your runway is a Boeing seven three seven. Report the previous departure in sight," the words tripped off my tongue like that of an auctioneer going for a big sale.

I barely acknowledged his readback before instructing the aircraft for the other runway to do the same. I watched the two aircraft start forward onto the runways immediately to comply with my instructions. *'Ah, good! The pilots are aware that it's getting busy and they are doing their part to help out.'* As soon as the previous departures were airborne I cleared the next two for take-off.

"United four thirty two, Runway one six left cleared for take-off. Wind one eight zero at five. Maintain visual separation with the previous departure until courses diverge. No delay in the departure roll, traffic on a two and a half mile final."

I repeated almost identical instructions for the aircraft on the other runway. I watched the two large jets climb into the sky, side by side, separated by only eight hundred feet, and it gave me goose bumps.

I used minimal spacing between airplanes until finally I cleared a DC-8 into position on the runway to await separation behind the previous departure. DC-8's were one of the first heavy jets. They were so old no one really used them for passengers but cargo companies loved them.

I watched the Cargo Tran aircraft lumber onto the runway and cleared him for take-off before the previous jet had lifted off. By the time the DC-8 lined up on the center line of the runway and throttled up the engines to start his departure roll, the previous departure would already be a mile south of the airport.

Cargo Tran started rolling down the runway and I put a Nationwide Boeing 737, into position to wait for his turn. I had to wait a bit behind the DC-8 because its powerful engines created enough wake turbulence to make it dangerous for any aircraft that took-off too close behind it. I was surprised to see the heavy cargo jet get airborne before it reached the midpoint of the runway. I figured it must be a light load and glanced down to read the call sign of the next aircraft.

I looked back out to check the progress of the DC-8 as it flew past the tower. My eye caught a flash of lighter color moving against the darker sky. It looked like it came from the direction of the cargo plane. I turned and stared at the area for a

13

moment to see if it appeared again. There was nothing out there except for the night sky.

"Did any of you just see that?" I asked, turning to survey the controllers in the cab.

"See what?"

I looked at Ben. He shrugged his shoulders. "I didn't see anything."

I was trying to figure out how to handle it when I realized I was tapping my pen on the console. I made myself stop and keyed the mike.

"Cargo Tran 165 I saw something large fly past as you went by the tower. Do you have any problems or did you hear anything unusual?"

"Negative, Tower. Everything looks fine here."

"Roger. Contact Departure. We'll pass it along if we learn anything new."

There were four or five aircraft waiting and I was tempted to clear Nationwide for take-off. I could feel the pressure of my training to keep traffic moving and it was almost instinctual to follow the programming. No one else saw anything. Ben was looking at me as if he thought I was nuts.

"It was probably just the reflection of the beacon, Cassie. Your line-up is getting pretty long," he prodded me.

I was winding my fingers around and around the lanyard I wore on my neck. I didn't know what I saw, but there was a little voice in my brain telling me not to ignore it. However, if it turned out to be nothing I'd be ridiculed for listening to the voices in my head. Finally, I keyed my mike again.

"Nationwide 225, I'm sorry for the delay sir. I saw something fly by as that DC-8 went past. I think it came off of them although they say everything is normal. For the moment I'm going to leave you in position on the runway and I'm going to get an airport operations vehicle out here to check. It's too dark for us to make out anything from up here. Again, I apologize for the delay."

"Nationwide 225, we're happy right where we are. Thanks for checking."

I asked the ground controller to call the operations vehicle out to check for debris on the runway. With a sigh and a shake of his head Ben called the Operations vehicle. I notified the TRACON to stop lining up arrivals for the runway until the check for Foreign Object Debris, known as F.O.D. was completed. Each airport operations employee had horror stories about the bizarre items they'd found lying around on runways and taxiways just waiting to be sucked into a jet engine.

It seemed like it took forever for the Ops Vehicle to come up on my frequency. Realistically, I knew it was only a few minutes but I was champing at the bit to get traffic moving again. Ops Four finally called and asked permission to enter the runway.

"Ops 4, all I saw was a flash of something when Cargo Tran flew by. He says everything is normal but it looked like it came from his aircraft. He was airborne between Taxiways Mike and Lima so you probably want to enter the runway at November and head north. Nationwide is holding in position. If you find anything I'll get him off the runway. Proceed on Runway One Six left."

The yellow operations vehicle turned onto the runway with its lights flashing. It hadn't gone very far when it slowed and started to zigzag from side to side up the runway.

"What is he doing?" I muttered to no one in particular.

I watched the vehicle continue its erratic journey northbound to the end of the runway. As the vehicle exited the runway I heard an open mike for a moment and then the operations vehicle operator finally found his voice.

"Tower, Runway One Six left is closed. There's debris all over the runway from at least Mike intersection all the way up to Hotel Taxiway. It had to come off the DC-8 and whatever it was, it was big. I can't believe they didn't notice anything. Someone needs to call them and let them know about this." I could hear the quaver in the ops driver's voice.

"We'll let him know Ops. Do you have any idea how long it will take to get the runway open again?"

"It'll take at least a half an hour to get all of the big pieces. And that's if I get a lot of help. Plus, we have to get the sweeper out here, so I figure at least an hour."

All of the controllers groaned. A single runway operation was going to delay everyone, arrivals and departures. I was focusing on how this was going to affect my traffic flow when I realized that I still had Nationwide 225 sitting on the runway.

"Nationwide 225, it's just not your lucky day. Do you have enough room at the end to make a hard right turn and taxi over to runway One Six Right?"

"Nationwide 225, yeah we can make the turn. And I guess it depends on your definition of luck."

"Thanks Nationwide 225. Turn right, taxi to Runway One Six Right."

The darkness was so complete that I could only tell the Boeing 737 was turning because his radar blip on the ground radar was moving. I could hear Ray in the back of the tower telling the TRACON the bad news about the runway closure. I heard him asking for extra spacing between arrivals so we could get some of our backed-up departures out.

"Tell him five mile holes will work for now. It doesn't look like we have any more heavy jets for a while. And make sure they contact Cargo Tran to let him know what is going on," I called out to him.

"Yes, Cassie, I figured that out," he said in a dry voice and rolled his eyes.

"Oops, sorry Ray, my therapist says I have control issues. Maybe there is something to that," I said with a laugh.

Ray snorted in response and finished his conversation with the TRACON supervisor. I watched the next arrival cross the threshold of the right runway then taxied Nationwide 225 into position behind it. Various operations vehicles were scurrying around the left runway. One of the men picked up a piece of metal and carried it to his truck. As he passed in front of the headlights I got a glimpse of it. I couldn't help the gasp of alarm. The piece of debris was huge.

"Oh, my God!" I was so amazed by the sight of the huge piece of metal that I didn't even realize I had spoken out loud until my coworkers responded.

"What's the matter?"

At first I couldn't even find the words so I just pointed at the man carrying the piece of metal. "Look at the size of that thing. He's putting it in his SUV and it barely fits. Look, it's hanging two or three feet out the back. Can you imagine what would have happened to Nationwide if he hit that thing?"

Ben stood next to me staring out at the ops worker trying to fit the large fragment into his truck, shaking his head in disbelief.

"Wow, how could Cargo Tran not hear that coming off their plane?"

Ray called out from the back of the tower cab where he has just finished another phone call. "Get this. Cargo Tran didn't want to come back to land. He wants to keep going up to Anchorage. He says all of his instruments look good."

"Tell him he's an idiot. Maybe if they describe the debris field he'll change his mind."

"I strongly suggested he might want to make another decision."

I finally dragged my gaze away from the clean-up and realized that the arrival had turned off the right runway and was waiting for clearance to cross the closed runway. I gave him clearance to cross before finally getting back to the Boeing 737 that had been waiting patiently to depart.

"Nationwide 225, I take it back, this is definitely your lucky day. I just watched them put a piece of metal in the back of one of the ops vehicles. It had to be six to eight feet long. It's sticking several feet out the back of an SUV. When you get to your destination you might want to buy a lottery ticket, Runway One Six Right, cleared for take-off."

After a moment of silence the pilot's voice came over the radio. "Well ma'am, I just might do that but only if you'll pick the numbers for me. We're rolling."

As I watched the aircraft accelerate down the runway I didn't realize I was holding my breath until it lifted gracefully into the air. I couldn't help contemplating what that sharp metal fragment would have done to the plane's wheels as I watched them stow themselves safely in the belly of the aircraft. My voice was a bit shakier than normal as I wished them a safe flight before telling them to contact the departure controller in the TRACON.

The bell sounded, announcing visitors coming through the door at the bottom of the stairway that led up to the tower cab. I glanced back to see a TRACON Supervisor and one of the radar controllers come up the stairs. Leave it to an emergency to bring everyone out of the woodwork. The TRACON controllers almost never came up to the tower.

"Did you guys make a wrong turn somewhere?"

"We came up to see what all of the fuss was about," the Supervisor responded. He was smiling but I could tell he thought I overreacted to the situation.

I was talking to aircraft steadily, trying to get caught up after the delay in departures so they just stood quietly and watched the clean-up work going on below.

"It's so dark out there. How did you see anything?"

"Well the halogen lamps help light it up but you missed the real shocker."

I couldn't resist telling them about the large piece of garbage that had already been carted away. Ray interrupted my storytelling to advise me Cargo Tran had changed his mind, and was returning to the airport, ETA 20 minutes. I just nodded in acknowledgement because the Supervisor was trying to get my attention.

"No, I mean how did you see the F.O.D. originally? It's pitch dark out there. How did you know to have the vehicle check the runway? Even with all of the lights out there now, you can barely see anything. How the Hell did you see anything without any lights?" he asked, shaking his head.

"Well it's difficult to describe. It was just a…a….vision of something moving that was lighter than the surrounding darkness. I almost didn't believe my own eyes. I'm just glad I didn't shrug it off and clear Nationwide for take-off." I couldn't repress the shudder that shook me at the thought.

The radar controller was a petite woman that I had spoken to several times in the break room. Her name was Grace and she was relatively quiet. I didn't know what I expected her to say but it certainly wasn't what came out of her mouth.

"You realize you saved all those people don't you?"

All I could do was stare at her; I had no idea how to respond to that. I felt embarrassed and I couldn't answer without stuttering.

"I… I'm just glad I checked before I cleared Nationwide. I was really tempted to just ignore it and keep the traffic moving."

"But you didn't. You did the right thing and now a whole plane load of people are safe because of you,"

I could feel everyone's eyes on me and it was an uncomfortable feeling. Sure, I was glad I did the right thing but it

23

wasn't like I was a hero or anything. I wished everyone would just go back to work.

"Thanks, but I think that anyone else would have done the same thing."

Grace just smiled at me and went back to watching the clean-up. The Supervisor was still shaking his head as he watched the half-dozen men work their way north on the runway throwing piece after piece of debris into the back of the slow moving vehicles in front of them.

"Well now we're going to have to widen the doorway downstairs so that our local hero will be able to fit her head through," Ben said loudly into the silence.

I could just kiss him right now. I glanced over at Ben. *Well, no tongue or anything but... on second thought, maybe a hug.* I was so relieved the mood had returned to the earlier jovial one. I was thrilled when a small arrival rush forced me to concentrate on getting the rest of the departures out without too much of a delay.

Finally, Cargo Tran came back on frequency and said that he would need the long runway for landing or he'd have to dump fuel. Ops told me they had all of the debris off the runway but they hadn't swept it yet. Cargo Tran still insisted on the long runway and the crew of vehicles exited to allow him to land.

I was able to relax a little when Cargo Tran turned off the runway without incident. When the DC-8 passed in front of the halogen clean-up lights there was no longer any doubt that this aircraft had created all of the debris on the runway. Both of the metal cowlings that normally covered the engines were missing on the left side. Such a large piece of metal coming off in flight could have done serious damage to the airplane. I was glad they decided to come back to be sure.

When I finally climbed into my car to head home I just sat for a minute. I couldn't bring myself to do anything but lean my head back against the seat and stare out the windshield. I figured I wouldn't be able to fall asleep very easily tonight, I could still feel the after affects of the adrenaline high. I forced myself to take a deep breath and let it slowly ease out of my lungs. I could feel my shoulders relax a little.

I knew Grace was proud of me but what she said embarrassed me. Only I knew how close I'd come to ignoring the little voice in my head. I didn't want to think about what could've happened. Any controller who thought too much about what could happen wouldn't be able to work airplanes for long. With a little shake of the head I turned the key in the ignition. As I drove out of the parking garage my overwhelming feeling was gratitude. I didn't really feel like I saved anyone. I was just glad I didn't kill them.

Chapter 2

On Wednesday, the last day of my week, I didn't get to work local until the end of the day. When I finally plugged in my headset to get the briefing, I felt like I imagined a junkie would feel just before getting a fix. Looking at all those airplanes taxiing out to the runway was a rush. What a great way to slide into my weekend.

I smiled as I keyed the mike and started my patter. I felt as if a low voltage wire was sending electricity through my body. Nothing compared to it. I said "move" and a hundred ton airplane obeyed. *How cool was that?*

A large jet floated across the landing threshold and set its wheels down with a little puff of smoke. Before he'd even touched down I was crossing the next jet behind him onto the runway. I couldn't seem to help rocking back and forth, heel to toe. It was like dancing with the pilots but I got to lead. I never had been a very good follower anyway.

"God, this is better than sex!"

Huh, did I say that out loud? I was so caught up in my Tango with the airplanes it took a minute for me to realize it was really quiet in the tower cab. Quiet was definitely unusual. I glanced at the ground controller and saw him biting his lip and trying not to laugh. *OK, maybe it was not better than all sex.*

"Well, it sure as hell is better than the sex I've been getting lately, which actually is not that hard to do since that would be none, nada, zilch, zippo."

I formed my fingers into a symbol for zero and thrust it at his face to give my statement the emphasis it deserved. The ground controller lost his battle and burst out laughing. He was laughing a little harder than the comment warranted.

"Hey, my lack of a sex life is not that funny. It's actually kind of sad… and pathetic….and frustrating, if you know what I mean."

Now he was laughing even harder. I had a really bad feeling. I looked at the clearance delivery controller and he was shaking his head, his eyes wide, pointing behind me. *Uh-oh.*

I didn't want to look. I turned slowly and glanced at the back of the tower. Two pilots were standing there grinning at me. I groaned and turned quickly back to the radar scope. I started working my traffic in earnest. When there was a break in the activity for a moment, I caught the ground controller's eye and asked in a stage whisper, "Are they gone yet?"

He laughed and replied, "They're here to see you, so I don't think you're getting off the hook that easily. You know, I do believe this is the first time I've ever seen you blush."

"I'm not blushing. It's just the exertion of working all this traffic."

"Funny, you've never felt 'exerted' before and I've seen you work a lot busier traffic," he responded with a grin.

I scowled at him. What I really wanted to know was why the two pilots were there. I continued to work my traffic while my mind cast about for a reason they would be waiting to see me. When my relief plugged in, I drew the briefing out as long as I could, trying to avoid the inevitable. Normally, I liked interacting with pilots but usually I hadn't just tried to eat my foot in front of them. Eventually, there was nothing else I could say and I had to unplug and walk over to put my headset away.

The supervisor, Tom, was just hanging up the phone as I walked up to his desk. He arched his eyebrows and asked, "What was everyone laughing about?"

"Let's just say it is better left alone. If I tell you, you'll just have to counsel me about a model work environment. So, why don't I just say I'm sorry and you tell me not to let it happen again and we'll leave it at that?" I asked hopefully.

"We'll talk later since we have visitors," Tom promised. Then he turned his attention to the two pilots who had been patiently waiting off to the side.

"Cassie these are the pilots who were flying Nationwide 225 the other night and they asked to meet you."

The Captain spoke. "Hi, I'm John Clay and this is first officer Steve Rayburn."

"Cassie Murphy, ... nice to meet you." I clasped the Captain's hand and was surprised at the tingle I felt at his touch. I really looked at him for the first time and saw what a striking man he was. He couldn't really be termed handsome. His features were far too blunt for that. But still, there was something about him. Maybe it was his eyes, which were the same gray as storm clouds with a dark outline. I felt like I couldn't look away.

With a start, I realized I was staring and still holding the captain's hand. I released it like I'd just learned it was poisonous and turned quickly to the co-pilot. Now, he was a good looking man. He could probably get a modeling job if he set his mind to it but for some reason I found myself looking at the Captain again.

"So, Captain, did you ever buy that lottery ticket?"

"It's John, and you never told me what numbers to pick so I didn't chance it," he replied, with a glimmer of a smile.

"With my luck, it's doubtful my picks would do you any good. It's probably too late now anyway. These karma things have a limited window of opportunity I think."

I did like a man in uniform but I didn't think that was why I was so drawn to him. Maybe it was his physique. He was really tall, probably three or four inches over six feet and, from what I could tell he looked to be all muscle. His shoulders were wide and solid. I had a thing for broad shoulders. I could picture myself grabbing onto them as I lay beneath him, straining against him.....*Oh my God, what the hell is wrong with me? I must have sex on the brain today.* I shook my head, trying to clear the errant thoughts from my mind. I prayed that he wasn't able to tell what I was thinking.

"Well, we came up here to thank you. You probably saved our lives the other night."

I was shaking my head before he even finished the sentence. "Well thanks but I didn't really do anything special. Anyone else would have done the same."

Steve Rayburn laughed. "Right, I went to school with Grace Welsh's husband. She told him the real story and he told me how pitch dark it was and even in the lights from the vehicles it was difficult to see anything. It's nothing short of amazing you saw anything at all. Believe me, we're grateful."

"Thanks again, but really, I was only doing my job."

Both of them looked as if they wanted to argue but finally John said, "Well my son is just glad to still have his Dad around. Are you going on a break? Can we at least buy you a cup of coffee?"

I hesitated because I was still processing the fact that he had a son, which meant he was probably married. *Of course he was married. Why wouldn't a sexy guy like him be taken?* I was surprised at how disappointed I felt about that and then I was disgusted with myself. I was awfully hard up if I was mooning over a guy I'd just met. Besides, even if he wasn't attached there was no way he would ever be interested in me. I'd accepted my limitations in the looks department a long time ago.

Some part of my brain was still functioning and I finally realized that they were waiting for an answer to John's question.

"I-I'm sorry, I guess I'm a little distracted today. I appreciate the offer and I know this is Seattle, but believe it or not, I don't drink coffee. And actually, I'm off work now and I've got to go pick up my daughter at school. She has gymnastics class today and I have to give her enough time to get changed before class."

I realized I was babbling and tried to rein in my runaway mouth. "But listen, I'll walk with you downstairs since you have to be escorted. I'll take a rain check on the coffee if I can exchange it for mint tea the next time you're in town."

I was surprised I'd had the nerve to ask for a rain check. Well what would it matter anyway? He was married. No harm in having tea with him, right?

John looked amused and gestured for me to precede them out of the tower cab.

"Actually, we're based here now. I just moved here from California and Steve came from the east coast. Finding our way around is an interesting proposition, sort of the blind leading the

33

blind," John said, as he waited for me to gather my stuff and sign out.

"Yeah, and neither of you will probably ask for directions either, huh?"

Great Cassie! That will definitely attract him.

"Boy I just seem to keep putting my foot in my mouth today," I said with a laugh.

And there I went again … sometimes I was such an idiot. I had to go and remind them of my earlier comment about sex. They both laughed at my discomfort.

"Don't worry. Your secret is safe with us," John said with a wink.

I groaned in embarrassment again. I figured when in doubt, get out; I started down the stairs, saying a general good-bye to everyone working in the tower.

"So, where did you guys move to?"

"We're staying at one of those long term hotels right now. We don't know enough about the area to make a decision yet." John said as he held the door for me and gestured for me to walk through.

"I guess it depends on what you are looking for. The more expensive areas and the worst commutes are generally from the north and the east. The west and south have more reasonable property values and an easier commute. I live down south in Federal Way, so I am biased. There are some nice areas near me and I make it in to work, door to door, in thirty minutes."

"Well I can't speak for Steve but my priority is a good school for my son. He's really sharp and I want to send him to a school that challenges him. Also, I can't be too far out in the sticks because of child care issues."

"I know what you mean. So, your wife works also, huh?"

"No, I'm divorced. My ex-wife is staying in California so I'm going to have to find childcare for when I have to layover. I bid this route because it's an experimental program with very few layovers but that doesn't mean it will never happen," he added with a worried frown.

I wanted to do a little dance of excitement. He was divorced. That gorgeous hunk of man was available and it wasn't even my birthday. He did seem worried about his son though and I felt guilty for being selfish.

"Oh, that must be so hard for both of you. I'm sure your ex-wife will have a difficult time being so far away from her child."

This time when John spoke it was with a tinge of bitterness. "Believe me; my ex can't wait for both of us to be out of her hair. She told me I have two weeks before she'll bring him up here herself and leave him on my doorstep."

His words had me stopping in mid-stride. "You must be exaggerating."

"Unfortunately, I'm not. Sharon doesn't have a maternal bone in her body. The real shame is that my son Josh is intelligent enough to understand how his mother feels about him."

"Why the Hell have a child in the first place? I just can't understand that mentality." I realized I was practically yelling and took a deep breath to calm down. "If someone separated me from my daughter Sam, I'd just shrivel up and die."

John nodded his head. "I'm with you. Josh is so amazing I just can't understand how someone can *not* love him, especially his own mother."

"So, how old is Josh?"

"He's just about to turn ten," John responded. "How old is...you said your daughter's name is Sam didn't you?"

"Yes. It's short for Samantha. She just turned six; six going on twenty-five that is," I said as I paused on the landing to turn and look at him. I couldn't help but grin when I thought of some of the adult things that came out of Sam's mouth.

John laughed. "I know exactly what you mean."

I realized I'd been pretty much ignoring Steve so I asked if he was married or had kids. He told me he was happily single.

John snorted. "More like blissfully single. I've only known him a few weeks and I've already seen him go out on at least a dozen dates. He has to beat them off with a stick."

I looked over at Steve, my eyebrow raised, querying the accuracy of John's statement. He looked amused and just shrugged his shoulders. He was really handsome. He had a mischievous twinkle in his eyes that gave me the impression that he would be a lot of fun to go out with. Still, I had no interest in him.

"Well I can definitely understand that," I said, smiling at Steve.

I was surprised to see John had a scowl on his face. Maybe he didn't approve of Steve's lifestyle. When he noticed me looking at him the dark look disappeared.

"Well I'm biased but I think you should look into Federal Way. It's got everything you need, including a great school for gifted children, Silver Creek. That's where my daughter goes. It's expensive but worth every penny."

"I'd be interested in any information I can get, and the sooner the better since school will be starting in a couple weeks."

"Where are you staying? Do you have a car?"

John told me he'd driven up from California but Steve was temporarily carless since he'd come from the east coast. They were both staying at the same extended stay hotel just down the road. An idea was beginning to form; a way for me to spend more time getting to know John and help him out at the same time.

"Are you home for a bit? I'm not trying to be nosy. I really do have a point to all my questions."

John didn't seem to mind my questions and just brushed off my explanation with a wave of his hand. "You're not being nosy. We just came back so we're off for the next three days. I'm trying to get my house hunting done during my weekends so I can save my vacation time for when I have to move into a new place and get Josh settled."

"Is your car here or did you walk?" I asked. I knew I should just come out with my suggestion but I was a nervous I was being too forward.

"We walked. Ok, now I am curious." John looked at me with a raised eyebrow.

I took a deep breath. I didn't even know these guys. We had arrived at the ticketing counter for Nationwide and it was either time to ask or walk away. Once we parted company I didn't know if I would ever see him again.

"You guys aren't axe murderers are you?"

They burst out laughing. "Well if we were we'd hardly tell you would we?" John said then added, "But no, we're not." Both men looked intrigued.

C'mon Cassie, have a little backbone. "Well if you'd like, I can drop you both off at your hotel. You can get your car and follow me to the school. There will be people there you can talk to until about 4:30. They have summer school going on so a lot of the staff is there."

I paused, and then continued before he could answer because I was afraid what the answer would be.

"I mean, that is, if you don't have plans. But, I figure, you said time was of the essence and I'm heading that way anyway."

He probably thinks I am completely desperate. Today must be national pick up a pilot day or something. I hoped he couldn't tell how fast my heart was beating.

"That would be great!" John responded immediately. "Are you sure you don't mind? You said you've got to get your daughter to gymnastics."

"I've got plenty of time. I'm just a little anal-retentive when it comes to getting her to the lesson on time. I think it's another one of my control issues but don't tell anyone."

John looked at his copilot as if to ask him if the arrangements were ok with him. Steve shrugged.

"Hey, I'm beat. I'm not going to turn down a ride home. I think I'll probably collapse and sleep straight through until tomorrow so I appreciate the offer," he said with a yawn

"Oh I didn't think about that. You're probably tired too," I said, turning back to John.

"I'm fine. I wasn't the one out carousing until late last night."

"Well it's settled then." I felt a flutter in my belly as I waited while they got their bags from behind the ticket counter. I figured I'd monopolized John for long enough. As we walked out to the parking garage I asked Steve about his life before Seattle. He told me he grew up in a little town in Vermont called Londonderry. What were the odds?

"You're kidding! I have family in Londonderry."

We spent the rest of the walk talking about the places we knew and seeing if we had any mutual acquaintances. I stopped at my minivan and turned to John to apologize about the mess in the car. Again, he looked less than thrilled and I wondered if I had pushed too hard. Maybe he was just being nice. Then I realized that he was probably still worried about his son.

"Don't worry; you'll get everything worked out in time."

John looked surprised for a moment, then a little sheepish. "I know. I was just thinking about some other stuff."

I apologized again as I spent several minutes tossing toys and dolls into the luggage area so they had a place to sit. John just laughed and made a comment about the joys of parenting. He claimed the front seat and let Steve share the back with the child seat. *Hmmm rank does have its privileges.*

Ten minutes later we pulled into the parking lot of the hotel. Steve grabbed his stuff and, with a wave, headed off to his room. Alone with John I was suddenly struck dumb. Luckily he didn't seem to be fazed at all. He asked if I would mind waiting a few minutes so he could change.

"I've been in this uniform for about eight hours and we were having trouble with the air conditioner on the plane. You can come up and have a soda in the living room while I change in the bedroom. It's one of those suite hotels."

I only hesitated for a moment and then agreed. I was usually a pretty good judge of character and I had no fear of John. If he could've seen my thoughts he's the one that would be barring the door against me. There was something about him that drew me. I knew a good part of it was physical but there was something else as well. It was one of the reasons I'd offered to show him where the school was. I didn't want to let him just walk out of my life.

His room was large even for a suite. It had a full living room with a little kitchen nook. The separate bedroom held a king sized bed and the bathroom was large with a jetted tub and shower. It had pretty bland coloring but it was a lot bigger than some of the apartments I'd rented in my younger days.

"This place is a lot nicer than I expected."

"Yeah, it's not bad, but it's not home either," he replied.

"Well, I've got a good book so if you want to take a quick shower you can. As long as we get out of here within a half an hour we should be fine. That's when the rush hour traffic starts and everything grinds to a screeching halt."

He looked relieved as he said, "Are you sure you don't mind? I could really use a shower. I take military showers. I'll be done in five minutes."

"No problem. I'll just curl up on the couch with my book. Go take your shower. Do you mind if I help myself to some water?"

He offered me soda but I said water was fine and shooed him off to the bathroom. I got a glass of water and settled down in the corner of the couch to read.

As soon as I heard the shower go on, however, all interest in my book disappeared. I read the same paragraph a couple of times and then finally closed the book in disgust. My mind kept shouting the same thing. *He's naked.... NAKED... unclothed, hot, wet male within a twenty foot radius.* I could almost hear the whoops of sirens sounding the sexy male alert. I wanted very much to see him in that state. All I'd seen were bulging biceps and forearms corded with muscle but my traitorous brain was quickly filling in the rest. Man, I needed sex. Obviously it'd been way too long since my mind seemed to be stuck in this groove. When I heard the water go off I sighed in relief.

My brain was not finished torturing me yet. It started flicking through images of him standing there with water beading up on those broad shoulders of his. Then I pictured him drying himself. *Oh, to be that towel.* With a disgusted grunt I stood and took my water glass over to the sink and washed it. I had to do something to get the images out of my mind before he came back out of the bathroom. I focused all my attention on cleaning the glass. Never had a glass been so clean. Finally, I forced myself to put it in the dish drainer and went back to the couch.

I'd just reopened my book when he walked out of the bathroom. Nope, it wasn't the uniform that attracted me. I think my mouth actually watered when I saw what a pair of faded jeans and a T-shirt could do for him. I almost groaned out loud. I covered myself by saying brightly, "Ready to go?"

He nodded and said, "Just let me get my shoes." I glanced down to see that he was only wearing socks and even that turned me on. I was completely hopeless.

He pulled on a worn pair of boat shoes and picked up his car keys. "Fifteen minutes exactly, not bad, huh?"

"I'm impressed. I take quick showers too. If we both took showers at the same time it would be a toss-up as to who finished first."

He raised an eyebrow and smirked. "I sure have a bad case of foot in mouth today," I said as I could feel the blush creeping up my neck.

"Don't worry, I knew what you meant. Plus, it's not like women have been lining up to jump in the shower with me," he said with an edge of sarcasm in his voice as he turned to open the door.

"That's hard to believe," I mumbled.

John whipped his head around and stared at me. "What?"

I almost choked. *Sheesh, Cassie! Is your foot permanently imbedded in your mouth today?* I thought as I beat my brain for a plausible response.

"I-I said it's time to leave." He hesitated as if he was going to call me on it but then just nodded and ushered me out the door. He pointed out his vehicle, a blue Jeep, and said he'd follow me. I started the car and backed out and waited for him to fall in behind. A couple of minutes later he tapped on my window and I jumped. I rolled down the window and gave him a questioning look.

"My car's dead. It's probably the battery. I've been putting off replacing it because I've had so much else to do. Now it looks like I'm paying for my procrastination. I guess I'll have to take a rain check."

I hadn't realized how much I was looking forward to spending more time with him until he said that. The hollow feeling of disappointment was swift and powerful.

Without thinking I said, "You can ride with me if you want. Sam's gymnastics class is about two miles from here. So, I can drop you off afterward but you'll have to sit through her class, which if you're not a parent of one of the participants can get really boring…"

"I don't want to take advantage. You've already been so great."

"It's no trouble, really. And you said yourself that you don't have a lot of time to make arrangements."

I felt a little guilty about using his concern for his son to convince him, but I'd get over it.

"If you're sure it's not a hassle?"

"Get in already," I said with a smile. "Time's a'wastin' and rush hour is heading this way."

"Yikes!" he said with a laugh as he walked around and climbed into the car. He never saw me doing the little happy dance in my seat.

Chapter 3

I turned out of the hotel driveway and wondered if inviting him along was such a good idea. His hair was still damp and I could smell his shampoo. I was so aware of him it felt as if an electrical field surrounded him, giving off little zaps like mini-lightning. I cast about in my mind for something to say and finally settled on the old stand-by.

"So how long have you been flying?"

"Pretty much my whole adult life … I got my private pilot license before I was 18, then I went on and got my multi-engine rating and IFR qualification. That just wasn't enough so I joined the Navy and became an F-18 pilot. I probably would've stayed in the Navy but I got married and Josh came along. I needed stability and better pay. It just worked out I got out right when the airlines were hiring. I've been flying for Nationwide ever since. I'm rated for the Boeing 757 and 767 but I fly the 737 because it was what was on this experimental route."

I could tell he loved flying by the glow he got in his eyes when he talked about it.

"I've always wanted to learn how to fly."

"Why don't you?"

"Sam came along and suddenly the thought of doing anything the least bit risky went right out of my head. I know, I know." I cut him off when I saw he was about to speak. "Flying is safer than driving a car. But it's hard to describe. I-I guess….Sam was so amazing, so perfect, and I couldn't figure out what I'd done to deserve such a great gift, so I had this horrible fear it was going to be taken away from me. I know it sounds crazy but it was like I'd gotten a lifetime's worth of good karma with Sam and I was afraid to tempt fate. Anyway, once I'd relaxed a little, the divorce happened and I didn't have the time or the money to indulge. So, I do the next best thing. I get to watch airplanes all day long, every day. Plus I get to indulge my control issues."

He smiled at me and I was relieved he hadn't belittled my reasons. I'd shown some vulnerability and he hadn't made me feel silly.

"Tell me about Sam," he said.

I spent the rest of the drive regaling him with stories of Sam's sense of humor and intelligence. As we pulled into the school parking lot, I stopped talking so he could focus on the school grounds and the atmosphere. It was a beautiful spot with lots of grass and small wooden buildings to house the different classrooms. There was even a creek running through the property.

"Wow. If the teaching lives up to the setting, this must be a great school."

"The class sizes are small, the student-teacher ratio is amazing and they genuinely care about every student. It's worth every penny. I would give up my cleaning lady before I'd take Sam out of this school, and if you knew how much I hate cleaning, you'd realize what a sacrifice that would be."

I took him over to the office to introduce him. While he was asking questions I walked over to collect Sam. I knew it would take a while to get her off the playground and I wanted a chance to explain John's presence.

After watching ten minutes of cartwheels, hanging upside down on the jungle gym and various other daring deeds, I was able to drag Sam away. Five more minutes elapsed gathering her stuff together. While we searched for her lunchbox, I told her about John. I kept it simple, telling her he was a pilot new to the area and had a son who needed to find a new school.

Almost twenty minutes after I left John at the office, I finally got Sam ready to go. We stopped at the office but they told me he'd gone over to the fifth grade classroom. The building was on the way to the car so we started walking toward the parking lot.

Sam and I swung our clasped hands back and forth as she told me about her day. She told me, in all seriousness, she would probably marry Gabe when she was older. Gabe was another six year-old in her class. She went quiet, suddenly, and frowned. I asked her what was wrong.

"We're friends but I always win when we play games and he said I was cheating because I'm a girl."

I saw John stepping out of the classroom. He looked so good it made me light-headed. I sucked in a breath to restore the oxygen to my brain. I smiled at him and held up a finger to indicate he should wait for a minute, and then turned my attention back to Sam.

"So, he thinks you cheated because you're a girl?"

"He said a girl couldn'a beat him so I must'a cheated. He made me real mad. So, I told him I wouldn't marry him until he got a brain."

I choked, trying not to laugh. Sam liked to be taken seriously and got really upset when she thought people were humoring her. John stepped up and I was glad to be given a reprieve. I didn't want to say the wrong thing to Sam and give her the impression what Gabe said was okay. But I also didn't want her to judge him too harshly. I was pretty sure he was just parroting what he'd heard another boy say. Gabe and Sam were best buddies and it wasn't like him to say mean things to her.

"Sam, this is Mr. Clay. He's going to come with us to gymnastics because his car broke down."

"I know Mom. You already told me," Sam said with a child's sigh of exasperation.

Sam looked up at John for a moment. She had to tilt her head all the way back. She studied him while I continued the introductions.

"John, this is Sam."

Before John could say hello, Sam cut in. "You sure are big."

John squatted down so he was at eye level with Sam. He held out his hand and said, "Hello Sam, it's a pleasure to meet you."

She studied him up close for a moment and then hesitantly took his hand. She barely made contact before she pulled her hand away.

"You sure do have big hands."

I started to speak but John cut me off. "You know, one day I just started growing and I grew and I grew. My Mom told me I'd better stop soon or the birds might mistake me for a tree and build a nest in my hair. Luckily, I stopped growing. I still get a little nervous when there are birds around so I cover my head so they won't get any ideas."

Sam studied him for a moment and then burst into giggles. "Uh- Mr. Clay you better watch out," she said as she pointed to a tree behind him where a large crow was sitting. John turned and looked at the crow, let out a little shriek and covered his head with his arms.

Sam's delighted giggles danced on the air and made me laugh out loud too. John held his cowering pose for a minute and then   grinned   at   Sam.
"Thanks for the warning. I don't think he saw me. I think I'm safe," he said in a stage whisper.

Sam giggled again. "You're silly." She reached out her hand to him and said, "Don't worry, I'll protect you."

John smiled and said thanks. He took her hand as he stood up and let her lead him to the car. I was dumbstruck. Sam was a friendly child but she'd never gotten comfortable with another adult as quickly as she had with John. She seemed to be even more reserved around adult men, but John had gotten right past those reservations with very little effort.

Great, not only was he sexy as Hell, he was a nice guy and good with children as well. All of those attributes would be great if I had a chance in Hell of attracting him but rarely did men look on me as girlfriend material. They all either wanted to be my buddy or have a quick roll in the hay.

"Earth to Mom, wake up, Mom; you have to unlock the car."

I shook my head as I opened the doors with the remote.

"Where do you hear this stuff?"

"T.V.", Sam replied with a self-satisfied smirk.

I strapped Sam into her car seat which brought on another spate of grumbling.

"Gabe is six and he doesn't have to use a car seat anymore."

"Sam, we've talked about this. I'm not comfortable putting you in the regular seat until the seat belt fits better. Gabe's Mom gets to make decisions for him and I …"

"I know, I know, you're the boss of me," she said, letting out a long-suffering sigh.

John smiled at me as I climbed into the driver's seat and started the car. He turned in his seat and looked at Sam.

"Is Gabe the one without a brain?"

"Yeah, he makes me so mad," she answered with a scowl of remembrance.

"Hmmm, is it all right if I tell you something about boys, Sam? I mean, I have a boy and I am one myself so I might have a little bit of an idea what's going on with Gabe."

Sam considered this for a moment and then agreed.

"Well, Sam, you are absolutely right, Gabe shouldn't accuse you of cheating just because he doesn't like to lose. Does Gabe get mad at anyone else when he loses?"

"No, he only gets mad at me."

"Well, there's a funny thing about that. Have you ever liked somebody so much you want them to be proud of you and think you're special?"

Sam thought about it for a moment, and then answered, "Yeah."

"I think Gabe really likes you a lot. So, he wants to show you how smart he is or how good he is at games so he can impress you. When he loses he thinks you are not going to like him and he gets mad and says things he doesn't mean."

"Well, I was right. He doesn't have a brain if he thinks I'm gonna like him for calling me a cheater."

"You're right. It's pretty silly to do something like that, but people sometimes have trouble talking about things that are really important to them. Then when they think they look bad they get mad and say mean things. Boys usually have a lot of trouble talking about their feelings because they think they have to be tough all the time."

Sam was quiet for a while as she mulled this all over. When she spoke she sounded confused. "I don't want him to feel bad but Mommy says I should always try my best."

"Your Mommy's right. You shouldn't lose on purpose just to make him feel better because then you'll feel bad. Maybe you could try a game where you and Gabe are on a team together. Then it won't matter whether you win or lose."

Sam looked intrigued by the idea. I was amazed at how much Sam was willing to accept from John. She got very frustrated with me when I tried to say similar things to her. It must be a mother-daughter communication thing. I looked back to see Sam staring out the window, deep in thought. I turned to John, smiled, and mouthed my thanks.

"So, what do you think of the school?"

"I'm really impressed," John said. "You're right, it is expensive but I think it would be easier for Josh to fit in here rather than a large, impersonal school. I asked for an application form and set up a tentative appointment for them to meet Josh."

"That's great. I think you'll be happy with it."

"If it works out it, really is a load off my mind. Now if I can just find a place to live, I'll finally be able to relax. Josh and I don't need a lot of space right now, so I think I'll just rent an apartment for the time being. You wouldn't happen to know any good ones would you?" he said half jokingly.

I burst out laughing. "You know, this is really bizarre but a friend of mine is moving out of her apartment. She wanted to be closer to her parents since they are getting older. She lives in one half of a duplex. There are three bedrooms and a nice backyard. It's not too expensive and the owner lives in the other side of the duplex. She is an older woman whose husband died a couple of years ago, so she has trouble keeping up on the maintenance. She just said the other day; if she could find a renter who could help with repairs she would give him a break on the rent. She owns the house outright and says she rents out the other half to make a little extra income but I think it's really because she's lonely. Her kids live far away and she doesn't get to see her grandkids often. She would probably love having a child around and, don't quote me on this, but she probably wouldn't mind exchanging a little daycare for Josh for maintenance work."

John's jaw was hanging open. He couldn't seem to form any words for a moment. Then he laughed loud and long.

"Is this a new reality show, "Find your Guardian Angel"?

I couldn't help laughing along with him. It was bizarre. I asked if he wanted me to call my friend.

"Are you kidding?"

"We'll be at the gymnastics center in about two minutes. I'll call when we get there."

The look on his face was priceless and I was glad I was the one who caused it. It was more like fifteen minutes before Sam got changed and out onto the practice floor. As soon as we were seated in the bleachers I dialed my friend Rhonda. I was surprised when she answered. She had been incommunicado for days, getting everything packed up for her big move. She sounded out of breath.

"Hi, Rhonda, it's Cassie. It sounds like you need a break."

"Oh, hi Cassie, I just carried a big box down the stairs. What's up?"

I explained John's situation and asked if Mrs. Sullivan, the landlady, had rented the apartment yet. Rhonda told me she was pretty sure it hadn't been rented but said she'd call Mrs. Sullivan and have her call my cell phone.

I smiled at John and crossed my fingers. We watched Sam practicing handstands and cartwheels. John commented on how good she was. I thanked him and told him it was a result of hard work. Sam had been doing gymnastics since she was three.

"The coaches say she is good enough to compete but she really has no interest in competing. I don't think she wants the pressure."

"That will probably change as she gets older," John said just before the phone rang.

I answered and talked to Mrs. Sullivan for a few minutes. I told her the situation and asked if John could come see the apartment. She said she had time the next day.

"She wants to know if you can see the apartment tomorrow and, if so, what time?"

"Any time that's good for her."

I passed the word onto Mrs. Sullivan and she agreed but asked if I would come along. I only hesitated for a moment. I could have pretended to myself it was because I wanted to see her but in reality it was a perfect excuse to see more of John. We spoke for a few more minutes and then I told her we would see her at 10:00.

After I hung up the phone, John looked at me with a raised eyebrow. "It sounds like you're coming with me?"

I blushed for the second time.

"I-I'm sorry. I didn't mean to invite myself along. Mrs. Sullivan gave me the impression she'd feel more comfortable with someone she knew there and I didn't want to mess up the opportunity for you. I'm sorry; it was rather presumptuous of me...."

"You're kidding, right?"

"I-I already said I'm sorry..."

"And if you say it again I'm really going to get mad."

At first I'd been embarrassed but then I was just confused.

"W-what?"

"I just met you..." He looked at his watch. "...three hours ago and you've already been more help to me than my wife was in eleven years of marriage. I wasn't trying to say I didn't want you around. I just feel guilty for taking up all of your time. I'm sure you have better things to do than lug me around everywhere."

If he only knew.

"Really, it's no trouble. Believe me, the only things I have to do tomorrow are things I'd like to have an excuse to put off."

He studied me for a moment as if he wasn't sure whether to believe me or not.

"Really."

"Okay, on one condition," he said firmly.

"Let me get this straight. You're putting conditions on letting me help you?" I asked with a laugh.

"Right! After gymnastics is over I get to take you and Sam out to dinner."

"That's really not necessary."

"Yes it is," he responded instantly. "I know your type."

"My type?"

"Yes! You're one of those people who is constantly doing things for other people and never asking anything in return. In fact, not only do you not ask but you probably rarely take it if it's offered."

"Believe me, I'm not noble." I said, shaking my head.

"Bull! You know how I know, because you're just like my sister."

Great! I reminded him of his sister. Way to go, Cassie. Just once I'd like some guy to think of me as irresistible or a naughty sex goddess but a sister? I'll show you sister, mister!

"Okay, we'd love to go."

He looked surprised I'd capitulated so easily but then he smiled and said, "Good, you pick the restaurant." I hesitated. "You're driving and I don't know any of the restaurants around here so it only makes sense."

"Okay, I'll try to think of a good one. Is anything off limits?"

"Absolutely nothing," he said and the look in his eyes made me wonder if he was just talking about food. Was he flirting with me? How about if I said I'd take eight hours of hot, sweaty, no-holds-barred sex? *Would you still be thinking about your sister, Mr. Sexier than Sin? Yeah, right! Like that would happen.*

By the time Sam finished her class and got dressed it was six o'clock. My stomach was growling and I was glad I'd agreed to dinner.

"How does Luigi's sound for dinner?" I asked Sam as we were heading back out to the parking lot.

Sam's eyes lit up. "Yeah, Mom, I love Luigi's."

I glanced at John to get his agreement but he just shrugged his shoulders.

"I'm starving; whatever you pick I'll eat."

Sam looked at John and asked, "Are you coming with us?"

John squatted down to her level again. Solemnly he said, "Yes, your Mom has saved my life three times so far so I thought the least I could do is take you two lovely ladies out for a wonderful dinner. Is that okay with you?"

Sam studied him for a moment and then replied just as solemnly, "Yes, thank-you for asking."

John stood up with a mischievous glint in his eye and said, "You should take lessons from your daughter."

I tried to frown at him but it came out as a laugh.

We got a table without a problem. John charmed Sam effortlessly. She giggled throughout dinner. When the waitress came by to see if we wanted any dessert, John ordered coffee for himself and a mint tea for me.

"Wow! I'm impressed," I said.

"Thanks but it's not impressive. You only told me a few hours ago."

"Believe me, it's impressive. I'm used to having to repeat things hundreds of times before they sink in."

Sam looked at John. "She's talking about my Dad. She won't talk bad about him in front of me so she won't say his name."

I almost inhaled my water and stared at Sam. John nodded to her. "That's right, because he's your Dad and you love him. Just because your Mom and Dad didn't stay married doesn't mean they should say bad things about each other."

Sam nodded. "Yeah, I know. Are you divorced too?"

I cut in. "Honey, it's rude to ask personal questions like that."

"I don't mind," he said to me then turned back to Sam. "Yes, I'm divorced too but my son is going to live with me instead of his Mom."

"Why?" Sam asked as if such a concept was completely foreign to her.

I started to interrupt again but John held up a hand to stop me.

"Well, you know how people are good at some things and not very good at others? Like, you're good at gymnastics but there are probably things you aren't good at also, right?"

"I'm not very good at going to sleep in a dark room."

"Exactly, I can understand that. Well, Josh's Mom just isn't very good at doing the things a mom needs to do. So we all decided it would be better if Josh lived with me. I'll be going to get him as soon as I find a place to live."

"You can live with us if you want. Daddy doesn't live with us anymore so it would probably be okay," Sam said and looked at me as if asking for permission.

"That's very nice of you Sam but I think Josh and I need a chance to live with just each other for a while."

"Josh will probably miss his Mom. I really miss my Dad."

I felt a stabbing pain in my heart. I'd worried about how the divorce would affect Sam. It hurt so much to see her sad. I wondered again if I should've tried harder to make it work.

"I'm sure your Dad misses you too," John said gently.

"Yeah, I see him a lot but he told me he was sad he couldn't see me more."

There was silence for a moment.

"Divorce is sad but sometimes it makes things better," John said.

"I know. Mommy isn't sad anymore and she almost never cries. That makes me happy," Sam said with the wisdom of a six year-old.

I was trying very hard to appear casual but having a hard time keeping the tears at bay. I smiled at Sam and once again counted my blessings for such an amazing child. Sam yawned and I looked at my watch. It gave me a moment to compose myself and I was surprised to see it was almost eight o'clock.

"I think it is almost bedtime for someone," I said as Sam yawned again.

"She means me," Sam explained to John.

John said it was his bedtime too and asked for the check. By the time the bill was paid Sam was yawning steadily and John asked if she'd like to be carried. She reached up soundlessly and John carried her out to the car. He put her in her car seat, strapped her in, and climbed into his seat with a yawn.

We were quiet most of the way back to his hotel but it was a comfortable silence. Finally, I looked in the rear-view mirror to check on Sam. She was curled up almost sideways in the seat sound asleep.

"Thank-you for what you said to her, being so understanding ….just everything."

John looked at me for a moment. "No thanks necessary. She's a great kid and, you're right, she is wise beyond her years but she still has a child's emotions and fears."

"She's right. I was a basket case before the divorce and I was terrified it was going to have some long term impact on her. I'm a much better mother now but I feel bad she's had to lose her Dad for me to get it together."

"Stop beating yourself up, I can almost guarantee you were not completely to blame for your marital problems. Sam's a happy, well-adjusted kid. If she's still that way after a divorce, I'm pretty certain you had a lot to do with it. Kids are resilient. They just need a chance to express their feelings and their pain and feel like they have a safe place to come home to and the rest pretty much takes care of itself."

"I wish I had your confidence."

"Hey, I was just as much of a basket case before my divorce. I could see what my ex's attitude was doing to Josh but I kept thinking it would get better. Finally, I gave up and got the divorce, thinking if I wasn't around to make her angry, she and Josh would get closer. What a big mistake. When I left, Josh felt he had been abandoned by both parents. I never realized how much he relied on me for security and love. He started acting out in school, getting in fights, deliberately failing his schoolwork. Then it got really scary."

John stared out the window for a minute as if he was reliving the experience. "Finally, I sued for custody. Sharon put up a fight but it was mainly only to make me suffer. She gave up pretty quickly because she never really wanted Josh. Hell, I had to beg and plead to get her to take him for a month or two so I could get settled here. As soon as I get settled I am going to go get him. I think it's dangerous to his mental well-being to be there any longer than he has to."

"Well, hopefully, you'll know by tomorrow."

"So now you know why I thought buying you both dinner was the least I could do. Besides, I had a great time."

His cell phone rang and he checked to see who was calling. His whole demeanor changed.

"Sorry, I have to take this."

He flipped his phone open and answered with a curt greeting. His shoulders tensed before my eyes.

"I really can't talk. I'm working as fast as I can. I have an appointment to look at a place tomorrow," he said in clipped tones.

He had been so happy just a moment ago. I wanted to reach out and rub my hand on his arm in support but it wasn't my place.

"It shouldn't be longer than a week, two weeks tops. Is he awake, can I talk to him?"

He dropped his head back on the head rest and sighed. He turned to me and mouthed his apology once again. I waved it away.

"Hey, bud, how are you? I think I might have a line on an apartment. I will find out tomorrow," he said in a loving voice. The difference in his tone was marked. He listened for a few minutes before he spoke again.

"Don't worry; I'll come get you soon. I have someone helping me out and I think I will have everything all settled in a couple of days. It's you and me, bud. You need to go to bed now, ok? I'll talk to you tomorrow. I love you."

He listened for a moment longer and then clicked the phone shut and dropped his head back against the head rest again. He sat there quietly for a minute, and then looked at me.

"Sorry about that. Sharon is getting a bit antsy to have her house to herself again."

He looked so miserable and worried I wanted to hug him. Throwing any rules of decorum to the wind I put my hand on his arm. When someone was in pain there were no rules as far as I was concerned.

"You don't have to apologize. Nothing is more important than your child. Don't worry you'll get everything settled," I said with a sympathetic look.

I released his arm to grip the steering wheel and turn into his hotel's parking lot. I stopped just across from his room and put the shifter in park.

He looked as if he were a million miles away. I just sat and waited. A moment later he roused himself and turned to me with an apologetic glance. I forestalled him with a wave of my arm.

"Really, it's ok. I'll pick you up tomorrow since your car is still dead. How about 9:30, will that work?" I asked, trying to take his mind off his troubles.

"That's great. Thanks again," he said as he opened the door and stepped out of the car.

He turned to close the door and then paused and just looked at me for a minute. I wondered what he was thinking but then he just asked for my cell phone number and gave me his. Again, he stopped and seemed about to speak and then finally just said good night and closed the door.

I pulled away with a wave. As I turned onto the main road I glanced back. He was just standing there as if lost in thought. I turned my attention to the road for a moment and when I looked back he was gone.

Flight to Forever

Chapter 4

John

I woke up to the sun streaming in through the hotel's bedroom window and my classic morning erection. Now, if only I could find something to do with it...the erection that is. The day stretched before me like a meadow of new-fallen, untouched snow. I couldn't quite put my finger on the cause for my anticipation until I remembered I would be spending at least part of the day with Cassie. Thinking about her was not going to make my stiff dick wilt any time soon. With a sigh of disgust I tossed the covers off but couldn't bring myself to crawl out of bed yet.

She wasn't classically pretty but something about her drew me. I'd heard her voice on the radio a lot since I'd started flying out of Seattle. She had one of those voices that made men think of sex. I figured it was one of those cosmic jokes, like the little old lady working at the 1-900 sex number. When we first walked into the tower cab and saw her, I congratulated myself for my insight.

Then I watched her for a while. When she smiled people couldn't help but smile in return. The men who worked with her seemed to respect and enjoy an easy camaraderie with her. She pushed the edge of the envelope and when she was angry about something she was a tiger. She was spitting fire when I told her about my ex-wife not wanting Josh. I wouldn't want to take her on when she was protecting someone she cared about.

Her eyes....there was something about her eyes. They were blue in some lights and green in others and they reflected all of her emotions. But it wasn't the color...it was the honesty in them. She looked at me and what she was thinking was right there for me to see....I trusted her because her eyes didn't lie.

Her body was great, tall and slender with sleekly muscled arms and shoulders. And those long legs made me think of how they would feel wrapped around my hips. Her movements weren't calculated like my ex-wife's. She was just naturally graceful and the way she moved made me think of sex.

I hadn't been with a woman since my ex and I split up. I hadn't wanted to after the number Sharon did on me. Cassie was so genuine and kind it made me feel like a lecherous heel, picturing her naked and sweaty beneath me. She brought out my protective instincts. She was so full of fire and determination but I sensed a deep vulnerability in her. Despite my insights I

76

couldn't seem to help an almost overwhelming desire to take her down to the ground and make her scream in ecstasy.

I was even pissed off at Steve when Cassie spent so much time talking to him on the way to the car yesterday. Steve was a babe magnet and I couldn't stand the thought of Cassie being another one of his conquests. I knew that wasn't fair to Steve because he wasn't a womanizer. He couldn't help how he looked or the fact women stuffed their phone numbers in his pockets every day. I just didn't want Cassie to be one of those women.

I wanted her all to myself. It was bizarre but there was nothing quite as sexy as seeing a mother with her child; probably some pheromone thing, designed to perpetuate the species. Whatever it was, I'd had to fight my instinct to touch her yesterday; wanting to kiss her right up until the phone call from Sharon. I hadn't even known her twenty-four hours yet, it would've scared the hell out of her. I had to keep my libido under control.

I looked at the bedside alarm clock. It was after 8, I'd better get my butt in gear if I was going to be ready when Cassie arrived. I climbed out of bed and looked ruefully at my boner. "Give it up. It ain't gonna happen," I said to that perpetually hopeful part of my body as I headed for the shower. *Great, she's got me talking to my dick.*

I checked the parking lot a couple of times. At about ten minutes after nine I saw Cassie pull in and walked out to meet her. She swung in a wide loop, coming to a stop right next to me. When I got in the car she looked a bit frazzled. I knew what it was like to try to get a child out the door in the morning and hoped she hadn't rushed for me.

"Sorry I'm late," she said before I'd even finished buckling my seatbelt. I held up a hand to stop her before she could continue.

"Let's make an agreement, okay? You're doing me an amazing favor. It's way more than I deserve, considering I've only known you about sixteen hours. So, you don't apologize for being late, or anything else, for that matter and I won't get mad and turn you over my knee, deal?" I said with mock severity. Then an image of having her naked bottom in my lap flitted through my mind and I almost groaned out loud.

"Oooooh, a spanking, huh, I'm not sure if that is a deterrent or not," she said and waggled her eyebrows.

My comfortable jeans were feeling a bit tight suddenly. She had no idea what a dangerous game she was playing. She dropped her head forward and pounded it against the steering wheel.

"Apparently that foot-in-mouth disease is a more than twenty-four hour variety," she said as she rotated her head slightly to look at me.

"I'm sor.."

"Ah, ah, ah, don't say it."

I slapped my palm against my leg lightly, indicating what the punishment would be. The flame that flared to life in her eyes caught me by surprise. I'd never spanked a woman but I was willing to give it a try if it would bring that light to her eyes. I think it surprised her also but for a moment she looked like she was going to tempt fate and test my threat. My jeans got even more constricting and I had to shuffle a bit in my seat. She was staring at my hands and it made me itch to reach out and touch her. The spell was broken when she dragged her gaze away and put the car in gear.

"We'd better get going. We don't want to keep Mrs. Sullivan waiting."

I was relieved and disappointed at the same time. I'd just been chastising myself about lusting after her. Then, within moments of getting in the car, I was threatening to spank her. I'd never been interested in spanking, or S & M, or bondage, or what

I thought of as 'alternative pleasures'. When I was around Cassie, however, my mind tended to make everything sexual. That flare of interest she'd shown made it even harder to behave.

I sure didn't need to get involved with anyone. My life was chaotic enough without adding a relationship. I'd already been burned and didn't want to put myself, or Josh, through that again. Just the thought of all of the pain we'd suffered as a result of Sharon's selfishness was enough to sober me and ease the stiffness in my jeans. No, I didn't need that.

But a little mind-blowing sex wouldn't be bad, my little brain chimed in. *Stop it, none of that!*

"How far away are we?" I asked in an attempt to stop my errant thoughts.

"About ten more minutes. We'll probably be a couple minutes late, but no big deal. Luckily, the traffic is going the other way."

I nodded and was quiet a moment. I wanted to explain the phone call the night before but I was hesitant to bring it up.

"What?" Cassie asked.

I looked at her in surprise. Was she a mind reader or was I that transparent?

"About the phone call last night, I shouldn't have put you in that position by taking it while I was still in the car. It must have been awkward for you. I'd just been trying to connect with Josh for a day and a half already."

"You don't need to explain. Nothing would keep me from talking to Sam, especially if I hadn't talked to her in over a day."

"Well, you shouldn't have had to witness my conversation with Sharon."

"It didn't bother me. Is Josh ok?"

"He was excited about the apartment. He's worried because his Mom is trying to unload him on her mother. It seems her new boyfriend wants to take her to Jamaica next week. Poor Sharon, her inconsiderate son is getting in the way of her enjoyment again. You know, I swore I would never be one of those people who constantly complains about his ex but she makes it so difficult to keep my mouth shut. And the worst part is Josh was sounding a little shaky; like he used to sound when he was having all of his troubles."

Cassie reached over and squeezed my arm. "It'll be okay. He'll be okay. Once he's back with you everything else will fade away. Remember, kids are resilient." she said, reminding me of what I'd told her the previous night.

I sighed and squeezed her hand that still lay on my arm. "You're right. Thanks. I just don't want him to hurt anymore."

When we pulled into the driveway of the duplex, I was glad to have something else to concentrate on. It was a nice place. It had a huge grassy back yard that backed up to a greenbelt. I thought I could even see a tire swing hanging from a massive tree in back.

Mrs. Sullivan came out onto the front porch as we stepped out of the car. She was a small woman, just over five feet, but she looked full of energy. She didn't look like her age was slowing her down much.

She smiled at Cassie and waved. "I've got water on for tea. Does your young man want coffee or tea?"

Cassie smiled at me. "I believe she means you."

"Tea is just fine, Mrs. Sullivan. Don't go to any trouble for me, Ma'am."

Mrs. Sullivan held the door open and waited for us to walk up the porch steps. She gestured for us to precede her inside but I took the door and said, "After you, Ma'am."

We sat at the kitchen table while Mrs. Sullivan fixed our tea. She set a cup in front of each of us and then put some homemade cinnamon rolls out. It was obvious the rolls were still warm because the frosting was melting down the sides. The delicious aroma of cinnamon and freshly baked bread permeated the room.

Mrs. Sullivan cut the rolls and placed one on a plate and held it out to me. "Would you like one, Mr. Clay?"

"John, please, and Ma'am, I wouldn't miss it for the world."

The older woman looked pleased and said, "all right John, and you must call me Mary."

Mary turned to Cassie. "Well dear, is this one of your weak days or one of your strong days?" she asked with an arched eyebrow.

Cassie laughed. "Kind of in the middle, I think. How about I split one with you?"

Mary nodded, cut a roll in half and put one half on each of their plates. Mary looked at me and indicated Cassie with a nod of her head. "She works really hard at taking good care of herself. She usually refuses any sweets but every once in a while she gives in and indulges."

Cassie laughed. "Well, Mary, the interesting thing is, it seems like I'm always doing my indulging here. Nothing else tempts me like your baking."

Mary smiled and patted Cassie on the arm, "Thank-you, dear."

My stomach was growling and my mouth was watering. With the first bite, cinnamon and sugar and butter exploded on my tongue and I think I groaned out loud. I made short work of the roll.

"So John, tell me about yourself," Mary said as she sipped her tea.

I pushed my plate away and leaned back with a sigh of contentment. "That was amazing Mary, Thank-you."

Mary beamed at the compliment and then attended to her own cinnamon roll while I told her about my job, a little about the divorce and a lot about Josh. I pulled a picture of Josh out of my wallet and showed it to Mary.

She got up to get the pictures of her grandchildren to show me. They were good-looking kids and I told her so. She patted my hand in thanks.

"So, how long have you known Cassie?"

"I met her yesterday."

Mary looked back and forth between us with a look of surprise on her face.

"Believe it or not, it's true."

"How did you meet?" she asked, unable to keep the curiosity from her voice.

"She saved my life."

Cassie sputtered and started to argue but I ignored her. I leaned toward Mary and said in a conspiratorial whisper. "She's way too humble, never takes any credit for anything."

Mary nodded her head. "Well that's the truth." She said with a knowing shake of her head. "But, what happened?"

Much to Cassie's consternation, I launched into the story of Cargo Tran and Nationwide. When I was finished with the story, Mary looked at her with new respect.

Cassie shook her head. "He makes it sound much more spectacular than it was."

"I don't think so dear." Mary said as she patted her hand. "You should be proud of yourself."

Then I told Mary about going up to the tower to thank Cassie; how she'd taken on all of my problems and within hours had most of them resolved.

"I'm not surprised. The giving instinct is very strong in her," Mary said with a nod toward Cassie.

"Hello..... I'm right here, you two," Cassie said in exasperation.

Mary smiled at her and patted her hand again. "Of course you are dear." Then she turned to me and asked if I would like to see the apartment.

I carried the dishes to the sink and followed Mary out of the room. Cassie, still shaking her head, fell in behind. Mary knocked on the front door of the neighboring duplex. Rhonda answered and introductions were made. Rhonda apologized for the mess and we all waved it away.

Mary showed me each room, telling me about any recent improvements as well as repairs she hadn't had time to make. I mentioned my older brother's construction company where I'd worked through high school and she beamed.

"Well, that about clinches it, I'd say. I think I'm a pretty good judge of character and anyone who worries about their child as much as you worry about your son is okay in my book. So the apartment is yours if you want it. Any repairs you make I'll deduct from the rent." Mary added and quoted a rental rate that made me wonder if I'd heard correctly.

"Mary, I'll take it. I'll be happy to make any repairs I can but that rent is so reasonable I'd feel bad deducting anything from it."

"Well, I'll tell you what. Once I've gotten a chance to know Josh, maybe we can work out an exchange of babysitting for repair work. I've raised four kids and helped out with nine grandkids, so you wouldn't have to worry about him," Mary suggested.

"It looks like I have two lifesavers here today. I have no doubt you and Josh are going to hit it off. Any help with childcare would be more than worth any repairs you need done," I said and felt the tightness in my neck and shoulders ease a little.

My next concern was finding out how long it would be until I could move in. Mary asked when I needed to be in and I hesitated before answering. "Well, originally I was supposed to get Josh at the end of the month but my ex-wife's new boyfriend wants to take her to Jamaica, so....well, suffice it to say, she'll go no matter what. I'm not always too happy with whom she chooses for child care. So, I'd feel better if I could go get him at the beginning of next week before she leaves on her trip." Mary looked upset so I hastened to add, "Of course, the couch at the hotel is a fold out bed and I can always move him in there until..."

"Nonsense, Rhonda said she would be out by tomorrow. You can move in this weekend if you need to. It's not my place but it sounds to me as if you're well rid of that wife of yours.....putting a trip to Jamaica ahead of her own child...well, I never..." Mary harrumphed in indignation.

We moved back out to the main living room and stood just inside the door. Cassie looked around her and said, "I know it doesn't look like it now but by the time Rhonda is done this place will be neat as a pin. You'll be able to move your stuff right in. Believe me, Rhonda is a neat freak," Cassie finished with a grin.

"I heard that," Rhonda called from the room next door.

"Well, moving in is going to be really easy. With my work schedule, I'm not going to be able to move our stuff up here for a couple of weeks. We'll just be bringing clothes and toiletries and camping for a while until we can get the furniture up here. I don't have a lot of stuff anyway. I was planning on buying new beds and some other furniture when we found a place."

Rhonda stuck her head in the room. "Did I hear you need a bed?"

"Well, I can make do until I buy one but I'd really like to have one for my son."

Rhonda crooked a finger at me. "Have I got a deal for you, follow me," she said as she headed up the stairs.

We all trooped back up the stairs and joined Rhonda at the doorway to the middle bedroom. She pointed at the double bed sitting under the window. "Will that do?"

I'd commented on the bed when we looked at the room. It had a bookcase headboard and looked like it wasn't very old. Josh would like a bed he could keep his books in because he always read before he went to sleep.

"It's great. How much do you want for it?"

"It's yours. All I want is the joy of one less thing to move. I had planned to put an ad in the paper but I never got around to it and now I don't want to deal with moving it."

"It's a nice bed. I've got to give you something for it."

Rhonda looked me up and down. "What are you doing tomorrow?" She asked with a devilish glint in her eyes.

"Not much. I have to put a new battery in my car but that shouldn't take long. Why?"

"Would you be willing to come over and help me move some of the heavy stuff? That seems like a more than even trade to me," she offered.

"Sure. That will work for me. Thanks," I said to Rhonda then turned to Cassie. "The list of things I have to thank you for just keeps growing and growing."

Cassie started to protest but Rhonda cut her off. "Just treat her right. It's about time some guy did."

Cassie looked mortified but Rhonda was unapologetic. "It's true, so don't deny it."

She groaned and put her head in her hands. "When did I lose control of my life?" she asked no one in particular.

"I don't think that's going to be a problem. It's getting her to let anyone do anything for her that's the problem," I said to Rhonda drawing another groan from Cassie.

Rhonda studied me a moment and then seemed to come to a decision. "The trick is to do things for her without asking permission. Just make it a fait accompli and she'll give in. That's what I do."

I nodded. "Thanks for the tip."

Cassie's jaw dropped. "Hellooooo....I'm right here. Could you stop discussing me while I'm in the room?" she asked with a look of disbelief. "Or, better yet, How about you don't discuss me at all?"

Mary patted her hand again and started back downstairs, offering Rhonda a cinnamon roll when she was ready to take a break. Rhonda heard 'cinnamon rolls' and decided now was as good a time as any for a break and followed us next door.

We sat around Mary's kitchen table and had more tea while Rhonda had a cinnamon roll and I had seconds. Cassie watched me eat my second roll with barely disguised envy. I held out a bite to her. "You know you don't need to lose any weight. You look great."

"I'm not trying to lose, I'm trying to maintain. I was heavy for most of my life. It's only since the divorce I've managed to get into shape and keep my weight stable," she said and waved away the bite. I didn't argue, just popped it in my mouth.

"Well, you've done a great job because I just assumed you've always been slender and active."

"Believe me, it's been a lot of hard work. But I think I've finally reached a point where my new healthy habits have become a way of life."

"I can attest to that. She works herself really hard and doesn't let herself slip backward, no matter how tempted she is," Mary added.

We talked for another half an hour. Rhonda finally stood up and said she had to get back to work. She waved good-bye and said she'd see us all tomorrow. I thanked Mary for everything and said we'd better get on the road also. Mary walked us to the door and told me she'd give me a key tomorrow. I promised to bring a check for my first month's rent.

Chapter 5

Cassie

I started the car and put it in gear before I realized I didn't know where we were headed. I hoped it wasn't back to the hotel. I was enjoying his company too much.

"So, where to?"

"Well, if you have things to do, you can drop me back at the hotel. If you're free and you're not too sick of me yet, I need a car battery."

"I know just where to get a battery," I replied while doing a little mental dance of celebration.

I took him to a small auto parts store where I knew the owner, Mike. I pointed him out as we walked through the door and waited for John's reaction. Mike was built like a wall. He was several inches taller than John and must have outweighed him by 50 pounds. Most people were a bit overwhelmed by his size but John just nodded. When Mike saw us he came over and gave me a big hug.

"Cassie, where have you been? I never get to see you anymore," he said as he lifted me off my feet and swung me around.

I gave him a kiss on the cheek and said, "Mike, I'm sorry I haven't been in but you did such a good job on my car that I haven't needed anything else."

"Well, darlin', you don't have to wait for your car to break to come for a visit. You know that. So what can I do for you?"

I introduced John and explained about the car battery. Mike nodded and said, "I'll take good care of him. Why don't you go on back and say hi to Trish. We'll come get you when we're done."

I hesitated for a moment, not wanting to miss any time with John. Then I mentally kicked myself. *Can you say 'stalker', Cassie? Sheesh,* I thought to myself as I walked to the back room calling out Trish's name.

Trish called out a greeting as I pushed through the door to the office. Her tiny form was almost hidden behind stacks of paper on the huge metal office desk. All I could see was a head of curly, brown hair and sparkling blue eyes.

"What the heck? It's not tax time. Are you being audited or something?" I asked incredulously as I took in the reams of paper on every available surface.

"No, I'm just finally getting everything computerized. It took me forever to drag Mike into this millennium," Trish responded with a laugh as she stood up to give me a hug.

"He is a bit of a Neanderthal isn't he? But you know just how to handle him don't you?"

Trish snickered and blushed a bit as she nodded, "Thanks to you."

"Nope, I just set him straight. The rest is all you. He's out front with a guy I brought in here to buy a battery. I hope I don't regret leaving them alone," I said with a rueful laugh.

"Guy? What guy? Did you meet someone new?"

Trish was suddenly completely focused on me and I almost wished I hadn't mentioned John. But then again, I wanted to talk to someone about him. He was all I could think about since I met him. I couldn't believe it was only yesterday. I quickly filled her in on what brought us together. I tried to downplay my reaction to him but she was having none of it.

"You really like this guy don't you? Don't try to fool me, it's written all over your face. I haven't seen you this excited about anything since.....I can't remember when."

"I feel a little foolish. We just met but every time I look at him I just want to....jump him," I finished with a self-conscious laugh.

"Nothing wrong with that, you deserve a little "me time". You don't ever do anything for yourself."

Trish actually shook a finger in my face as she scolded me. It was funny that such a petite woman could command attention with so little effort. She was right. I wanted him bad and if anyone deserved a little indulgence, it was me. The thing was he had to want me back for that to work.

. . . . .

John

When Cassie walked away Mike turned to me and said, "No need to scowl at me like that. Cassie and I are friends. She saved my marriage and I love her to death, but just like a sister.

I was surprised at the man's bluntness but appreciated it. "I'm not involved with Cassie. I just met her, although she has already saved me too."

"You may not be involved but you want to be." Mike replied. "You were bristling like an angry dog there for a minute."

When I started to argue, Mike cut me off and gestured for me to follow as he walked across the store to the batteries. He picked out the best one and handed it to me.

"Cassie and my wife are friends. A few years back, I was screwing up big time. I was going out all the time, drinking and carousing, having a grand old time and pretty much treating Trish like shit. I love my wife but I wasn't sure how to be a good husband. So I fell back on what I was familiar with. I acted the way my dad acted with my mom. All I remembered was my dad's 'rule the roost' attitude. I forgot the sadness I saw in my mom. Anyway, apparently Trish told Cassie she was going to leave me. Cassie asked her to wait a week and if I didn't straighten out she'd help her pack." Mike paused and shook his head as if remembering how close he had come to losing his wife.

"Cassie marched on in here and got in my face. I mean, she grabbed a step stool, climbed up it so she could look me in the eye, grabbed my shirt, and nose to nose, she gave me what for. The place was full of customers but that didn't stop her. She told me that Trish had fallen in love with me, not my father, and that if I didn't want to lose her I'd better remember how to act like the man she fell in love with. She also gave me hell for not letting Trish work in the store. She told me I was a Neanderthal and stupid to boot since I was paying someone to do a job that Trish was already trained to do. She told me I had one week to straighten out and convince Trish I was serious or she was gonna help Trish leave me. She said she'd already reserved a moving truck." Mike laughed.

"Then she said she'd appreciate it if I could get my shit together at least 24 hours before the one week deadline was up. If she had to cancel the truck, she didn't want to lose her deposit." Mike shook his head and laughed again. "She was magnificent; trembling with righteous rage. Then she let go of my shirt, climbed down the stool and put it away. Everyone in the store started clapping and cheering. I kicked 'em all out and closed the store and just sat in back and did some serious thinking. Apparently, I'm not beyond help because Trish didn't leave me and I am thankful every single day."

Mike ushered me up to the cash register to pay for the battery.

"That's a great story but I'm not sure why you told it to me."

Mike rang up the battery, and then folded his massive arms across his chest. "Well, you've got that look in your eye. Whether you'll admit it or not, you want her bad. There's something about Cassie that makes men think with their dicks. Most of them don't take the time to get to know her and see what a treasure she is. So, she married a guy who wanted a mother instead of a lover and then was surprised when she was miserable. She has always lacked confidence about her looks, which amazes me because I think she's beautiful. Then that bastard husband of hers had so many screws loose he made her feel completely undesirable. She has no clue how she affects men. She doesn't believe that anyone ever really wants her."

I started to speak again and Mike held up his hand. "I'm almost done. The reason that I'm telling you all this is to let you know there is a lot going on under the surface. Cassie gives and gives and gives. She is everyone's biggest protector. But she never protects herself. She's been hurt a lot and I don't want to see her hurt again. You're both adults and you can both make your own decisions, but know this..." he paused and leaned forward. "If you break her heart I will find you and I will hurt you. Do we understand each other?"

I studied him for a moment. I wasn't really worried about getting my butt kicked but I respected his protective instinct.

"Message received."

"Okay" Mike said and his body relaxed again. "So, how did she save you?"

For the second time that day I found myself telling the same story. Then I explained how she'd found me a school for my son and an apartment in less than twenty-four hours.

Mike clapped me on the back as he led me to the back office to retrieve Cassie. The friendly blow almost knocked me off my feet. I decided that I wouldn't want to piss him off if I could help it. No matter what Mike said, I wouldn't stay away from Cassie just on his say so. If I ignored the attraction it would be because I didn't have anything to offer her. *Who was I kidding? I wasn't going to stay away, the more I saw her the more I wanted her.*

Cassie's cheeks were pink when Mike and I walked into the office and I wondered what she and Trish had been talking about. She looked at me and looked away as the color in her cheeks darkened. Hmmm, that was interesting. I would just have to finagle a way to spend the rest of the day with her to investigate that blush.

Mike went over and kissed Trish and introduced us. I could see the difference in Mike when he was around Trish. He was very gentle and tender and it was obvious that he adored her. Cassie had done a good thing keeping them together.

Mike and Trish walked us out to the front door. Mike told me to come back if he needed anything else. I smiled. "Well I've got a Shelby I'm restoring."

Mike's eyes lit up. "You're kidding."

"Nope, I'm about halfway done. It's stored at my brother's house until I get settled. I'll probably go get it in a month or two. Good thing my brother could keep it for me. My ex said if I didn't get it out of there she would send it to the junkyard."

The look of horror on Mike's face was almost comical. I told him he'd probably be seeing a lot of me once I got the car up here. Mike told me he'd help him in any way he could. He looked envious and Trish patted him on the shoulder consolingly. As we got into the car, I glanced back at Mike and Trish. Mike was kissing Trish and she was wrapped around him like a second skin. As I watched, Mike locked the door, flipped the sign to 'closed', lifted Trish into his arms and carried her off toward the back room. Cassie laughed and I saw she'd been watching the lovers also.

"They're terrible. This store has the closed sign up a lot during the day," she said, shaking her head in exasperation.

"They're lucky," I said quietly.

She gazed at me a moment and then said, "Yes they are."

After a moment Cassie started the car and glanced at me. "Any other errands?"

"Yup, taking you to lunch."

"You don't have….."

I never let her finish, holding up my hand and speaking as if I were instructing a small child. "Repeat after me, Thank you John, I'd love to."

"Okay, okay, thank you John I'd love to," she said with a laugh.

"I'd like to see the gym you work out at too. I've been going crazy with the tiny fitness center at the hotel. Since it looks like I'm going to be living in here, I might as well check out the gym now."

"I'd rather work out before we eat, if you don't mind waiting. Actually, I can get you in on a guest pass for a couple bucks, but you don't have anything to wear," she said. Before I could respond she added, "If you don't mind swinging by my house, I think I have something that would fit you. If I grab an extra towel you could take a shower afterward. Then you could spot me and I wouldn't have to bug the other guys at the gym."

"Sounds like a plan."

It only took her about ten minutes to get home. She introduced me to her dog Keesha, a playful golden retriever, and then gave me a quick tour of the house. She found the sweats and was pleased to see they fit me perfectly. The T-shirt was tight but that didn't bother me since I caught her eyeing my chest and arms a couple times. I might have even flexed a couple of times ....all's fair.....She grabbed her workout bag and an extra towel and we were back on the road in under a half an hour.

When we walked into the gym, the woman at the front desk greeted Cassie like a regular customer. Cassie gave me the guest pass, told the woman to have Travis come help me with a possible membership, then headed off to the locker room to change and put her things away.

"Tell Travis he's my friend, if he tries to price gouge him, I'll take it personally."

I was standing by the water cooler with Travis as he finished up his sales pitch when I realized I hadn't heard anything he'd said for the past five minutes. I couldn't take my eyes off Cassie.

She was wearing Lycra shorts and a sports bra with a tank top over it. She had finished her run on the treadmill and was doing some stretches. Her skin had a fine sheen of sweat and she was glowing with vitality. She looked good enough to eat. Apparently, I wasn't the only one who noticed because for the past five minutes, practically every guy in the gym had stopped to talk to her.

"It's amazing isn't it?"

"W-what is?" I glanced at Travis and saw that he was also watching Cassie.

"It's like bees to honey. It's like that every time she's here. Guys can't help wanting to be around her," Travis said in a

106

bemused voice. Then he turned back to me and asked, "How long have you known her?"

"Since yesterday," I answered and watched Travis' jaw drop.

"You're kidding! That's interesting." He added and looked thoughtful.

"Why?"

"Well, Cassie started coming in here about two and a half years ago. She used to come here with her husband, every once in a while, but mainly by herself. She never talked to anyone. She wasn't rude. It was just like she was closed off from everyone else."

He paused for a moment as if trying to decide if that was the right way to explain it. He must have been satisfied because he continued on.

"Then, a little over a year ago, she got divorced and within months she was a new person. She became friendly with everyone. Personally, I think it was her real personality coming through, finally. But she still gave off these vibes like, 'don't try to get too close'. All of the guys think she's great but she never dates any of them. You're the first guy she's ever brought here."

107

He finished and looked at me with a raised eyebrow. I didn't comment on his story as I watched Cassie interact with all the guys. I asked what kind of deal he would give me for the gym membership. Travis quoted a reasonable price so I told him to write up the paperwork and I'd sign it when I was finished working out.

I made my way between the guys standing around talking to Cassie. Stopping in front of where Cassie was stretching on the floor, I smiled and held my hand out. I could feel all of the men's eyes on me. I ignored them and pulled her to her feet when she put her hand in mine. Cassie introduced me around and I nodded politely.

I kept her hand in mine as we walked across the gym. Like a big dog peeing on a tree, I'd just marked my territory and didn't care what anyone thought about it. I refused to analyze it any further than that.

"So what are we working on today?" I asked her when we reached the free weight portion of the gym.

"My schedule calls for chest and triceps and a little abs thrown in."

"Sounds good to me, why don't we just do your regular workout? I'll do whatever you do and we'll just trade off spotting each other."

Cassie happily agreed. She seemed a little self-conscious at first. I lifted weights fairly regularly and could easily out lift her but I tried to put her at ease. Soon, she relaxed and we got into the business of building muscle. I made some suggestions without talking down to her and she readily accepted them.

I was impressed. Cassie had great form and she really pushed herself. She bench pressed ninety pounds. I knew a few female, professional, body builders who benched the same amount. Cassie wasn't there to play around or pick up men. She was there to stay in shape and it showed.

I was the one having trouble keeping my mind on what we were doing. Her Lycra shorts were form fitting and showed off her ass to perfection. More than once I'd had to study the wall for a moment to get control of myself. I figured it wasn't all one-sided, though. She kept sneaking little glances at my chest and arms. I pretended I didn't notice. At one point I thought she was going to reach out and rub her hand down my chest and my pecker started to come alive again. It was time for another dick-talk.

I pushed her to bench press one hundred pounds for a few repetitions. She managed five reps at the hundred pound weight. When she got off the bench she threw her arms around my neck and hugged me in her excitement, squealing about a new record. The hot woman, that I'd just spent the last hour fantasizing about, pressed up against me and I froze. Wanting to grab her hips and pull them against my rapidly hardening dick, I forced myself to put my hands on my hips and leave them there. I felt it when she went from warm, soft woman to a rigid piece of plywood and stepped back away from me. I could have kicked myself.

She didn't look at me. She walked over to the matt to work on abdominals. I grabbed my towel and hung it in front of my lap to hide my reaction to her. I could tell I'd hurt her feelings. I'd wanted to touch her everywhere, wanted to mold her body to mine and cup that great ass with both hands. God, she'd felt so good. She was all sleek muscles and soft skin. Her breasts had flattened against my chest. I wanted to feel those breasts naked against my skin.

Then she pulled away and the feeling of loss scared the hell out of me. I could tell by the way she avoided my eyes she was embarrassed. It was obvious she'd jumped to the wrong conclusion. How could she not know how incredibly sexy she was? Every male eye in the place had been on her at one time or another during the entire workout.

She was lying on the floor doing leg lifts and abdominal crunches. Her face was red from the effort and I could see beads of sweat trickling down her chest and disappearing behind her tank top. I wanted to follow that trickle of sweat. I was envious of its path over her breasts. I yearned to follow its path with my tongue and taste the salt on her skin. I almost groaned out loud as I pushed the thoughts away. If this kept up I would be holding a towel in front of me every time I saw her.

"I think I'm going to skip the abdominals and go hit the showers," I told Cassie hoping that the shower would give me time to get myself under control.

Cassie found me later at the front desk. I was just signing the credit card slip for the purchase of my membership. She'd been in the locker room a long time and if she hadn't come out when she did I was about to go in after her.

She still didn't say anything all the way across the parking lot. A couple of times I thought she was going to speak but she seemed to change her mind. When we got to the car I stopped at the driver's door and waited for her to look at me. She made me wait a while.

"Cassie, I'm sorry, I…"

She cut me off. "No, it's no problem. I was excited because I've never been able to bench that much weight and I just wanted to share it with someone. I wasn't trying to push myself on you. I know you think of me like a sister." I started to speak and she cut me off again. "I mean, you are a good looking guy and I'm well aware of my limitations in that regard, guys don't view me sexually, it's all right, I'm used to it but…"

I could feel my blood pressure rising. I was pissed as hell. I was surprised at how much I wanted to find the person who'd made Cassie doubt herself and punch him in the head. She must have noticed the look on my face because her voice trailed off in the middle of a sentence.

"Bullshit!"

"W-what?"

"For a smart woman you are pretty fucking clueless." I ground out through gritted teeth. I wasn't angry at her but I was pretty sure it was coming off that way. I took a deep breath and tried to calm myself.

"I-I…"

"Cassie, every straight guy in there is panting after you. You're like a walking guy magnet."

"You're crazy!" she exploded. "Those guys are all my friends. That's all they want from me," she said indignantly.

I couldn't help it, I burst out laughing. "You really don't have a clue. Believe me; each of them would jump into bed with you in a second if you gave off the least little vibe that you'd be willing."

When she started to respond, this time I didn't let her talk.

"You don't have a clue about how I view you either. Believe me; I don't look at you like a sister."

"But you even said that I reminded you of your sister."

"No, Cassie, you only hear what you expect to hear. I said that your giving personality, never doing anything for yourself, reminded me of my sister. Nothing else about you makes me, even remotely, think of my sister."

"Oh…"

"Yeah, Oh," I said as if she was finally getting a clue.

"But, you...when I hugged you, you..."

It had become patently clear that I was not going to be able to talk sense into her so I would just have to show her what I was talking about. I stepped right up to her and she backed against the car. I crowded close to her until we were almost touching. I spoke softly but frustration gave my voice and edge.

"I froze because I'd just spent the last hour trying to keep my hands off of you. When you pressed up against me all I could think of was how I wanted to strip off your clothes and feel you skin to skin all over. I wanted to touch you....I want to touch you with my hands and my mouth and the urge to drive myself inside you is the most primal thing I've ever felt."

Cassie swayed on her feet and I saw her shudder, her nipples hardening enough to raise the tight fabric molded to her chest.

"Y-you want to....do that to me?" she asked in a trembling whisper.

"To you, with you, on you, under you, in you for hours," I breathed each word through gritted teeth. "I had to cut the workout short because when you hugged me I got so hard I was afraid I was going to embarrass myself."

Cassie shook her head in disbelief and my control snapped. "Oh Hell," I ground out before I gave in and pulled her into my arms. I stared into her eyes for a moment looking for acceptance or agreement. Then my eyes dropped to her mouth. She parted her lips and that was good enough for me.

My body was demanding that I ravage her but I didn't want to scare her away. I kissed her tenderly, moving my lips gently over hers, memorizing her softness. I ran my tongue lightly over her bottom lip and she melted into me. Her mouth opened under mine, her hands slid up my chest as she moaned low in her throat and I was lost.

I wrapped my arms around her and crushed her to my chest. With a slight turn of my head I slanted my mouth across hers and thrust my tongue past her lips. Her tongue met mine and played a game of advance and retreat. I groaned deep in my throat as her nipples pressed into my chest. I stroked slowly down her back, cupped the cheeks of her ass and pulled her against me so she could feel my erection pressing into her belly. Cassie ground her hips against me and I dragged my lips from hers. I leaned my forehead against hers, trying to get my breathing under control.

"Do you believe me now?" I asked in a husky voice.

She pressed her hips into me again. "Well the evidence is quite apparent," she said with a sigh.

I pulled my hips back. "Hey I'm right on the ragged edge here. Don't tempt me."

"Why not," she asked with a serious look on her face.

Yeah, why not? I cupped her face in my hands and tenderly kissed her then stepped back with a sigh.

"Believe me, I would like nothing better than to find a bed and make you come until you scream uncle," I said with a shudder at the pictures that flashed through my mind.

"But?"

"But, my life is complicated right now and I can't make any promises to you. Hell, I don't know if I'll ever be able to make promises again. Sharon really did a number on me and I'm gun shy. You're an amazing woman and you deserve better."

"Hey," she said as she placed her palm against my cheek. "I'm an adult. It's not your responsibility to protect me from myself. I have my own demons that make me gun shy. I'm not asking for any promises, just honesty. I'm a little freaked out that

I just met you yesterday and I feel this out of control so quickly."
I started to speak and she put her hand on my mouth to stop me.

"Let me get this out. My marriage made me believe a lot of things about myself that I'm just beginning to realize might not be entirely accurate. I don't know what is going to happen a month from now. But I'm trying to get to the point in my life where I make decisions based on what I want and not based on someone else's idea of what is right for me. And what I want is you.....anyway I can have you."

I sucked in a breath and lightly kissed the fingers that were resting on my lips. My brain was saying, *take it slowly* and my dick was saying, *what are you waiting for?*

"How about I take you to lunch; give us a chance to gain some rationality back. After lunch we see what happens, okay?"

She gave me a smile that made something warm curl in my gut but she just said, "Okay, what do you want to eat?"

Visions of her draped across my bed, with her legs spread apart by my shoulders, while I used my tongue to drive her into a frenzy, flashed through my head. I sucked in more air to compensate for all of the blood going to my nether regions.

"You decide. I don't know what's available." I said as I wisely stepped away and walked around to the passenger side of the car.

Cassie chose a local restaurant that had great salads. By a kind of mutual agreement we didn't discuss any more about where we would go from here. We talked about family and everything else but getting naked and crazy. It was all I could think about. Half way through lunch I knew I wouldn't be able to resist her.

Neither of us spoke during the trip back to the hotel. When we pulled into the lot, Cassie parked and we sat for a minute. As much as I knew that I was complicating an already complicated life I finally turned to her and looked into her eyes.

"Do you want to come upstairs?"

"Yes."

Chapter 6

Cassie

Somehow I got from "Yes" to his living room but I don't remember the journey. I was looking at everything but him, suddenly shy, when he took my purse, tossing it onto the couch. He used a finger under my chin to slowly coax me to raise my head and meet his eyes.

"Hey, I won't hold it against you if you change your mind," he said with a kind smile that overshadowed but didn't quite eradicate the look of desire in his eyes.

"I won't change my mind," I said softly, my gaze locking with his.

He stood in front of me running his hands lightly up and down my arms. My entire being seemed to focus on those hands. He rubbed one thumb against my breast, never breaking eye contact. I sucked in a breath as goose bumps broke out on my arms. I glanced down to where his thumb continued its sensual assault. My whole body was flooding with warmth as I felt a flush of moisture between my legs. He reached out and tilted my chin back up so I would look at him.

"Are you sure?"

I stared at him for a moment but finally managed to croak out "Y-yes." I cleared my throat and tried again. "Yes, it's just been a long time and I'm afraid I'm not very good at this. I-I just hope I won't disappoint you."

"Where do you get the idea you're not very good at this?"

The second warm flush I felt was of embarrassment. I was at a crossroads. I could keep the armor protecting me from all past pains firmly in place or start trying to put those demons to rest. I squared my shoulders but my voice still shook a bit as I spoke.

"My husband….. didn't …um…want me very often. When he did……. I always seemed to do something to turn him off. If I talked….or laughed while we were….. it bothered him and he rarely touched me ….sexually. He would kiss me and then just…just…"

"You weren't ready for him?"

"Yes," I was so grateful he understood it made it easier to continue. "He would complain I was too…too dry and too tight."

I closed my eyes for a moment, afraid to see his expression. "Hey," he said gently. I finally opened my eyes and saw his were filled with tenderness. "All of those were his failings, not yours."

"Y-you really think so?"

"Mmmhmm, and I'm going to prove it to you."

He reached up and cupped my face with both hands, sliding his fingers into my hair.

"How much time do you have before you have to pick up Sam?"

"I have to leave in about three hours."

"Pity, that's not nearly enough time but it will have to do for now."

I watched his mouth descend toward mine until my eyes closed of their own volition. I sighed into him as his lips closed over mine. His hands held my head in a softly padded prison. He nibbled along my lower lip and then laved it with his tongue, soothing the light sting. Strong fingers wound tightly through my hair and held me fast for his marauding mouth. All of my being was centered in the small part of me fused with him.

121

I whimpered, momentarily bereft, as his lips left mine. But he continued down the side of my face to my throat where he sucked an earlobe into his warm moist cavern. I trembled as goose bumps erupted all over my body and my knees sagged, threatening to give way. I tunneled my trembling fingers through his hair, holding him against me, silently begging him to continue the onslaught. His hands slid down to my shirt and began working the buttons. I felt cool air on my skin followed by his hot breath.

I was so drunk on feeling I didn't notice when he pulled back for a moment. Then the loss of his body heat snagged my attention enough for me to open my eyes to locate him. He stood before me, his cheeks flushed with color. Eyes, darkened with passion, followed the line where the swell of my breast met the satin edge of my bra. His finger traced the same trail as I swayed on legs that barely supported me.

He pulled the shirt down, trapping my arms against my side. His delight at discovering the bra fastened in front made me smile. When he unclasped the plastic catch my breasts swung apart a bit but lay, still covered like a present waiting to be opened. He peeled the cups away with an expression bordering on reverence. When my nipples were uncovered he rubbed his thumbs lightly over them until my breathing hitched in my throat.

He looked back up at my face for a moment. I don't know what he saw but he quickly stripped the shirt and bra off my arms and then, once again, threaded his fingers through my hair and gently pulled my head back. This forced me to arch my back and thrust my breasts out like offerings to the gods. He slid one arm behind my back to support me and quickly took what I offered.

When John's mouth closed over my nipple I moaned and arched toward him. Little bolts of heat flashed through my body. The warmth seemed to be pooling in the breast he was laving with his tongue. I felt boneless, leaning all of my weight on his arm. He switched to the other breast and slowly lowered me onto the bed, his mouth and tongue never ceasing their assault. My arms came up, seemingly of their own accord and held him in place.

He disappeared for a moment, removing my shoes and socks. My reality became a kaleidoscope of sensations. I felt his hands at the button of my pants and then the pants being peeled down my legs. Shyness returned as I realized I was lying there almost naked. But then his hands were moving on my body and once again all I could do was feel.

Floating in a fog of erotic images, the only reality that cut through the mist were the jolts of pleasure my nerves were sending to my brain. He slid my panties down my legs and then

123

his fingers were sliding through the curls at the juncture of my thighs. His middle finger pressed deeply into my core. He groaned and said, "You are so wet. Do you know how much it turns me on that I can make you this wet?"

His fingers skimmed lightly over my clit and I arched as if I'd been touched by a live wire. I spread my legs in an unconscious invitation. I felt his lips kissing my legs and thighs and, realizing where he was headed, frantically started pushing him away and trying to close my legs. He held them open but rose up to look at me.

"What's wrong?" he asked quietly.

"I-I…You don't have to do….that. I know it's ……I-I don't expect it," I said with an embarrassed flush, once again, creeping up my neck.

"Do I hear your ex's voice again?"

I closed my eyes, unable to look at him while the shame consumed me.

"H-he said the smell made him feel nauseous."

He didn't speak for a moment; when he did it sounded like he was talking through gritted teeth.

"Your ex is a seriously repressed, fucked-up individual."

I still couldn't open my eyes and I wanted to crawl under the bed.

"Cassie, honey, you smell like a woman; a beautiful, sexy, aroused woman. There is no bigger turn on for a man. As for how you taste, I'll have to let you know."

Slowly I opened my eyes. I hoped he was right but I was glad when he raised his hands off my thighs and said, "Scoot up, will you?"

He folded a pillow in half and put it behind my head. It raised me up so I could look down my body. He left the other pillow on the bed next to my thighs. He quickly took his clothes off; he couldn't have picked a better way to distract me. All of those mouthwatering muscles made me want to lick him all over. When he took off his boxers and his erection sprang free, all I could think was how much I wanted him inside me. He straddled my hips, ripping open a condom before handing it to me.

"Will you help me put it on? I want to feel your hands on me," he said huskily.

I was intrigued but uncertain. He put the condom on the tip of his cock and then took my hand. "Just roll it down the sides."

At my first contact with the head of his cock I saw him shudder and arch involuntarily. By the time I was finished he was breathing hard and his hands were trembling.

"You almost made me come just putting on a condom. When I actually get inside you I might just die on the spot."

His words touched a part of me that unleashed a flood of liquid. He leaned over and kissed me, gently at first and then he turned up the heat until I was writhing underneath him and struggling to get closer. Slowly he started down my body giving my nipples lots of attention again. My breathing was raspy and my breasts were swollen and hard by the time he continued on down toward my stomach. He kissed and tongued his way down my belly. I stiffened up a bit. I couldn't bear it if he felt the same way George had. He kissed around one side of my mound and down my leg. I relaxed a bit and started enjoying the sensations once more.

He lightly stroked my belly and thighs with his fingertips while he continued to kiss and lick my legs. His fingers skimmed over my pubic hair, just lightly brushing the outer lips. Almost against my will, my thighs parted and he pressed down and rubbed the wetness all around. His fingers found my clit again and I thrust helplessly against his hand. He teased me, skimming just out of reach of where I wanted him most, making me writhe. While his fingers kept me occupied, he pressed my thighs wider until he could hold them open with his shoulders. I was open and pink and wet right in front of him but I was so involved in the sensations I hadn't even noticed.

"Lift your hips, Cassie," he commanded.

I obeyed without thinking and he slid the pillow underneath my hips. In one swift move, he wrapped his arms around my thighs, pulled my legs open wide, spread me open with his fingers and drove his tongue into me. I think I stopped breathing for a moment as an electric jolt I had never felt in my life crashed through my body. I pressed my hips toward his face, rather than pulling away again. His tongue made my thighs quiver as if assaulted by freezing temperatures but I was oh so warm.

He raised his head and softly commanded, "Cassie, open your eyes. I want you to watch what I do to you."

I had to pry my eyes open but the sight was worth it. His tanned arms were wrapped around my pale thighs. His fingers splayed across my auburn curls while his mouth drove me to distraction.

He locked eyes with me while he ran his tongue up and down and around. When he wrapped his lips around my clit and sucked gently, my hands went into his hair to hold him there. I couldn't believe only moments ago I was trying to push him away. A warm flush started at my toes and moved up my body.

My eyes closed and I started chanting, "Oh my God, Oh my God, Oh my God."

"Come for me, Cassie. I want to feel it," he whispered and then closed his lips around me again.

The pleasure was so intense I was almost afraid. I pressed my heels down into the bed, trying to pull away from his mouth before I shattered like glass. A moan started low in my throat and built with the pressure. My involuntary cries seemed to drive him to work even harder at making me come apart. When I gave in and went over the edge it was with a keening cry wrenched out of my very soul. The pulsing, clenching, climax consumed me and scattered my thoughts like leaves in a windstorm.

John kept suckling on me, trying to draw out the climax as long as possible. When he finally released me, he pressed a quick kiss to my still pulsing core and then moved up and drove into me.

"God, you're so tight," he ground out. I could still feel my warm moist heat clenching and releasing his hard length. It felt so good and so right I didn't want it to ever end.

John looked down at me and saw I was crying. "Hey, hey, hey, what's this?" He whispered as he kissed my tears. "I didn't hurt you did I?"

More tears shimmered in my eyes as I shook my head, "N-no."

"Cassie, when I said how tight you are...you know that's a good thing, right? You're like a warm glove squeezing me all over. I stopped because I want to make this last."

He just waited for me to answer even though I knew he must be suppressing the urge to move.

"You didn't do anything wrong, you've done everything right. I've spent so many years feeling ...ashamed of my body. Finding out there is nothing wrong with me, that I'm a normal woman, and you could get such enjoyment out of...of...my...out of doing that to me...."

I couldn't think of how else to explain it but my smile must have said it all because I felt him getting even harder inside me. Desire flared in his eyes as he slowly began to withdraw. My blood pulsed through my veins like molten lava. He slid back into me just as slowly until he was buried to the hilt. Then he did it again, keeping a slow, teasing pace.

He dropped his mouth to mine and kissed me deeply. I thrust my tongue into a mating dance with his. When he started to pull back I grabbed his head and held him in place, licking my way around his lips.

"That's what I taste like?"

"Yeah, I love the way you taste," he said softly as he gazed into my eyes.

"I love the way I taste on you," I whispered.

His control snapped. With a sound like a roar, he withdrew and slammed back into me. His eyes darkened and seemed to lose focus as I lifted my legs and wrapped them around him. I pressed my heels into the muscles of his ass, needing him to get even closer.

He braced himself on his arms, angling his thrusts to rub against my already swollen center. I felt the coiling, tightening, build-up begin again. I dropped my head back and let out a long cry as the feelings built to a crescendo. I tried to grip his thrusting hips with my legs, but they were trembling and weak. They fell back on the bed, opening me even wider to his thrusts. A sob was torn from my throat as I hung at the precipice.

"Open your eyes, Cassie," John demanded. "I want to see you come apart."

I opened my eyes to a beautiful, sweaty man above me. Every muscle was straining, his arms were trembling. My gaze locked on his as the first contraction ripped through me. Then I couldn't keep my eyes open any longer as I gave myself over to the sensations with a ragged cry. With a growl, he dropped his head and thrust once, twice, then on the third thrust, with a shout he erupted. He collapsed onto me, his breath chugging like a freight train.

When he recovered enough he started to lever himself upward to roll off of me. I gripped his hips with my thighs. "Don't move yet, please. I like the way this feels."

He dropped back down to his elbows and said, "I just don't want to crush you."

"You're not crushing me, you're filling me."

131

He groaned. "Do you have any idea how the things you say make me crazy. If it wasn't a physical impossibility, I swear…"

I smiled and waggled my eyebrows. "You swear what?"

"Never mind," he said with a growl. Then as if he couldn't help himself, he dropped his head and took one of my nipples into his mouth.

I sucked in a breath and said, "Watch it buddy, you're playing with fire."

"Hmmm?" was his only response as he switched to the other breast and began nibbling his way to the crest.

"Two can play at that game." I said as I clenched my vaginal muscles around him and heard him suck in a breath.

"Okay, Okay." With a laugh as he rolled off me.

I pouted, "You didn't have to leave me."

"Condoms have a limited useful life, and then they start to leak. Come on," he added as he grabbed my hand. "How much time do we have?"

I looked at my watch. "About an hour and a half," I answered as I was pulled into the bathroom.

After disposing of the condom he turned on the water, testing the temperature and adjusting until it was just right. He pulled me into the shower and turned me under the spray. When I was completely soaked he squirted shampoo onto my head and worked it into lather. It was one of the most luxurious things I'd ever felt. His strong hands worked my scalp until I was on the verge of collapse.

He tilted my head back and rinsed my hair out. Then he turned his attention to my body and my nipples hardened instantly. He soaped me all over and gently ran his hands between my legs, washing me and arousing me at the same time. My legs began to tremble and I grabbed his hands.

"My turn."

I handed him the shampoo bottle. "Some other time I'll treat you to an amazing scalp massage but I can't reach your head in here." I gazed down his body. "Well, I can reach the head I'm really interested in," I said with a lascivious look. He groaned and his cock lengthened right before my eyes. He started lathering his hair while I took the soap and worked up suds in my hands. I stood there for a moment just enjoying the view. I'd seen Michelangelo's statue of David when I was in my teens. John wasn't far off as far as I was concerned.

"God, you are beautiful," I whispered.

When he finished rinsing the shampoo out he left his hands interlocked behind his head. "I'm all yours."

I turned him so he was not in the spray and pulled his hands down to his sides. I soaped his shoulders, kneading the muscles at the base of his neck.

"Do you remember when we first met and we were talking about lottery tickets?"

"Mmmhmm," he replied with his eyes closed, head leaning back against the shower wall.

"All I could think about was how I'd like to grab onto these broad shoulders of yours while you were deep inside me."

A moment later my hips were pulled up against his hard length and his eyes were smoky grey as he growled, "You're asking for it woman."

"Ah, ah, ah," I said as I grabbed his hands and removed them from my hips and then used one finger in his chest to push him backward. "Back up big boy, I'm in control here."

Heat flared in his eyes at the challenge in my statement but he stepped back and left his hands at his sides. I soaped his chest, raking my nails gently over his nipples, watching them contract into hard points. I kept moving down over his firm abdomen. Goose bumps erupted on his skin when my hand skimmed his lower belly. His cock was jutting straight out and I ran my hand lightly up the length of it. I heard him suck in his breath but I didn't look up. I was enjoying watching my fingers encircle him and soap up and down the length of him. I ran my thumb over the sensitive tip and a bead of fluid escaped.

I could feel him trembling with the effort of standing there without touching me. I cupped his balls for a moment, but didn't spend a lot of time caressing them because, suddenly, I wanted him in my mouth. I wanted to give back to him what he'd given to me. I soaped down his legs and then told him to turn around and rinse off.

I was still kneeling when he turned back around from rinsing off, which put his throbbing cock right at mouth level. I didn't hesitate, I grasped him with one hand and swirled my tongue around the head. I felt a jolt go through him as his breath hissed out between clenched teeth.

I licked and kissed my way down the length of him and then gently swirled my tongue back up to the tip. I could hear his breath hitching as I took just the head in my mouth and sucked, tapping the top with my tongue.

Finally, I pressed downward, taking as much of him as I could deep in my mouth. His fingers were in my hair; his hands trembling. I withdrew, sucking softly, and he groaned deep in his throat. I swirled my tongue around the head and then tightened my lips and thrust down again. His fingers closed around my head. I withdrew again, sucking a little harder on the way up.

I released him for a moment and looked up at him. His head was tilted forward, resting on his chest, eyes blazing with passion as he watched me take the head of his cock in my mouth. I maintained eye contact as I swirled my tongue around and around.

"Cas-s-s-ie", he hissed when I took in his whole length and pressed him against the back of my throat. I sucked hard as I pulled back and with a groan he pulled away and brought me to my feet. He turned off the water and took me into his arms. He slanted his mouth across mine and our tongues began a duel.

When I was weak-kneed and leaning into him he released my mouth and whispered against my lips. "I want to be inside you when I come."

He lifted me into his arms and stepped out of the shower. He set me down on the counter, pressed my thighs open and fell to his knees in front of me. I made no protest when he wrapped his arms around my legs and buried his face in my warmth.

I fell back against the mirror. Minutes later my thighs were trembling and I could feel the coil tightening. I pushed him away and slid down from the counter, pulling him up to his feet.

"I want you inside me when I come," I whispered against his lips.

"Stay right there," he ordered.

He walked into the bedroom and came back with a pillow and a condom. He rolled the condom on and then turned me to face the mirror. He pulled me back against him until I could feel his hard hot length pressed between the cheeks of my ass. I watched his tanned hands cover both of my breasts and lightly pinch the nipples. As his tongue traced lightly up my neck to my ear a gush of heat and liquid made me slick with need. I leaned my head back against his shoulder and turned to lightly bite his chin.

His hand lightly caressed its way down my belly and the anticipation of his touch, where I ached for it most, made me moan.

"Spread your legs for me," he ordered against my ear. I felt like I was watching someone else as his hand dipped between my spread thighs. Then his finger parted my outer lips and teased me, skating on the edge of my most sensitive spot.

"So wet, so hot, God you make me crazy", he sighed against my ear. "Do you want me inside you?" he whispered to me.

"Y-yes," I croaked through a, suddenly, dry throat.

He slid a finger inside me and I clenched around him, trying to draw him deeper. My chest flushed pink and my breasts swelled. I writhed, pressing my hips into his hand. "More….please," I said huskily, as my head fell back against his shoulder again.

He slid the first finger out, brushing across my swollen nub and I cried out. He brushed across it again as he pushed back inside me with two fingers. I clenched again, pressing frantically

138

against his hand. He ran his tongue around my ear and then dipped it inside. His breath cooled the moisture and made me shiver as he said; "Tell me what you want."

My embarrassment at asking for something so intimate warred with my need. The need won. I raised my head and caught his eye in the mirror.

"I want you to fuck me until I scream."

He grabbed my shoulders and pressed me forward, positioning the pillow over the edge of the counter to protect me. He spread his legs slightly and guided the head of his cock to my opening and pressed in about an inch. Then he grabbed my hips so I couldn't work him any deeper. He pulled back and again thrust just barely inside me. He rocked back and forth working just the head in and out of me.

I was straining against his hands, trying to take him all the way inside. I let out a whimper and he pressed in a little deeper. But still he just went in about two inches before withdrawing. He watched me but wouldn't give in until I met his eyes in the mirror again and said, "Please."

"There's the magic word," he said as he plunged forward while he pulled my hips back to meet his thrust. My mouth opened in a silent "Oh", as he slid all the way into me. He reached around front and pressed his hand hard against my clit as he drove in and out causing friction from inside and outside. We were participants and voyeurs at the same time and it heightened all of my senses.

When I bucked back against him for the last time the cry I let loose seemed to come from my toes. My head dropped forward and my insides clenched around him as my feet came up off the floor. This drove him even deeper, wrenching another cry from me. All I could see was my white knuckles gripping the pillowcase to keep me from falling off the edge of the earth.

I glanced in the mirror and watched John watching himself thrust into me. With a hoarse shout he threw his head back and pinned me to the counter as his explosion seemed to go on and on. Finally, he collapsed forward over my back.

My first conscious thought was how good it felt to have his weight bearing down on me while he was still inside me. My tremors had subsided and my breathing had returned to normal. I sighed in contentment. When he lifted himself off and out of me I felt the cool air and shivered but wasn't sure I could move. He stood behind me and removed the condom then lightly caressed my ass.

He spanked me lightly and said with a wry grin, "I think another shower is in order, but in the interest of surviving until tomorrow, I think we should both wash ourselves."

I pushed myself to my feet and turned to him.

"Thank-you," I said softly.

"For what?" he said with a lecherous waggle of his eyebrows.

"For making me feel desirable again."

His grin became a tender smile and he leaned forward and kissed my forehead.

"You're welcome, believe me, it was my pleasure." He leaned back and the lecherous grin returned. "And the next time you get a case of the undesirables. Just let me know and I'll work really hard to cure you again."

"I'll keep that in mind, Doctor," I said with a laugh.

He turned on the shower again and adjusted the temperature. I leaned forward toward the mirror rubbing some make-up out from under my eye. My hair was mussed and I could see where his whiskers had left red marks on the sensitive skin of my breasts. I glanced back toward him and caught him staring at me. The look in his eye made something clutch low in my belly.

"This is kind of scary," he said in a husky voice.

"What is?"

His eyes drifted down my body and then back up to my eyes. "I want you again," he said with a helpless shrug.

My knees went weak and I sagged a bit against the counter. His words started a reaction in my head that spread like a wave through my body. I glanced down to see he was, once more, hard as a rock. I licked my lips and his cock actually twitched in response.

"My God, you are going to kill me woman," he growled. "Okay, your penalty for tempting me beyond reason is you get to shower by yourself."

I turned toward him and with a pout that was belied by the gleam in my eye; I ran my hand lightly over one breast and rolled my fingertip around the nipple.

"Shit," he was almost yelling but he couldn't take his eyes off my hand which was now skimming across my belly and heading for the triangle of soft curls at the juncture of my thighs. "I've created a monster," he groaned.

Some last little bit of reason surfaced in his oxygen deprived brain and he wrenched his eyes away from the hand between my thighs. "Get in the shower, now!" he growled.

"If you insist," I said as I stepped into the shower. Just before I closed the curtain I turned to him and slid my finger into my mouth and slowly withdrew it. When his brain registered that the finger I was sucking on was the one I'd just had between my legs a loud "Aaargh", was wrenched from his lips and he almost ran out of the bathroom, slamming the door behind him.

The heady feeling of feminine power was a new and exciting experience for me. I ached to have him inside me again, despite how extra-sensitive I felt when I washed myself. I felt as languid as a cat, a well-loved cat.

When I walked out into the living room John was standing in the kitchen in his boxers. I wondered if I would ever look at him without feeling a flare of hunger. Not likely, now that I'd experienced what his body could do.

He handed me a cup of mint tea.

"You like mint tea?"

"I got some last night. I walked down to the store after you dropped me off. I was out of a couple things and when I was getting more coffee I saw the tea." He shrugged as if it was no big deal.

It was certainly not a declaration of undying love, which I didn't want anyway, I reminded myself; but it said that he'd planned on seeing me again.

"You can come over for dinner tonight if you'd like," I said without planning to. "I-I mean, I just figured that eating in restaurants must get old and it doesn't look like you have much available here for making gourmet meals."

"Thanks, but can I take a rain check?"

"Sure," I said and could've kicked myself. Nothing like pushing, Geez I'd never learn. He'd already told me that he didn't have anything to offer other than friendship and sex; amazing, wonderful, mind-blowing sex but still, just sex.

"I have to install the battery in my car tonight to be sure it works before I drive over to Rhonda's tomorrow. Plus, Josh is supposed to call later so I can tell him about the apartment," he said as he leaned back against the kitchen counter and sipped his coffee.

Flight to Forever

"Oh, that's right, I forgot about the battery,"

His simple explanation made me feel so much better.

"Well I should get going. Sam gets worried if I'm late."

John put his coffee down and walked me to the door. I wasn't sure how to act. *That's what I get for going to bed with a guy I've only known a day,* I chastised myself. He pulled me into his arms and kissed me. I sighed with relief.

"Whatever conclusions you're reaching in that head of yours, they're probably wrong," he said with an amused look.

"Really," I said with a smile. "And I was thinking what an amazing lover you are, pity."

He dropped his hands to my hips and pulled me against him. I was stunned to feel he was still hard.

"I'm going to make you pay for that," he growled in my ear. "And for the way you teased me in the bathroom."

"I can't wait."

He groaned and said, "Get out of here. I'll see you tomorrow at Rhonda's house... actually; I guess it's my house now."

Chapter 7

I spent the evening catching up on the housework I'd neglected during the day. I helped Sam with her homework, then, after several games of Chutes and Ladders and a half an hour of Sam's other nightly delaying tactics, I was finally successful at tucking her into bed.

With no other duties to attend to, I wandered around the house for a while feeling strangely unsettled. I rarely watched television and had no desire to watch it now. Reading was one of my favorite pastimes, but the thought of losing myself in a book held no interest.

I poured myself a glass of wine and carried it up to my bedroom. Placing the fluted glass on the bedside table, I went into the bathroom to get ready for bed. As I was putting on my nightshirt I noticed the red marks on my skin. It took me a minute to realize it was beard burn. There were marks on my breasts, belly, and thighs. The marks on my thighs made my mind flash on the activity that put them there. My skin heated with the remembrance and my nipples tightened. How quickly the thought of John aroused me. And here I was with no way to relieve the ache.

I finished washing myself and brushing my teeth and all of my other nightly ablutions. Then there was nothing else to do but go crawl in bed and try to relax enough to go to sleep. I propped a couple of pillows behind me to raise my head high enough to drink the wine.

I took a sip of wine and shuddered at the suddenly bitter taste. It was my own fault for brushing my teeth before drinking the wine, I thought sourly. God, I just couldn't get comfortable in my own skin. I scowled at the wall and tried to figure out what was wrong.

Oh, quit kidding yourself. You know damn well you want to jump in the car and drive like a crazy woman down to his hotel, bash the door in and jump his bones. Yes, I wanted more, more kissing and touching and loving and......orgasms. *Who the hell doesn't want more orgasms?* I just wanted more John, any way I could have him.

"You are in trouble, girl," I said aloud. "Yeah, especially because I'm talking to myself," I spoke to a picture on the wall. "Even worse, I'm answering myself," I said aloud again and finally had to giggle.

"Great, a little sex for the first time in....in....geez, how long has it been?"

I gave up on normal and just decided to keep on carrying on a conversation with the various objects in my room. Maybe it was the wine, I thought, but then dismissed the idea. I wasn't a lightweight when it came to alcohol.

"It's been over five years since I had sex," I said to the bedside lamp.

I decided saying it out loud was like therapy. Kind of like those things you say out loud to make you feel better about yourself. What were they called? Oh yeah, affirmations. I was really losing it. "A little sex and....well, actually it was a lot of sex and it was amazing sex so maybe it's like cocaine and now I'm addicted," I said to the telephone.

"Yup, it's all downhill from here," I said with a giggle. "Stealing money out of my daughter's piggybank to fund my next orgasm, I can see it now," I said to the fan in the window. This struck me as so funny I laughed out loud. I could just picture my first meeting of Oversexed Anonymous. *Hi, My name is Cassie and I'm a sexaholic.*

"Okay, you've lost your mind. Time to go to sleep, maybe your mind will return sometime during the night," I said aloud as I turned out the light.

A moment later I turned the light back on and went to brush my teeth again. When I crawled back in bed I was grumbling to myself. Then I lay there and stared into the darkness.

Damn, I couldn't turn my brain off. Pictures of John, above me, behind me, between my legs, driving me crazy, making me scream in ecstasy. All of the pictures crowded into my mind, keeping me aroused, keeping me awake. I wanted him here right now.

I twisted and turned, trying to find a comfortable position. It wasn't my position keeping me awake but I figured it was a harmless lie. I looked at the clock. It was 9:30. It wasn't late. Maybe I should give in and watch TV because the images in my mind were driving me crazy.

The phone rang. Who would be calling? It was too late for a telemarketer. My mom never called this late. The phone rang again. It was probably my ex-husband, George, making arrangements to get Sam this weekend.

Finally, I answered and there was silence on the other end. I said hello again. I was about to hang up when John said, "Did anyone ever tell you what a sexy voice you have?"

"No, why don't you tell me about it?" I laughed into the phone.

"It's especially sexy when you're moaning my name, but it's sexy all the time. In fact, at work I've heard other pilots talk about the fantasies they get in their heads when they hear your voice."

"That's not true," I said in disbelief.

"Yes it is; I wonder if there is a regulation or order somewhere about not giving pilots a hard-on while they're flying. What do you think?" John asked and I could hear the amusement in his voice.

"I don't believe you," I said primly.

"I didn't wake you did I?" he asked with a laugh.

"No I was just lying here, tossing and turning. I can't seem to shut my brain off," I said in exasperation.

"Hold that thought, I need to ask a favor."

"What do you need?"

"I talked to Josh and he's pretty upset."

"What's wrong?" I asked. I hadn't even met him but I was already worried about him.

He sighed before he spoke. "Just Sharon being Sharon, really, I don't know why I'm surprised by anything she does anymore."

He paused for a moment then continued. "Anyway, I told you she wants to go to Jamaica next week, right?"

"Yes, and she was trying to find someone to watch Josh."

"Right, well she found someone to watch him. Only problem is, it's her mother. Her mother isn't a very stable person. To tell you the truth, I'm surprised Sharon survived her childhood."

I bit back a catty remark about the apple not falling far from the tree and waited for him to continue.

"The other problem is, her mother lives in Colorado. So, unless I can get Josh by next Tuesday, he's going to be winging his way to Colorado to spend three weeks with his crazy grandmother. I don't even want to go into all of the problems it creates if I have to go get him in Colorado. Sharon's mother isn't too fond of me," he added in a dry tone.

"I've been on the phone since I hung up with Josh. That's why I'm calling so late. I got a buddy to swap with me. He'll take my flights on Tuesday if I can take his flights on Thursday. So, now I can go get Josh on Tuesday. I got a hold of Mrs. Sullivan. She's a great lady, by the way," he added, but didn't wait for me to respond before he continued.

"She said she would be fine keeping an eye on him Wednesday but she has a couple of Doctor's appointments on Thursday so she can't watch him then. I'm assuming you're off next Thursday, also, so I'm hoping you won't mind watching Josh for me. I know this is really pushing it, but I don't know what else to do. I managed to get some time off starting Friday, to get settled in, but Thursday is still an issue, so…"

"John….John….John," I repeated, trying to get his attention. He was angry and upset but, finally, the third time I said his name he paused.

"Yes, of course, I'll watch him for you. I don't have any other plans other than working out and I'm sure I can work it in somewhere. Even if I have to miss it, Josh is more important," I assured him.

"He's more important to you than he is to his mother and you haven't even met him yet," he said in disgust.

"Did the possibility of a trip to his grandmother's upset him?"

"I think that was part of it. He was so upset it was hard to understand everything he said but I think Sharon is playing mind games with him again. He said something about her telling him she'd changed her mind and was going back to court to get custody."

"Will she really do that?"

"Hell no, he cramps her style. But she does things like this to keep him under her thumb."

"You're kidding," I cried out in indignation. "How sad using your own child like to make yourself feel better. I try to give people the benefit of the doubt but she sounds like a Class A bitch."

"Uh-oh, I woke up mama tiger. Sharon has no idea how lucky she is you live so far away," he crowed.

"You've got that right. I'm not a violent person, but I have an amazing urge to slap her right now," I replied through gritted teeth.

"She tends to bring that out in people. But enough about her, I don't want to let thoughts of her ruin my night. There was something else I wanted to ask you?"

"What do you need?"

"I need to take you up on my rain check. I was wondering if you and Sam and I could do dinner tomorrow night. The twist is if you aren't afraid to let me into your kitchen, I'd like to make dinner for you."

"You don't need to. I mean, I'd love to have you over for dinner but you don't have to cook."

"Don't be afraid. I haven't killed anyone yet. Besides, I like to cook," he insisted.

"Okay, as long as you like to cook. Just don't do it because you think you owe me something."

"Why, the hell not?" he asked and he actually sounded angry. Before I could say anything he continued. "Cassie, you do amazing things for people all the time. You haven't even met Josh and you agreed to give up one of your days off to watch him. It's not fair to me, if you don't let me do things for you too. It makes me feel like a taker and I don't like feeling like that."

By the end of his diatribe his voice had softened a bit but I was still surprised at the strength of his feelings.

"I-I'm sorry. I've done everything for myself for so long, I guess I forgot how to accept help. Can we do that over again, please," I asked earnestly.

"Cassie, can I make dinner tomorrow night for you and Sam?" he asked promptly. He sure didn't hold a grudge, I thought. I realized how sick I'd been of the way George had pouted, sometimes for days, about a disagreement or some imagined slight.

"Why thank-you John, that would be lovely. Can I help in any way?" I asked in a pleasant voice.

"Good for you, you're a quick study," he said with a laugh. "You can help by telling me what time you'd like to have dinner and by letting me know if any foods are a no-no for you or Sam."

"Why don't we say five o'clock since I'm not sure if George is going to pick Sam up on Friday? If he calls I'll just tell him he can pick her up at seven and she can eat with us."

"Don't you have a set schedule for visitation?"

"Well he takes her most weekends because I work evenings on the weekends but I'm never sure if he's going to pick her up Friday night or Saturday morning until the last minute," I explained.

"How can you make plans?"

"Plans, what are plans?"

"I look forward to meeting your ex," he said grimly.

"He's actually a nice guy. Most people like him. He's a good father too; he's just not good husband material," I said matter-of-factly.

"You'll pardon me if I reserve judgment," he said with a snort.

"So, I should probably let you go and get some sleep," He said when we'd finished discussing all our plans for the following day.

"If I can sleep," I mumbled.

"Oh yeah, that's right. What's going on in your brain you can't turn off?"

I hesitated, feeling a little vulnerable about telling him it was images of him keeping me awake.

"Come on, let Dr. John cure your insomnia," he said coaxingly.

"Hard to be the cure when you're the cause," I grumbled.

He didn't say anything for a moment and I wanted to kick myself for opening my big mouth again. Then his deep voice rumbled in a near whisper, "Hmmm, I believe I do have the cure for what ails you."

I could almost see the lecherous twinkle in his eye.

"Yeah, and its thirty minutes away," I grumbled again. I just couldn't seem to help myself.

"You know what I keep thinking about?"

The husky rumble of his voice reached down into my belly and kicked the butterflies back into motion. He hadn't said anything suggestive but the timber of his voice started a low burn in my bloodstream.

"I keep seeing you bent over the counter with my dick sliding in and out of you. I get hard every time I think about it."

My breath left me in a whoosh. His words were like gasoline on a spark and suddenly I was on fire.

"You are not making it better!" I groaned.

"Yes, but anticipation is the key. Just think of what I'll do to you the next time I see you. I can't wait to get inside you again and I want you ready for me," he said in a gravelly purr.

"Now turn out the light and dream of me. The Doctor will see you tomorrow."

"Okay, I'll see you tomorrow," I said with a sigh of frustration.

"Count on it," he responded softly. "Sweet dreams."

Despite my inability to settle, eventually, I slept. My night was filled with erotic images of John's naked body intertwined with mine in every conceivable way but the dreams never awakened me. In the morning I felt like I'd been the victim of several hours of foreplay with no corresponding release. I lay there wishing I could roll over into John's arms, but I would see him in a couple of hours. The thought forced me out of my warm cocoon into the cool morning air.

I enjoyed a long shower, taking extra time shaving my legs and conditioning my hair. I felt like a royal consort being prepared for an evening with the king. It gave me a little thrill of naughtiness. Normally I would be rushing to complete my morning ritual but today I felt like being pampered. I just couldn't seem to stop smiling. Even when Sam woke up cranky my smile never dimmed. I teased and cajoled and tickled her until she was just as sunny as me.

Right before heading out to the car to take Sam to school I remembered to call George to find out about his plans. I called him at his office and managed to catch him at his desk.

"Hi, George, you're actually in the office, huh?"

"Who's this?"

I almost laughed out loud. He liked to play games but I was in too good a mood to let it bother me. "It's Cassie, George, you remember me don't you?" I asked with a laugh.

"Oh, Cassie, I guess I didn't recognize your voice," he said and I rolled my eyes.

"I'm calling to see when you are going to come and get Sam. I'm about to take her to school and I want to be able to tell her what's happening."

160

I knew if it was for Sam, he would be a little more forthcoming with his information.

"I was planning on picking her up tonight but I can't get there until after dinner. How about eight o'clock?"

"That's fine, I'm having a friend over for dinner and we won't be finished until about seven o'clock anyway."

"Really, anyone I know?" George asked and I could've kicked myself for saying anything.

"No, no one you know. I've got to go George or Sam will be late for school. See you tonight," I said, cutting him off from any further interrogation.

As I strapped Sam into the car seat I told her about her father's plans to pick her up after dinner. She was happy because her father had promised to take her to the zoo the next day. I always missed her when she was away but I was glad she was going to be able to do the activities she loved.

"So, Sam, guess what?" I asked as we turned out of the driveway.

"What Mommy?"

"You remember John Clay?" I asked and looked in the rearview mirror to see her nod.

"Well, he's going to come over and cook dinner for us tonight. What do you think about that?"

"What's he going to make?" she asked in the typically pragmatic way of a six year-old.

I told her it was a surprise. Sam chewed on my response for a second and then asked, "Is he your boyfriend now?"

"He's a friend and I really like him. But we don't know each other very well so we want to spend some time getting to know each other," I answered after an initial moment of panic.

She seemed to take me at my word. I figured while we were on the subject I might as well tell her about Josh.

"Did I tell you he has a son? His name is Josh."

"Yeah momma," Sam responded as she looked out the window.

"Well Josh is moving up here next week to live with his Dad and I'm going to watch him on Thursday since his Dad has to fly. He'll probably have dinner with us."

I watched Sam in the rear view mirror, trying to gauge her reaction to the news.

Sam shrugged and said, "He's a boy. Boys aren't fun to play with."

You won't always feel that way but I hope it's not until you're at least thirty.

"Well he's moving to a new place and he's going to a new school, your school, by the way. So, he might be a little nervous. It would be nice if you could make him feel welcome, Okay?"

"Okay, momma," Sam replied. I wondered if Sam had taken in even a third of what I'd said but decided to let the subject drop.

After leaving Sam at the school I made a quick stop at the local coffee shop. Rhonda would certainly need a coffee this morning after all of her hard work yesterday. Fifteen minutes later I pulled into her driveway and parked behind John's Jeep.

I carried the drinks inside and called out Rhonda's name. There was no answer. I set the drinks down and walked upstairs to check around. No one was there either. Just then I heard the front door close.

I went back downstairs and still didn't see anyone. I walked toward the kitchen and suddenly a hand reached out and spun me around. I landed against John's chest. His eyes were lit with a devilish glint.

"The Doctor will see you now."

The last word was said against my lips as he covered my mouth with his own. Within seconds I was wrapped around him like a second skin. My body already knew the contours of his and seemed to automatically fit itself against him like an interlocking piece of a jigsaw puzzle. I slid my fingers through his hair and held him in place, giving in to all of my pent up passion.

His hands slid down to my waist and then onward to cup my bottom, pulling me snug against him. He was already hard and the feel of his firm length was enough to send my body into overdrive. I moaned deep in my throat and my nipples hardened against his chest. A flame leapt to life deep in my belly as I felt warm wetness moisten my underwear.

The sound of the door opening and closing brought us to our senses and made us spring apart. Both of us were gasping for breath and flushed with desire. The time it took for Rhonda to walk around the corner to where we were standing, was enough to get our breathing under control. But it was not enough time to mask any of the other signs of what we'd been doing.

"Hey Cassie, what's up? John thought you had come over here. We were next door having some of Mary's coffee cake and he said he'd come and let you know...."

Rhonda's voice trailed off as she took in the state of our clothes. John's hair was showing evidence I'd been passionately running my hands through it thirty seconds earlier. My lips felt swollen and I was sure my face still had the flushed look of someone who had been thoroughly kissed.

"I see he found you," Rhonda said with a little smile playing around her lips. "I guess I should have had another piece of coffee cake," she teased.

My already flushed face heated even more. "I-I brought coffee," I said in a desperate attempt to change the subject. John just stood there, not in the least embarrassed. In fact, he looked slightly amused at my blush. I walked over and got the coffee and gave one to each of them. I took a sip of tea, more for something to do than anything else.

"So, what can I do to help?" I asked when I felt sufficiently composed.

"Well my brother Carl isn't here with the truck yet; no big surprise there, huh?" Rhonda asked with a laugh. "I was thinking since it's such a beautiful day out we could stack everything in the yard. It will give us a better idea of how everything will fit in the truck. Plus, then loading the truck should go really quickly once Carl deigns to show up," Rhonda ended with a sarcastic dig at her brother. Rhonda adored her brother but his tardiness was legendary.

"Sounds good to me, where do you want me to start?" I asked as I looked around at all of the boxes and furniture.

"Normally, I'd wait for Carl to get here for the big stuff but since I've got two strong fit types right here, let's move some of the heavy stuff while we still have some energy," she replied and started up the stairs.

Chapter 8

John

I thought it would be better to wait for Carl to get there before we started lifting heavy things but figured I should keep that to myself. I smiled when I thought of the reaction I'd probably get from Cassie if I told her to let the men take care of the heavy stuff. I was tempted to say something just to get a rise out of her. I settled for following her up the stairs, watching her delectable ass sway back and forth just out of my reach.

By the time Carl showed up with the truck we'd emptied out the upstairs and made a good-sized dent in the downstairs. The front yard was three quarters full of furniture and stacks of boxes. Rhonda was very organized and had numbered the boxes in order of the likelihood she would need the contents.

I was impressed with Rhonda's organization, but I was more impressed with Cassie. She was unstoppable. She lifted and carried anything asked of her. She worked just as hard as me and with no complaints. She made helpful suggestions but didn't insist things be done her way. Sharon would have sat around, insisting on directing everything and generally creating confusion.

Cassie was so easy to work with I didn't even realize how much we'd accomplished in a little over two hours until I took a look around the yard. My muscles were sore so I knew hers must be, but she stood there, rocking back and forth on her feet, waiting for new instructions. When Rhonda called for a break for lunch I walked over to Cassie and started rubbing her shoulders.

"Oh boy, I'll give you about two hours to stop that." she said with a smile as her head collapsed forward onto her chest.

"Sore?"

"A little bit, but it's a good type of sore. It just feels like I've been physically active. I like that feeling."

She groaned as I hit a particularly sensitive spot between her shoulder blades. Then she just stood there quietly and enjoyed my ministrations. Finally, with a little stretch she straightened and said, "Enough, you'll put me to sleep. Besides, it's your turn."

I relinquished her shoulders and she turned and directed me to sit on a chair in the yard. She started kneading my shoulders and I moaned in contentment. I had large dense muscles and she really had to work at them. She used her elbows

Flight to Forever

to make up for the lack of strength in her fingers and my muscles started to relax.

"God, you're good at this," I said as I slumped in my chair.

I would have let her continue forever but Rhonda dragged Carl over to meet me. "This is my brother Carl, you can tell because he's the one who showed up right at lunch time," she said by way of introduction.

Carl held a hand out for a shake. "Just good planning as far as I'm concerned," he said with a laugh as he shook my hand.

He wasn't quite as tall as me but he was muscular and good looking with dark hair and light eyes. Couldn't any of Cassie's acquaintances be ugly? Carl turned and enveloped Cassie in a bear hug.

"Cassie, how are you. I haven't seen you in ages."

Cassie smiled and hugged him back. I could tell they were good friends by the easy camaraderie between them but I couldn't help a jolt of jealousy as Cassie rocked back and forth in Carl's arms for a minute.

169

"I know Carl, and now that Rhonda's moving are we ever going to see you up here again?" she asked as she stepped back from his hug.

"Now, you know I would walk across a burning desert in bare feet just to see your lovely face," he answered with a twinkle in his eyes.

Cassie snorted. "You must have Irish blood in you because you are full of blarney."

"Cassie I am hurt, deeply hurt," he said in mock indignation with his hands across his heart.

"Yeah, yeah, yeah, save it for someone who will be taken in by your lines," Rhonda cut in with a laugh. "It's time for lunch. Some of us have worked up an appetite," she added as she poked her brother in the shoulder.

Cassie offered to drive since she had a minivan and her car was the last one in the driveway. Rhonda declared she who drove got to pick the restaurant. Carl headed toward the front seat but with a little conspiratorial smile at Cassie, Rhonda grabbed him and asked him to sit in back with her. Cassie blushed when she realized Rhonda had purposely maneuvered it so I would sit up front.

She took us to a restaurant at the mall known for its quick service and its large selection of foods. As we were walking across the parking lot, I took her hand in mine and held it until we got inside. Then I ushered her into a seat in a booth and slid in next to her. She looked surprised but didn't seem to mind. Carl caught my eye for a moment and tipped his head at me with a little smile. Message received.

I knew I was establishing my claim on Cassie in the eyes of Carl and any other male in the vicinity. It was stupid and somewhat Neanderthal but I couldn't seem to stop myself. I wondered if Cassie would be angry or amused if I admitted my caveman tendencies. Hell, I would be amused by the whole thing if it didn't scare the hell out of me. Where she was concerned I couldn't seem to help myself.

Lunch was relaxing and fun. Carl kept everyone amused with tales of his latest hunting trip. Then I told some bizarre, believe-it-or-not stories from some of my flights. By the time I was finished Rhonda swore she wasn't sure if she would ever fly again. I told her after listening to Carl's stories I wasn't sure if I'd ever go in the woods again.

Finally, sore from laughing, we gave in and headed back to the house to finish loading the truck. Despite all of his statements about avoiding work, Carl was a very hard worker.

He and I started loading the truck after Rhonda explained her numbering system. The women continued to empty the house and let us devise the loading strategy.

The truck was loaded and the house empty by three o'clock. Rhonda kept things clean as she packed so a little sweeping was all there was left to do. By half past three they were ready to get on the road. Mrs. Sullivan came out and she and Cassie said a tearful good-bye to Rhonda with lots of promises to keep in touch. Carl and I stood around watching the leave-taking with a good amount of eye-rolling.

Carl finally said good-bye to everyone and climbed in the truck. He told Rhonda they really should get on the road since they had a long trip ahead of them. Rhonda handed the house keys to me. "You take good care of everything, you hear, and I'm not just talking about the house," she said with no compunction about her meddling.

I shook her hand and nodded. "I'll treat everything with tender loving care."

Rhonda held onto my hand for a moment and then must have decided I was sincere and released me to say one more good-bye to Cassie. Finally, Carl honked the horn and threw up his hands in exasperation. Cassie and Rhonda broke apart laughing. Mrs. Sullivan and Cassie and I waved as they drove away.

Cassie gave me a couple of suggestions on supermarkets before heading off to the school to pick up Sam. I was pulling into her driveway by four thirty. She came out the door as I stepped out of the car and helped me unload the groceries. I found I enjoyed the homey feel of Cassie greeting me at the door then quickly banished the thought from my head. No complications, that's what I wanted. Right?

She gave me a brief tour of the kitchen cabinets, poured me a glass of wine and then asked if I wanted her to make herself scarce.

"Well, if you have something to do then I don't want to keep you from it but if not, I'd like the company. I like to talk while I cook and I might just put you to work."

She told me she'd be right back and went to check on Sam. She came back laughing, wondering aloud if Sam even knew she existed when the television was on. She pulled out a stool at the center island and settled in with a glass of wine to watch me create. I started chopping vegetables, my knife practically flying. I'd gotten so used to using a knife expertly I'd forgotten how it appeared to others until Cassie spoke.

"You've done this before," she said drolly.

I glanced up from the cutting board for a moment and smiled. "Well it started as an attempt to achieve marital bliss."

She arched her eyebrow enquiringly and waited for me to continue.

"Are you sure you want to hear this? I feel like I'm always ragging on Sharon and I don't want to be one of those people everyone avoids because they never stop complaining."

I continued to chop with my eyes on my fingers until I finished speaking and then looked up to gauge her response.

"Actually, I think you've been very circumspect about Sharon. You've only discussed her when you've had to explain the background of various problems you're having." She hesitated for a moment, and then continued. "I know what you mean, though. I was so hurt and angry by the time my marriage ended I found it difficult to even mention George's name without being nasty. It took me a while to let go of the anger." She paused for a moment of introspection before continuing.

"I realized the real problem we had was we were too different and we wanted different things out of marriage. Once I realized everything George did wasn't a deliberate insult to me, it

174

became easier to relax. He does play games still but I think it is more a passive aggressive response he has to his hurt. I divorced him and he hasn't gotten over the rejection. I mean, I don't think he was any happier than I was during the marriage; but since I filed for the divorce it still rankles."

She watched me slice steak into thin slices for a moment. I didn't say anything, figuring she would continue when she was ready. She seemed to spend a few moments contemplating what she wanted to say before she spoke again.

"The difference I see here, though, is George has always tried to do what is best for Sam. He never puts her between us. If he wants to be angry at me and aggravate me, fine, as long as he doesn't hurt Sam. But, from what you've told me about Sharon, she deliberately puts Josh between you and that I can't stand. Children's psyches are so vulnerable to their parents' attitudes. To devastate a child, just to get back at the other parent, is indefensible as far as I'm concerned," she said fiercely.

"I agree. Sharon's treatment of Josh was the last straw in our marriage."

I paused for a moment, reliving the deterioration of my marriage in my mind. I never wanted to have to go through such pain again.

"You don't have to tell me anything you don't want to, but I'll listen. And I am curious about your culinary expertise," Cassie said with an encouraging smile.

I wasn't sure where to start so I didn't say anything for a few minutes. She just waited quietly for me to continue.

"I should probably give you a little background. I knew Sharon in high school. Well, I can't say I really knew her. I wasn't one of the popular kids and Sharon was probably one of the most popular kids in school. She was beautiful, a cheerleader, homecoming queen, the whole enchilada. We knew of each other, but we didn't really know each other, you know what I mean?"

I glanced at Cassie and she just nodded.

"I went into the Navy and became a fighter pilot. I also grew about a half a foot, put on about sixty pounds of muscle and got a little confidence in myself. So, I went back home to visit and Sharon practically fell all over me. I think she was excited about seeing the world and she enjoyed the cachet of being involved with a fighter pilot. I was so flattered by her attention. I mean, she wanted me when she could have had anyone. I just ignored all of the warning signs....and there were a lot of them."

I had to shake my head at the thought of all the signs I'd ignored over the years just hoping things would get better. I put aside all of the chopped meat and vegetables and started making batter for fortune cookies while I collected my thoughts.

"Anyway, by the time I realized what a mistake I'd made, Josh had arrived and I tried even harder to make things work. Sharon was completely self-involved. Everything was always about her. I spent a lot of time thinking if I just did this or just did that, then things would get better. I got out of the Navy because she was so angry when I was always gone. But then she didn't like losing the cool factor of being a fighter pilot's wife."

I beat the batter until it was smooth before continuing. "She was always trying something new, always searching for something, and I was willing to try anything to make things work. Cooking was one of those things. Sharon got it in her head she wanted to be a gourmet chef and she signed up for all of these classes. I was still trying to prove ....well I don't know if I was trying to prove anything. It was more along the lines of trying to find something, anything that would bring us closer together, for Josh's sake mostly. But half way through the classes I could tell she was already bored with the whole thing."

"It was really no surprise; I knew it would happen all along. You know those little lies you tell yourself and hope they'll turn out to be true?"

Cassie just nodded. She was a good listener. She didn't push; just let me tell my story in my own way.

"Anyway, the big surprise was I loved the classes. It was fascinating to me and I discovered it was a great form of relaxation. Sharon didn't mind, at first, because it was one more thing she didn't have to do. But after a while she began to resent it because it was something I enjoyed and it had nothing to do with her."

I finished stirring the batter and set it aside. All of the fixings were ready so I leaned against the counter and took a sip of wine before continuing my story.

"Sharon got worse and worse with Josh. He was becoming a timid kid; afraid of his own shadow. So, we got divorced. I figured it was me she was angry at and once I wasn't around, her relationship with Josh would improve. I was also out of town a lot on layovers, so it just made sense Sharon should get custody. God, what a mistake!"

The devastation I felt must have been plain on my face because Cassie got up and walked around to give me a hug. She just held me for a minute without speaking. I liked the comfort it gave me so I rested my cheek against the top of her head and continued. "I'll never forget when his teacher called me. She was worried about a story Josh had written. She'd already called Sharon but she just dismissed it as unimportant. The teacher thought it was important enough to follow up on so she went and got the emergency locator card from the office and called me. Thank God for her."

I shuddered at the remembered terror I'd felt on receiving the phone call. Cassie must have felt it because she gave me a squeeze and started rubbing my back.

"So, I went in to meet with the teacher and she showed me this paper Josh wrote. It was so surreal. It was in this little kid's handwriting, he was just eight, but it was all about suicide."

Cassie made a small gasp of alarm but still she didn't say anything.

"He wrote it like he was telling a story about someone else. It's about this boy who knows no one loves him but he's heard God loves everyone so he figures if he dies and goes to live with God he'll finally be loved. I was so petrified. I felt like I couldn't move fast enough."

My hands trembled at the memory. I couldn't believe I might have lost him.

"I called a friend who was a lawyer and told him the whole story. I told him I wanted custody and I didn't care what we had to do as long as we didn't hurt Josh. I didn't want him to feel any more pain. My friend said he'd file the paperwork. Then I went to Sharon. I told her I was suing for custody and I would do whatever I had to do to win. I was like a crazy man. I had always been relatively easygoing with Sharon but not this time. I think she knew I was deadly serious. She really didn't want Josh anyway, so she didn't put up much of a fight. I went right into Josh's room and told him he was coming to live with me. He just crumbled, he cried for hours."

My voice cracked and I had to pause to compose myself. I couldn't believe the retelling of the story was almost as painful as the event.

"I got him into therapy right away and he made a quick turnaround. I had to do some really fancy footwork to adjust my work schedule and find daycare for him but it's amazing what you can do out of desperation."

I kissed her on the top of the head and released her. I was a bit embarrassed I had gotten so emotional. Cassie just went up on her toes to give me a little kiss and then poured some more wine before returning to her seat.

"Everything has been great. He has really blossomed into an outgoing wonderful child and it's hard to tell he was ever fragile. That is until now. I made this move because it was the only place where I could be guaranteed to be home almost every night and still be able to fly. I still have some layovers but it's not anywhere close to a normal crew schedule."

"So, I had to come up here to get established. The last place I wanted to leave Josh was with Sharon but they've been doing pretty well together. Josh said he actually wanted to stay there. His therapist said, since it was temporary, it was okay and it would give him a chance to work through some issues with his mother. But when I talked to him last night it was almost as if the last two years never happened."

I knew I'd had no other choice and I'd done everything I could to mitigate any problems that might come up but I also knew if anything happened to Josh I would never be able to forgive myself.

"When I told him this morning I was coming to get him on Tuesday he seemed to get some of his confidence back. I just hope he hasn't lost a lot of ground because of this."

Cassie finally spoke. "John, I'm not just saying this to make you feel better. I really think once he gets here with you and has love and stability again instead of selfishness and uncertainty, he'll bounce right back. You said the change before was remarkable but now he has the added bonus of being able to look forward to building a new life here. He can really put all of the past behind him," she said earnestly.

"I hope you're right. But hey, I just meant to tell you about cooking. I didn't mean to drop all this other stuff on you. It just proves you're a good listener."

I was grateful to her for listening but now I'd gotten it all out of my system I hoped she didn't see me as a candy ass crybaby.

"I know how important it was to me to have someone to talk to after my divorce. Rhonda and Trish were always there for me and my friend Jasmine was a big help too. I'll listen anytime you need to talk."

I couldn't believe she just dropped the subject. She let me get it all out, offered support and didn't beat the subject to death. *Where they heck was she ten years ago?*

"In a few minutes I'll have a fun job for you and Sam if you can tear her away from the TV."

"Hmmm, sounds interesting, I'll go see what I can do," she said and headed off to the TV room.

It actually took about ten minutes to coax Sam away from the TV and get her into the kitchen. She grumbled a little as she came through the doorway but I just ignored it and smiled at her.

"Sam, I am so glad you can help because you are perfect for this job."

Sam's frown didn't disappear completely but she looked like her interest had been piqued.

"You see, I have big clumsy hands and this job requires small graceful hands."

I continued as if she was already enthusiastic about helping. I'd learned with Josh it was all in how you approached things.

"I noticed when I watched you at gymnastics the other night you have just the kind of hands I need. So do you think you and your mom could help me out here? I'd really appreciate it."

Sam looked at me with barely concealed curiosity and asked, "What do I have to do?"

"You're going to make fortune cookies."

Sam's eyes widened. "Really?" she asked in excitement. Cassie looked as if she thought it was pretty cool herself.

"Yes, Ma'am," I nodded. "I'll show you how to do the first one and then you and your mom can finish the rest, deal?" I asked and stuck out my hand for a handshake.

Sam was practically bouncing with excitement when she shook my hand. I pulled a step stool over so Sam could reach the counter with ease. I separated out a bit of the batter and set it aside. Cassie gave me a curious look but I just smiled at her.

"Okay, this is what you have to do. Sam, have you ever heard of crepes?"

Sam shook her head. "Well crepes are French and they are like really thin pancakes. This batter is almost like crepe batter but a few of the ingredients are different so, instead of staying soft like crepes, these will get crunchy like fortune cookies. Do you understand?" I asked and waited for her nod before I went on.

"Okay, the first part your mom will have to do because it's the hot part," I said and showed them how to smear the batter into the pan in a very thin circle.

"The first one will take a little longer because the pan is not as hot but it'll get faster and faster as you go along, okay?"

Sam was mesmerized and nodded again.

"Now Sam, here is your part. Are you ready?"

I stood behind Sam so I could guide her fingers.

"See, we flip this little pancake out onto the counter. Then we give it a few seconds to cool off so we don't burn our fingers." I touched the unformed cookie and danced around like I'd been burned. It was evident from my expression I was kidding and Sam started giggling.

"Okay, give me your hands."

I reached out and took her hands in mine.

"You don't want to wait too long because then it will harden before you fold it. You take one of these fortunes and you put it in the middle then you fold the cookie around it like this." I showed her how to fold it and Sam crowed with delight when she saw the result looked just like a fortune cookie.

"Do you think you and your mom can handle it now or do you want me to show you one more time?"

Sam asked me to demonstrate again and was just as delighted at the result. I left them to it after a glance at Cassie to make sure she was comfortable with it.

I put some rice on to boil and then began assembling the ingredients I'd chopped to get ready to stir-fry. I asked Cassie if she had a large frying pan. She glanced at the ingredients and asked if I'd rather have a wok.

"You've got a wok?"

"When I started trying to get in shape and lose weight I learned all about the benefits of stir-frying," she said by way of explanation and pointed at the cabinet where she kept the wok.

They were making the cookies faster and faster and she didn't have a moment to get it for me. I found the wok without a problem and was impressed with its quality. She'd obviously cured it and kept it well oiled. I hadn't had a wok since the divorce and looked forward to using one again. I glanced over at Cassie and Sam and had to smile when I saw they were getting sloppier and sloppier as the speed picked up. They were also laughing harder and harder trying to keep up and their joy in the simple made me laugh also.

When Cassie and Sam finished, amidst peals of laughter, I asked them to find serving bowls for me and set the table. When I had everything ready I shooed them upstairs to wash up for dinner. While they were gone I quickly made a few extra fortune cookies with special fortunes in them and then hid them before Cassie and Sam came back.

I wasn't sure how Sam was going to react to the food but she had two helpings. I figured it was always easier to get a kid to eat something they'd helped create. After her second helping she begged to have a fortune cookie.

The dinner was a success. Cassie looked relaxed and happy and my fortunes had Sam giggling with glee. She didn't even complain when her Mom asked her to bus her dishes and help load the dishwasher. The cleaning was almost as much fun as the dinner. All of us ended up with soap bubbles in our hair and damp clothes. My abdominal muscles were sore from laughing so hard. The only thing missing was Josh.

It was only five after seven when I saw headlights and heard a car driving down the driveway. Cassie sent Sam upstairs to get her stuff. She was shaking her head when she dried her hands and headed for the door. When I asked what she was thinking she laughed.

"Well, I just find it interesting George couldn't get here until eight. Then he heard I had a mystery guest coming for a dinner that was supposed to go until about seven and surprise, surprise, here he is at five after seven."

"We could give him a show." I said as I grabbed her hand and twirled her into my arms.

She kissed me lightly on the lips and said, "Behave, I would love to give him a show but I hear Sam coming and I don't want to confuse her."

I thought that was a strange thing to say but I let her go to open the door. Before she had a chance to say anything, Sam came racing past her and leapt on her father, yelling, "Hi Daddy."

George swung her around in a big hug saying, "How's my favorite daughter?"

Sam giggled. "I'm your only daughter, Daddy."

The greeting looked like a well known ritual. George put Sam down and turned to Cassie. "So you actually cooked dinner, huh?"

Looks like old George is looking to get his clock cleaned. Just talk to Cassie like that one more time in my presence.

Sam answered for her. "No, Mr. Clay cooked dinner and it was yummy. Mommy and me made the fortune cookies. They're really funny and I brung some with me. You can have one, they're really good. Mommy and me did a good job but they look kind of funny because we had to work so fast," she said, seemingly all in one breath.

Sam's remark made me laugh along with everyone else. I figured I couldn't very well knock George out in front of Sam anyway, although when Cassie introduced us I probably gripped his hand a little harder than I had to. When George asked how we knew each other I was tempted to tell him it was in the biblical sense but opted for the truth.

"I'm a pilot for Nationwide. Cassie saved my life a while ago and I came up to the Tower to thank her. The rest, as they say, is history."

The expression on George's face was comical. Even Cassie had a smirk on her face.

"Mr. Clay told me mommy saved him three times," Sam said with a solemn look on her face.

It was obvious he wanted to know more but he couldn't bring himself to admit it so he fell back on sarcasm. "Well, it seems Cassie is quite the hero. So, gratitude gets you a home cooked meal, huh?" George said with a smirk.

I saw the look of pain flash across Cassie's face and I revisited the idea of punching him out. I could almost see her drawing back into her shell, feeling unattractive and unworthy of male attention. I'd be damned if I was going to let this prick ruin all my hard work.

Cassie stepped back almost as if she'd been slapped. I stepped behind her and wrapped my arms around her from behind in a very possessive gesture. I pulled her back against my chest, effectively halting her escape, and gently rubbed a hand up and down her arm.

I could see George recognized the gesture for what it was. I was staking my claim and making sure he knew it. I was also silently establishing that I was protective of Cassie. George understood the silent communication even if Cassie was completely unaware of the signals. I knew he got it but I wasn't going to leave anything to chance. There would be no misunderstandings.

"Gratitude only goes so far. It got me into the Tower. Everything afterward is a direct response to Cassie's other attributes. She is warm and caring and beautiful and sensual. Now I'm just grateful she is willing to spend time with me. But I'm sure you are well aware of how amazing she is, after all, you were married to her," I said with a smile.

George looked nonplussed. I could tell he knew he'd been outmaneuvered and decided it was time to retreat. He mumbled a response and then told Sam, who was completely oblivious to all of the adults' power struggles, they had to get going. Sam gave her mom a big hug and a loud smacking kiss on the cheek. Then, to my surprise, she reached for me and repeated the embrace.

"Good-night Mr. Clay, thank-you for teaching me how to make fortune cookies," she said very politely.

My heart turned over in my chest and I hugged her back and ruffled her hair.

"If it's ok with your mom, you can call me John, if you want to," I said as I looked at Cassie for approval.

"Sure that's fine with me." Cassie said with a smile.

Sam grinned in delight and said, "Good-night John." She puffed up with importance when she said it.

We stood at the door and waved as Sam walked to the car. When George began to back out of the driveway Cassie shut the door. She looked self-conscious now that Sam was gone and she was alone with me. I wasn't going to let us go backwards. I wasn't sure what she was coming up with in that head of hers but I was pretty sure it was not even close to what I was thinking. It was time to lay everything out on the table. I wasn't going to let her use George as an excuse to pull away from me.

I grabbed her hand and pulled her back into the living room.

"You and I have to talk."

Chapter 9

Cassie

I followed along behind with a sense of foreboding. John grabbed my shoulders and guided me down onto the couch and poured us each some more wine. Then he sat on the coffee table facing me rather than on the couch next to me. Before he could say anything I leaned forward and spoke.

"I really appreciate what you said to George. It was nice of you to stick up for me. I just want you to know I won't hold you to....I mean it was great of you to say all those nice things about me but I don't want you to worry that I think it changes our relationship or..."

I began to stammer and my voice faded as John's expression changed from amused to incredulous to a complete lack of any expression at all. The only evidence he was feeling anything at all was a muscle ticking in his cheek.

"Cassie I can't quite decide if I'm angry or insulted or just frustrated I didn't punch George when I had the chance."

"W-what," I asked uncertainly.

"I felt your reaction when George made the crack about gratitude. You really believed his bullshit. I think a part of you knows he was just trying to yank your chain but you fell for it anyway," he said with a disbelieving shake of his head.

"Well you are grateful to me, you said so yourself," I cut in.

John sighed. "Cassie how do you see our relationship? I mean what do you think we are doing here?"

"Well it's hard to define," I said with a shrug. "I mean, I know we're friends, but it's more because...well.... we sleep together, but I already told you I'm okay with it because you let me know up front you didn't want anything more."

"Christ!" John ground out as he leapt to his feet. He paced back and forth for a moment before he stopped suddenly and looked at me with a frown.

"Cassie, are you interested in seeing other people. I mean, do you see me as just someone to take the edge off every once in a while?" he asked bluntly.

What type of person did he think I was? I jumped to my feet and got in his face and told him exactly what I thought of his insinuations. After a moment he grabbed my arm to try to get me to stop and when that didn't work he finally put his hand gently but firmly across my mouth.

"Cassie, I'm not trying to insinuate anything, I'm just trying to make sure I know what you want from this relationship. No more assumptions, okay? I'm going to tell you straight out where I'm coming from all right?" he asked and waited for my acknowledgement.

John cupped my face with his hands and said gently. "I did not say all of that stuff to George to be a nice guy, honey. I meant every word of it. And I never said I didn't want a relationship with you. I said my life was complicated and I couldn't make any promises. I meant long-term promises. I consider us to be a couple for as long as it lasts. When I say couple I mean exclusive couple. When I sleep with a woman she is the only one I'm sleeping with, no matter how old fashioned it is, and I expect the same from her."

He paused for a moment and when I started to speak he forestalled me with a finger against my lip again and continued.

"I'm angry because it pisses me off an incredible woman like you should be so insecure as to think I would make love to you out of gratitude. I'm insulted because, even though you've only known me a short time I feel like you know me well enough to know I couldn't make love to you the way I did without caring for you. And, I want to punch George because he is a selfish son of a bitch who deliberately hurts you to make up for his own inadequacy," he said and his fury was evident as he finished the statement.

"But I made sure tonight George very much sees us as a couple. I see us as a couple. Despite your worry about confusing Sam, I think she sees us as a couple. What I need to know is how you see us and what you want because I'm feeling pretty vulnerable here?" he finished with a wry smile.

He didn't remove his finger from my lips, almost as if he was afraid to let me speak, afraid to find out what my answer would be. Finally, I kissed his finger lightly and pulled it away from my mouth.

"Yes," I said simply.

"Yes, what?" he asked and it killed me to see the uncertainty in his eyes I felt responsible for.

"Yes I want us to be a couple, I want it very much," I answered and had to look away because my eyes were filling with tears.

"Thank-God," he breathed as he finally pulled me into his arms. He just held me, rocking back and forth. I was surprised by how much it seemed to mean to him, surprised and happy.

He stepped away for a moment and sat down on the couch then pulled me into his lap. He picked up his glass of wine, handed mine to me, and leaned back against the back of the couch. He seemed content to just sit there, with me on his lap, and sip his wine.

I couldn't stop touching him. I traced the contours of his face with my fingers. I touched him as if I couldn't quite believe he was real. It was as if I was trying to reassure myself he was really there, and he wanted me. I kept waiting for the other shoe to drop. But then I decided I would enjoy this while it lasted and try to stop thinking about the future.

I put my wine down and took his hand in mine. I splayed my fingers against his, comparing our hands, reveling in the differences. His large strong hands dwarfed my smaller more delicate ones. But I knew how gentle his could be and I shivered as I remembered how they had looked against my pale skin.

Something hot flared in his eyes and I just knew he was remembering the same thing. He had said no more assumptions. It was difficult for me to make myself vulnerable. I'd protected myself by erecting a wall and never giving anyone the key. But he had gone out on a limb so it was only fair I should climb out there with him. I smiled at him and said, "Will you stay with me tonight?"

"I was hoping you'd ask. I checked out of my hotel this morning. I figured there was a bed in the apartment but I was really hoping to stay here with you." He raised my hand up to his mouth and kissed my palm.

He locked eyes with me and slowly swirled his tongue around my index finger. He sucked the finger into his mouth and then slowly released it. "Do you trust me, Cassie?" he asked softly.

"Yes," I answered without hesitation.

He smiled at me. "Well, I planned some activities for tonight." He hesitated a moment. "They are probably a little kinky. I want you to know we won't do anything you are uncomfortable with and I'm hoping you know me well enough to know I only want to please you. Are you willing to put your body in my hands, no questions asked, and trust I'll take care of you?" he asked in a husky voice.

I was a little nervous but also surprised the thought of giving up all control to him made me very aroused. I was not worried he would abuse my trust. I was more worried I would somehow, fail to satisfy him.

"Yes, I trust you."

His eyes darkened with desire. "Thank-you," he said simply. He lifted me to my feet, told me to wait right there and went out to his car. He came back with an overnight bag. He took my hand and led me toward the kitchen. He took some fortune cookies out of the cabinet and handed them to me. I gave him a puzzled look but he just took my hand again and led me upstairs to my room.

John set his overnight bag down on a chair and put some soft music on my stereo. He turned to me and the look in his eyes was enough to make me shiver in anticipation.

"These are special fortune cookies I made just for us. Each one contains a fantasy of some kind. You choose one and read the fortune which determines what we do. I know I'm asking a lot for you to agree sight unseen. If anything gets uncomfortable for you, just say the word. Ok?" he asked softly.

"I'm all yours."

The heat flared again in his eyes as he held out the plate of fortune cookies to me. I selected one and started to open it. He stopped me for a moment and said, "I just want you to know I'm not expecting you to do all the trusting here. Next time it's my turn to choose a fortune, okay?"

I smiled at him and broke open the cookie. I unfolded the paper and read aloud.

"I am your captive."

John didn't speak. He just reached forward and started unbuttoning my blouse. He pulled my blouse off and his eyes smoldered when he saw I was wearing a black satin and lace teddy that barely covered my nipples. He lightly ran his fingers over them, coaxing them to harden even more. I shivered and arched my back at his touch.

John unbuttoned my pants and slid them down my legs. He knelt in front of me and helped me take them off along with my shoes and socks. He ran his hands up my legs to the swell of my ass and held me there as he pressed his face to the thin fabric covering me.

"I can smell your desire. It's the most beautiful smell in the world," he said as he dropped a light kiss at the vee of my legs.

He led me over to the bed and told me to lie in the middle. He went to his bag and brought back some silk scarves. He tied me to the four posts of the bed so I lay before him spread eagled and completely captive.

John stood at the side of the bed and gazed at me for a moment. I squirmed a little under his intent perusal. He took off his shirt and pants. His erection was making a tent out of his boxers.

"You see what just looking at you does to me?"

I shivered again. He stood in front of me and rubbed his hand up and down his cock through the fabric of his shorts. "Is this what you want?" he asked in a whisper.

"Yes," I said, already pulling against the bindings.

He turned back to his bag and removed one more piece of silk. He put it around my eyes.

"But I want to see you," I said plaintively.

"Later, first you are going to be completely attuned to the sense of touch. I don't want you to know where I'm going to touch you next." He spoke softly against my ear after he'd finished tying the blindfold. His breath tickled my ear as his words stoked my desire and I squirmed again.

Then he began touching me. I would feel his fingers on my belly, then his lips on my knee, and then his tongue swirled around my nipple right through the fabric of the teddy. I was completely submerged in an ocean of sensation. I had no warning where he was going to strike next but my body reacted to every touch. At some point I felt the snaps at the crotch of the teddy give way. Within minutes I was arching off the bed at his touch and sobbing out my need.

All of my nerve endings were on fire. Tremors wracked my body. When I felt his tongue separate the lips of my vulva and his teeth graze the sensitive nub of my clitoris I exploded with a shriek. I arched all the way off the bed and John grabbed my hips and held on while he buried his face in my wetness. He used his tongue and mouth to make my climax last as long as possible. I could feel his lips against my pulsing flesh and wondered what it must feel like for him.

I collapsed on the bed with a sob. Tremors left me boneless and weak. John gently kissed his way up my body to my mouth. I could taste myself on him and there was something about it that I felt all the way to my soul. It was a primitive feeling of having marked him with my scent.

His lips disappeared and I felt him moving around the bed. Then I felt something press against my lips. I realized it was the head of his cock. I swirled my tongue out and around the head before he could pull back. He shuddered with reaction and moaned softly.

"Please let me taste you?" I asked beseechingly.

He quivered in response. He leaned forward, straddling me just below the shoulders.

"Please hold my head up so I can reach you."

He lifted my head up and supported my neck and I swallowed him whole. His legs started trembling. He was deep in my mouth and I was sucking on him, gently at first and then more firmly. I wondered what he was seeing. My face was almost completely covered by the blindfold. The only thing left uncovered was my mouth and I was using it to drive him to the edge. I could taste his salty pre-come and with a strangled cry he pulled away from me. All I could hear was harsh breathing for several minutes and then the sound of a condom being torn open.

A moment later his hands were back on my body and his fingers were once again delving into my moist heat. Soon my head was rolling back and forth as I begged him to take me. Finally, I felt his weight on me and his cock probing my opening before sliding home.

"Please, I want to see you when I come. I want to look into your eyes and see what I'm doing to you," I whispered.

John removed the blindfold and then the scarves at my legs. He wrapped his arms around my thighs and spread my legs wide, pushing my knees up and outward. He started slowly but built to a frantic pace. As he plunged into me his eyes never left mine. I was so close and I could tell he was right there with me. He stopped and released my legs. I groaned in frustration, closing my eyes.

"Open your eyes!" He demanded.

I opened my eyes and looked into his. He reached between us and stroked my sensitive nub for a few moments. He switched hands and caressed me until I thought I would die from the feelings building inside me. He was a master of keeping me right on the edge, building me to a fever pitch. He slid his hand out from between us and cradled my head with it, dropping his thumb against my lips and resting on his elbow. He put the fingers of his other hand into his mouth and sucked the length of them.

I realized he was tasting me and pressing the same wetness into my mouth with his thumb. He thrust once, twice and I went over the edge with a loud cry. Right before I closed my eyes I saw his eyes lose focus. I heard him shout while I was sobbing out my own release.

When he recovered enough to move he released the two remaining scarves and wrapped me in his arms, rubbing my arms to ease any soreness from the restraints. He cradled me against him. Tremors raced through my body every few minutes. "Thanks for trusting me," he said softly as he kissed the top of my head.

I sighed in contentment and burrowed into him further. I lightly kissed his chest lying under my cheek. "I should be thanking you. Every time I think it can't possibly get better....it gets better."

"Yeah, kind of scary, isn't it? When my mind comes back into focus it's hard to believe I felt so much and the rest of the world wasn't even affected. I feel like at least the lights should flicker or something," he said with a laugh.

Languid warmth filled my body and I wanted to lie there, wrapped in his arms forever. Unfortunately, forever only lasted ten minutes, John slid out from under me, smiling when I protested. He assured me he'd be right back. I heard him relieving himself and then running the water in the sink. He came back into the bedroom with a warm wet washcloth and slowly bathed me. It felt wonderful and I moaned and stretched like a cat.

I wondered what amazing thing I'd done in my life to deserve him. For once, I decided I wouldn't question it, I wouldn't deny the possibility, and I wouldn't look this gift horse in the mouth. I was going to grab onto this horse with both hands and ride it until it threw me. I just hoped it would not completely devastate me when that happened. I pushed the thought away and forced myself to live in the present.

. . . . .

John

I watched Cassie's naked body stretching on the bed and the picture was seared into my brain. Who was I kidding; I didn't think I'd ever get my fill of her. Just seeing her lying there, content and warm, marks from our recent lovemaking still on her skin, made me feel such a fierce sense of belonging it was staggering.

I wanted to spend years proving to her what a naturally beautiful and sensual woman she was. Suddenly, I knew I wanted a life with this woman almost as much as I wanted to continue breathing. *My God, I love her* How had this happened so quickly? A part of me was afraid to trust the feeling. Maybe I was just so much in need of someone who actually cared about me I was assigning more importance to this feeling than was really there. My rational mind kept coming up with arguments of why it wasn't possible to love her yet. But in the back of my mind, the quiet, sure voice of my heart said, "You're toast."

"So, when do you choose your fortune cookie?" she asked with an arched eyebrow.

I laughed out loud. "You are going to kill me," I said in disbelief. "I think I'm probably going to need a little time to recover. I am a mere mortal after all. God has a sick sense of humor. He gave men a constant desire for sex and then didn't include the wherewithal to take advantage of the desire."

"What a shame to be such a mere mortal," she said with a wicked gleam in her eye as she began to caress her breasts. This woman was a siren. I couldn't resist her. I watched as her hands continued down her belly and finally dipped between her thighs. She drew her knees up and let them fall open so she was displaying all of her feminine warmth and wetness for my viewing pleasure.

I forced myself to stand there watching. I couldn't help the breath that hissed out of my lips. She was boldly watching me getting hard, thickening and lengthening with desire. She reached for the plate of fortune cookies and handed them to me. I selected one and cracked it open. I unfolded the paper and smiled.

"I am dessert."

She looked at me, raising a questioning eyebrow.

"You can interpret that anyway you like but if you want to know what I had in mind we need to go down to the refrigerator."

"You stay right here. Just lie on the bed and I'll be back in a minute," she said as she walked out of the room naked.

When she walked back into the bedroom I was sitting on the bed, leaning against the headboard with my fingers laced together behind my head. Cassie set her treasures down on the bedside table and smiled at me

"All of my favorites; Hot fudge, Butterscotch and whipped cream. You know, I don't get to have dessert very often, so I am going to enjoy this immensely. I think I want to make it last a long, long time," she said as her eyes ran up and down my body.

I smiled a lazy smile and wondered if my face gave away how turned on I was. She directed me to slide down until I was lying on the bed.

"You can have a couple of pillows behind your head so you can see, if you want, but leave your hands behind your head," she ordered, enjoying her role as director.

I did as she asked. She looked like a kid in a candy store; the possibilities were endless and she didn't know where to start. Finally, she opened the butterscotch sauce and dribbled some on her lips and pressed her mouth to mine. The heat and moistness made the sweet concoction even stickier and fused our mouths together.

Cassie kneeled on the bed above me. She straddled me and lowered herself to her elbows and braced herself there with her breasts rubbing against my chest. Her nipples hardened as they brushed against the hair on my chest. I plundered her mouth with my tongue, enjoying the sweet and hot sensation the butterscotch created.

Cassie rested her thighs lightly just below my waist. My cock pressed up against the cleft between the cheeks of her ass. Her wet heat was pressed into the skin of my lower belly and I felt, rather than heard, her moan deep in her throat. She wrenched her lips away and lightly licked the rest of the sweetness off my lips.

I stared into her eyes for a moment, enjoying the passion that burned there. I was completely focused on her as she reached for the bottle of butterscotch again. The look of carnal intent in her eyes made me shudder with reaction. When she slid down my body and straddled my thighs I thrust upward, grinding my pelvis against her. She just smiled at me, slowly drizzling butterscotch across my chest.

Beginning at my shoulders, she swirled her tongue around and around, sucking and then lightly biting my hot skin. She acted as if the combination of sweet sauce and salty skin was a gourmet meal. She reached one of my nipples and suckled it and then lightly blew on the wet skin. I shivered. She lightly grazed her teeth over the nipple and I arched against her with a low moan.

Slowly working her way lower, she teased me. She spent a lot of time cleaning me all off and nibbling all around my lower belly, her tongue meandering just along the edge of the thatch of hair that surrounded my hard shaft. She sat up and grabbed the chocolate syrup and the whipped cream. With deft artistry she turned my throbbing cock into a hot fudge sundae with a whipped cream topper.

She started by licking all of the whipped cream off of the head. She swirled her tongue around and around and I had to grip the headboard to keep from grabbing her head and thrusting into her mouth. She slowly worked her way down to the base of my shaft. She seemed fascinated by every inch of the velvety soft skin covering such a hard steel interior.

Reaching the base she slowly sucked each of my balls into her mouth one at a time before working her way back up. She lightly grazed her teeth over the tip and I started to reach for her. I forced my hands down and gripped the bedspread until my knuckles turned white as she repeated the light caress of her teeth.

When Cassie pressed her mouth down over the head of my dick I almost shouted. My muscles were straining as I tried to keep from pumping my hips. She sucked gently and swirled her tongue around and around the head and my hips came up off the bed a few inches. She continued the gentle sucking as my breathing quickened and I gripped the bedspread as if it were the only thing keeping me tethered to earth.

Suddenly, Cassie thrust downward, taking my whole length deep into her mouth. I cried out and helplessly arched my back, pressing my head back into the pillows. She slowly released me, sucking gently as she moved upward. She cradled my balls in her hand as she plunged downward again. I felt my balls tighten and knew I was close to losing control.

She gripped the base of my shaft with her hand and squeezed upward, her hand following her mouth's ascent. She began to pump a little faster and suck a little harder. I continued to arch upward as if my dick was forced to follow the warm caressing wetness of her mouth every time it retreated.

I was gasping for air and I knew I couldn't hold off any longer. I yelled out a warning and rocked my head back and forth on the pillow. She moved faster surrounding me with heat and sucking wetness. My body trembled as the feelings inside of me built toward an eruption. I wrenched my hands off the bed and grabbed her head. I made a feeble attempt to pull her away as I gasped, "Cassie, I can't hold back much longer."

She released me from her mouth for a moment but kept up the squeezing caressing motion of her hand. I watched her lick her lips and almost lost it. She locked eyes with me and whispered, "I can't wait to taste you."

She plunged downward with her mouth again pressing me into the back of her throat. My hands that had been trying to pull her away were now guiding her head. I was lost as she made love to me with her mouth. My fingers pulled her hair slightly and it only seemed to drive her onward. As she pulled back she sucked hard as if her mouth didn't want to let go. With a shout I erupted, pumping my hips toward her receding mouth and shooting my seed to the back of her throat. I growled low in my throat as I helplessly thrust my hips upward over and over again.

When I finally collapsed on the bed in a boneless heap, she slowly released me from her mouth. She gently kissed the head of my cock and my body jerked involuntarily.

"Now that's what I call dessert!" She said softly as she crawled back up my body and snuggled against me. I pulled her tightly to my chest and dropped a trembling kiss on her hair. I waited until my breathing slowed before speaking.

"Cassie you have no idea how...how earth shattering that was. I really thought my heart was going to stop."

"It's the one thing I know I'm good at, I got plenty of practice during my marriage," she said with a rueful laugh.

I stared at her for a moment. I was surprised at my irrational jealousy of her ex-husband. But my main emotion was fury and disgust. "Let me get this straight, he wouldn't go down on you but there was nothing wrong with you doing it for him?" I asked incredulously.

"For the last few years we had sex it was about all we did," she admitted with an embarrassed shrug.

"I should have hit him. I should have locked Sam in another room and punched him," I said with barely restrained fury.

"Hey, it's okay. I'm sorry I brought up his name. I'm actually glad I had the knowledge to make you so crazy. I'm glad I was able to give back a small sample of what you've given me. Besides, this was the first time I really enjoyed it," she said with a contented smile.

I groaned. "Oh, don't tell me that. I'll be dreaming about it all the time. I don't know if I can fly a plane with a hard-on."

"I don't even know how to describe how you make me feel," she said with a thoughtful look. "You make me feel.....wanton. I want to make love to you until we pass out. I want to make you come again and again. I just can't seem to get enough of you. I've never reacted this way with a man before," she said with a helpless shrug.

I smiled at her and lightly kissed her lips. "It's nice to know I'm not the only sex addict here. I was beginning to think there was something wrong with me. My first thought when I wake up is wondering when I can make you come again. When you come apart in front of me and your eyes go out of focus, it just....I can't wait to do it again,"

A little while later I pulled her upright. "I think a shower is in order," I said as I peeled my hand off her arm. Cassie looked at the cover on the bed which had swirls of chocolate, butterscotch, and whipped cream splotched on it.

"Good thing we didn't get under the covers," she said as she stripped the bedspread off the bed.

"Come on, leave it. We'll get to it after the shower." I said as I pulled her into the bathroom.

Cassie turned on the shower and adjusted the temperature. When she turned to me I was watching her with a mock scowl on my face. "Promise you'll behave or you're getting in there by yourself," I said and crossed my arms.

Cassie laughed and then pouted. "You're no fun."

"I'd like to live, at least, until tomorrow."

"Okay, if I have to," she said with a whine although it was evident she was trying not to laugh.

The shower was relaxing. We washed each other gently and when all of the sticky syrup was gone we got out and dried off. I climbed into bed while she ran downstairs to put the bedspread in the washing machine. I think I dozed while she was down there because the next thing I knew she was snuggling up next to me. I pulled her tight against me and threw a leg over her thigh. As I drifted off to sleep I felt like I was where I belonged.

Chapter 10

Cassie

I woke up on the verge of an orgasm. It was disorienting because I hadn't slept in bed with a man since my divorce. But my body already recognized the tongue pushing me toward the pinnacle. I struggled to reconcile the change from what I thought was a really great dream into what was actually a really incredible reality, I slid my hands through his hair, holding him in place. Within minutes of awakening, I toppled over the edge of the earth with a husky cry.

I gave myself up to the sensations throbbing through my body. I was still breathing hard when he slid up my body and entered me with one savage thrust. I cried out again as his head appeared from under the covers. His hair was mussed and his lips shone with wetness and I didn't think I'd ever seen anything so wonderful in my life.

"Breakfast of champions," he said with a gleam in his eyes before his mouth descended and captured mine.

He set up a slow rhythm. His tongue in my mouth kept time with the thrust of his hips. I felt as if my whole body was on fire. I opened my thighs wider, trying to draw him in as deep as I could. He thrust in deeper but still kept up his slow cadence. He rested on his elbows and framed my face with his hands.

"I love watching you when we make love. Every time I do this," he said as he slid back inside me. "Your eyes widen a bit and I can hear a catch in your breath and you moan. Your pussy grabs on to me as if it never wants to let go and just before you come your eyes get all hazy like your brain disconnects from your body."

His whispered words drove me higher. I could feel the pressure building. I grabbed onto those shoulders I had fantasized about the first day I met him and locked my feet behind his hips, pulling him toward me. I could never get close enough. I wanted to make him a part of me.

"Do you know how hot you make me?" He asked with a groan as he slowed even more. I cried out in frustration.

"I had to force myself to put on a condom this morning. All I could think about was feeling you against my skin. Nothing in between us, you, squeezing me, milking me, until I want to scream," he groaned.

I grabbed onto his face with both hands forcing him to look me in the eyes. "John, please fuck me now. Fuck me hard," I said, half demanding, half begging.

I watched the heat flare in his eyes, saw his control snap as he began to thrust into me. I grabbed onto his shoulders, meeting him thrust for thrust. Less than a minute later we were both crying out as he thrust one last time.

Several minutes later he rolled off me with a groan, pulling me on top of him. He wrapped his arms around me and sighed in contentment. I was happy to stay right there. I was running my fingers over his chest muscles, appreciating his body.

Neither of us seemed to be in any hurry to move and then John's stomach growled. We laughed. I raised myself up on an elbow and smiled at him.

"My turn to cook. I make a mean omelet," I offered with a raised eyebrow.

"Sounds wonderful," John said with another sigh but he didn't move.

"I'll let you take the first shift in the shower. The omelet should be ready by the time you're finished."

"Okay," he said but still he didn't move.

"Oh Jo-ohn," I called in a sing-song voice. "I'm having visions of sitting on your face while I suck on your cock. If you don't get your delectable body into the shower I don't know if I'll be able to control myself," I said only half in jest.

John rolled out from under me instantly. "Back, back, you witch. You're like one of those sirens aren't you? Beautiful voices luring sailors to their deaths," he laughed as he backed toward the bathroom. I stalked him for a moment but couldn't keep a straight face. I laughed merrily as he backed into the bathroom. I laughed even harder when he locked the door.

"Take that." I heard him say through the door.

I put on my robe and practically skipped down the stairs. I hadn't felt this lighthearted since....since I couldn't remember when. I perused the contents of the refrigerator and decided the stir fry leftovers would make great ingredients for the omelets.

John walked into the kitchen as I slid his omelet onto a plate.

"Smells wonderful," he said as he sniffed appreciatively.

I poured him a cup of coffee and a glass of orange juice and then sat down across from him to dig into my own omelet. "I cheated a little. I used the leftovers from last night. So, you helped with the omelets whether you knew it or not."

"Wow, this is great. I never knew I could cook like this," he said with a teasing glint in his eye.

We must have worked up an appetite because neither of us spoke until out plates were empty. I sipped my tea and enjoyed just looking at him. I enjoyed having him in my kitchen. He asked about my plans for the day. I told him I had to work out and leave for work by 3:30 but other than that my day was free. When he offered to work out with me I happily agreed. He could have offered to remove one of my teeth without Novocain and I would have agreed if it meant spending more time with him.

"Then if you really don't have anything else planned, maybe you could help me buy a new bed."

I stopped with my cup halfway to my mouth and raised an eyebrow at him.

"I really don't like the mattress I have. It's a hand-me-down. Sharon kept our mattress. So, I need your help to find a good place to buy a mattress," he said with a shrug.

"Oh, okay."

"Besides, I plan to have you in my bed as often as possible so it only makes sense for you to help me choose the mattress."

I wasn't sure how to react. I was happy he intended to continue our relationship but I didn't want to read too much into it. I hadn't even met Josh yet. I'd known John just three days. I felt like I'd known him a lot longer and I already cared for him a lot more than I was comfortable with. Despite what he said about us being a couple I was sure he would tire of me. I knew I would be devastated when it happened if I let myself care anymore than I already did.

"Hey, I didn't mean to push. You're not tired of me already, are you?" He smiled but the smile didn't quite reach his eyes.

"Tired of you?" I asked incredulously. "I find it hard to believe I'll ever get tired of you. It's just....I don't know. For me, these last few days have been perfect. I've never just clicked with someone so completely before. I can't believe I've only know you for three days. But, I haven't met Josh yet and I....I keep wondering what I did to deserve you and I can't think of anything so....I guess I'm just waiting for the other shoe to drop." I finished with a shrug.

John took my hand across the table. "Well, see that's where we differ. I can't figure out what I did to deserve you either so I just stop worrying about it and enjoy it. I think what's really going on here is George trashed your self-esteem so much you have a hard time believing someone really wants you. So, I'm making it my special assignment to convince you otherwise." He paused and grinned at me. "I know you have 'issues' with control but, for once, try to just trust things will work out. Okay?"

He pulled my hand to his mouth and kissed it. I gave him a saucy look. "If you convince me any more I'm not going to be able to walk."

He laughed but he didn't let my hand go. "Very funny, but you know I'm not just talking about sex. We already had that discussion last night." He squeezed my hand and then let it go.

I realized I was borrowing trouble where there was none. He was right. I shouldn't try to analyze everything. I should just enjoy it. "Okay, I'd love to help you pick out a mattress. I know just the place."

John laughed. "I thought you would. You sure are wired to this town."

I ran up to wash. I'd save the shower for after the workout but if I showed up at the gym without washing everyone would be able to tell what I'd been doing.

John grabbed some sweats out of his car and rode to the gym with me. Travis was working at the front desk when we checked in. He gave me a raised eyebrow and then a wink when he saw John holding my hand.

We had a great workout. Normally I got interrupted a lot by guys stopping by to talk to me but no one did more than wave. John pulled me into his arms and kissed me silly a couple times during the workout. I wondered if that's why so few men stopped by.

I met him at the front desk after we showered, and he took my hand again to walk out to the parking lot. I was beginning to really enjoy the attention. It was even worth the looks Travis was giving me.

The warehouse I took John to had miles of mattresses. By the time we were finished it seemed like we'd tried everyone. We laughed a lot. We finally settled on a king size mattress and box spring we both thought were comfortable.

At my suggestion, John called Mary to ask if she would accept delivery of the bed for him. She agreed without hesitation. I took him to a small bistro for lunch. He was so easy to talk to; I was always surprised how easily he got me to open up. I found myself telling him things I had never told anyone about my parent's divorce.

"I know I didn't have anything to do with it, in my head at least. But in my heart I think I felt if I'd just been better somehow....I don't know. I guess I had to come up with some reason why he would leave. So, being a child, you know everything revolves around you. I decided somewhere along the line if I'd been a better daughter he wouldn't have left." I shrugged, embarrassed at having revealed so much about myself.

John seemed to sense my embarrassment and took my hand. He held it, palm up, and lightly traced the lines in my palm with his finger. "Tell me about your dad, what is he like?" he asked as he continued to study my hand.

"He's.....I guess....kind of larger than life in a lot of ways. He feels very strongly about equality for women and people of different races. He was very involved in the civil rights movement in the sixties. He's looked up to by pretty much everyone who knows him. He always taught me to try to do the right thing, to try to leave the world a better place. He was always trying to make things better for people. I really admire him."

"But what was he like as a dad?" John pressed.

"Well he was gone a lot. He wrote editorials for several papers. He wasn't very touchable. I mean, we didn't hug or talk about our emotions much. He could be strict too. I remember making a lot of choices based on what his reaction would be. I guess I basically worshipped him from afar." I shrugged.

"Sounds kind of lonely," he said quietly.

"It's hard to be lonely with three loud rambunctious brothers always driving me crazy."

"But it wasn't your brothers you wanted to notice you, was it? It sounds like you spent all of your time doing anything you could to win your dad's respect, to get his attention. No matter how many times your attempts were dismissed there was always the possibility the next time it would work. Then he left....the ultimate dismissal."

His words cut through all of my carefully constructed reality about my father. Tears flooded my eyes and I blinked several times to try to hold them back. John looked at me and squeezed my hand.

"I'm sorry Cassie. I shouldn't psychoanalyze you. Lord knows I have enough problems of my own."

"No....it's all right. Really," I added softly when it looked like he was going to apologize again.

"I....I just realized how many times I've....I mean I'm still trying to please him, isn't that crazy?" I shook my head and laughed softly. "Do you know how long I stayed in a bad marriage because I was trying to 'do the right thing'? I was so miserable and I convinced myself it was my fault. I wanted too much, or I just couldn't be satisfied, or I wasn't trying hard enough. My God...... even George understood." I was incredulous as reality hit me square in the face. "I just realized every time I started demanding things get better, George found some way to bring up my Dad. What a manipulative bastard."

John brought my hand up to his mouth and lightly kissed my fingers. The he pressed a kiss into my palm. He sat quietly, supporting me, letting me get it all out of my system. No one had ever done that for me before.

"I was so terrified if I got a divorce, then Sam would be hurt as badly as I was hurt by my father. Finally, I realized it wouldn't hurt her any more than a mother who was a basket case. And I certainly didn't want her to learn to let people manipulate her or walk all over her. So, I got the divorce and prayed I could make her understand. The one thing I have to give to George is he's never put Sam in the middle. He has always told her our problems are ours and she isn't to blame for any of them."

I laughed bitterly. "My father never blamed me but he never explained anything to me either so it was left to my child's imagination. You know children see everything in the world in relationship to how it affects them so, of course, in my mind I had to be at fault."

I paused and just stared at our clasped hands for a moment. Suddenly I was hit by a stroke of pure joy as a new realization hit me.

"I just realized something else too. I just realized now I know why I've been doing all the things I've been doing, I don't feel compelled to do them anymore. I mean I still would like to do the right thing but I just realized the only person I really have to please is me. Not that I don't want to please other people but what a feeling.....I feel.....free..."

I felt like the Grinch, as if my heart had grown ten times that day. John smiled at me and the caring in his eyes warmed my soul. The waiter stopped by to make sure everything was all right. We looked down and realized we hadn't touched our food. Laughing, we waved him away and dug into our meal.

When we got back to the house he followed me inside to get his bag. I remembered I hadn't put the bedspread in the dryer so I went to do that while he went upstairs to get his things.

He came and found me in the laundry room. I was folding clothes I'd forgotten in the dryer. I'd been pretty absent-minded the last few days, I mused to myself. John set his bag down and began helping me fold laundry. I started to protest and then realized I liked doing things with him.

After a few minutes I realized he had mostly folded underwear and bras. I raised an eyebrow in inquiry. "Do you have an underwear fetish?"

"Only your underwear," he replied with a smile. "But this underwear is a little different from the delectable creation I saw you in last night," he said as he held up a pair of plain cotton panties.

"I used to wear sexy underwear and garters and all those kinds of naughty things. Hell, I even used to sleep in the nude. I guess the less desirable I felt, the less important that stuff was."

"What about what you were wearing last night? What was that thing called?" The appreciative look on his face was almost comical.

"It's a teddy. I bought it on a whim a little while after my divorce. It was a present to myself when I'd been at my goal weight for a year. It was kind of a silly purchase because I didn't have anyone to wear it for. But sometimes I'd wear it anyway just to enjoy how it made me feel." I felt my face flush with the admission.

John put the underwear down and turned to me. He took the shirt I was folding and dropped it into the laundry basket. Taking hold of my arms he pulled me up against him, and then backed me up against the dryer.

"How did it make you feel, Cassie?"

Just that quickly, his touch and his soft question brought my body to life. My nipples hardened against his chest and I felt a flutter in my belly. It felt like there wasn't enough oxygen in the room.

Flight to Forever

"It made me feel feminine and sexy the way the silky fabric rubbed against my skin." I said in a breathy whisper.

"Did it feel like a caress? Did it feel like this?" he asked in a husky voice as his hands lightly caressed my breasts making them swell and ache for his mouth.

"Yes," I whispered as I arched my back, pressing my breasts into his hands.

He dropped his mouth to one peak and laved it right through my blouse and bra. The moist fabric rubbing against my nipple made me tremble. He stepped back just long enough to pull my shirt off over my head. Then he was licking and lightly nipping the tops of my breasts as his hands went behind me to unhook my bra.

My bra fell away and he closed his mouth around the peak of my breast. He flicked his tongue over the nipple and sucked lightly while his fingers caressed the other nipple. I was bent backward over the dryer while he feasted on me. He switched his mouth to the other breast and I moaned in encouragement.

I couldn't believe how quickly I was lost in desire. A minute ago we were folding laundry. Just the sound of his voice

231

had my nipples hardening. A suggestive look and I was wet and ready for him. I could feel his erection pressing into my belly and I couldn't wait to get him inside me. John lifted his head for a moment and I groaned and reached for him, trying to bring his mouth back to the tight bud that already felt bereft.

He looked at his watch and even though I was the one who had to be somewhere, I didn't care. I caressed his hard shaft through his jeans. He shuddered as the snap gave and the zipper descended. I reached in and pulled him free of his boxers, reveling in the feel of his silky, soft, skin covering solid steel. He groaned as I lightly squeezed and caressed him.

He fumbled with the snap and zipper on my jeans. His hands seemed to take forever. I needed him. I wanted his hands on me. I wanted him buried deep inside me.

His hands were trembling when he finally got my jeans undone. He yanked them, along with my underwear, down over my hips, lifted me onto the dryer and punched the on button. I could feel moisture seeping out of me onto the dryer as the machine vibrated against my naked bottom. John was like a crazy man, pulling my shoes, jeans and underwear off with a growl and flinging them out of the way.

He grabbed me around the hips and started to pull me forward toward his rigid cock when he stopped and let out a string of curses. I grabbed at him to keep him from turning away.

"Condom," he said, gasping, holding me off as if it took all of his strength.

"It's ok. I'm really irregular and I tried to get pregnant for almost a year and I couldn't. I think we're safe." I said, pulling him toward me as I slid forward toward the edge of the dryer. The dryer vibration had me on the edge of an orgasm and I couldn't bear being without him for another moment.

"Are you sure you want to chance it?" He spoke through gritted teeth as he held me off.

"Yes, John, please I need you now." I pleaded as I grasped his cock and pressed it against my swollen wet flesh.

John gave in and with a loud groan he thrust inside me. I yelled out and came almost instantly. John was so aroused he couldn't even pretend control.

"Hang on," he growled out as he grabbed my hips and thrust forward.

I wrapped my legs around him and grabbed onto his shoulders. I urged him on with words and gasps of pleasure. His hips were thrusting forward like a jack hammer. I could feel my breasts jiggling with his thrusts. I looked down and saw his rock hard cock thrusting into me and then coming out again covered in my juices. John's fingers were white where he gripped my hips. He threw back his head and all of his muscles grew taught with his effort.

"John, I want to feel you come inside me." I gasped out.

That was it. With a roar, John bucked, spilling his seed deep inside me. He was half lying on top of me, pressing me into the dryer but he couldn't seem to stop thrusting. Finally, with a loud groan, he collapsed on top of me. His legs were trembling so badly I wondered if they would support him.

John's legs eventually stopped trembling and he was able to put a little more weight on them. Suddenly, I was laughing almost hysterically. John looked at me strangely. I was hoping he would understand. I wanted to stop but I couldn't. He stood up and pulled up his boxers and jeans. Then he stood there and waited for me to explain. I sat up and leaned against him, shaking with mirth. After a couple of minutes I stopped laughing long enough to speak.

"I'm sorry, John. I was just lying here thinking you'd done it again. You make me come until I scream. Then I realized I've just been fucked to within an inch of my life on top of a dryer, of all things. Here I am lying here with your sperm dripping down my leg and suddenly I was wondering if my dad would consider this 'doing the right thing'. It just struck me as funny. Then I realized I don't give a fuck." I giggled. "Well, obviously, I do give a fuck, and a pretty good one I think. But what I meant to say was for the first time I really don't care what my dad would think. It just makes me feel so good that I couldn't stop laughing once I got started." I shrugged but still couldn't stop grinning.

John smiled but he didn't seem particularly amused.

I reached up and cradled his face with my hands. "You know I wasn't laughing at you, don't you?" I asked and my grin softened to an intimate smile as I caressed his cheek.

His smile turned rueful. "Well I have to admit that my ego took a hit at first. Then I realized I was taking myself a bit too seriously. After all, having sex on a dryer is humorous when you think about it. I guess I just flashed back to Sharon for a moment there. She had a tendency to find my most vulnerable point and exploit it." he said with a shake of his head.

"Other than the birth of my child, making love with you is the most amazing experience of my life. Believe me, there is nothing in that area that you have the least bit to be vulnerable about. And if Sharon thought there was then she is stupid as well as cruel."

I kissed him lightly on the lips and hopped off the dryer. I laughed again as I realized I was only wearing a sock and a watch and nothing else. This time John laughed with me. I checked the time and realized I'd have to kick it in gear to get to work on time.

"I've taken more showers in the past few days than I don't know when. But it looks like I need another one."

"I'll take one when I get home. Otherwise, you'll definitely be late to work," he said as he helped me gather my clothes and then followed me out of the laundry room.

I glanced through the kitchen window, making sure I wasn't going to shock anyone by standing there naked.

"I know you'd probably like some time by yourself by now but you are welcome to spend the night here since your bed won't be delivered until Monday," I said when we reached the door.

"I'm in no particular hurry to be by myself but you won't get home until after midnight and I have to be at the airport at six am. We both know we won't get any sleep at all if I come over here. I'll just sleep on Josh's bed. But I'll be thinking about you," he whispered against my lips as he kissed me good-bye.

I kissed him back and then stepped back to stay out of the view of the windows. "As a matter of fact, I'll be thinking of you just like this," he said as he perused my naked body one last time before walking out the door. I locked the door and watched him walk to his car, then ran upstairs to take a shower.

Flight to Forever

Chapter 11

I made it to work with one minute to spare. My least favorite Supervisor was working but nothing he said bothered me, I just smiled. I think it drove him a little crazy and that made it even better. By half way through the shift the other controllers were remarking on my good mood.

"Cassie, what's up with you? Did you win the lottery?"

"Maybe she finally got a little...."

I just smiled at all the nods and winks. If they only knew how I did my laundry....

My relationship with John was too new to share, plus I didn't want to jinx it. Maybe, in the back of my mind, I was still convinced he would tire of me and move on. If no one knew and things didn't work out, then I wouldn't have to deal with a lot of painful questions.

I got to work the evening rush on local. The heavy traffic put me in an even better mood. I was 'in the zone'. A few pilots told me 'good job' right over the frequency.

Just as I was getting off local to go on a break, the phone rang in the back of the tower cab. I wasn't expecting any calls so I was surprised when the Supervisor handed the phone to me. I couldn't help the delighted smile that flashed across my face when I heard John's voice.

"Hi, I'm sorry to bother you at work. You're not going to get in trouble for this are you?

"No problem. Every once in a while they let us speak to people on the phone. They even let us use the bathroom if we're really good."

"Ha, I'd hate to be up there when everyone is being bad. I have a big favor to ask if you're able to do it."

"What do you need?"

"Well I realized that you need to meet Josh before I drop him on you on Thursday. And I wondered if it would be possible to bring him up to the tower when we get in on Tuesday. Our flight lands about one o'clock. If you can get permission Josh would love the experience. Plus, I get the added benefit of seeing you."

"Well I'd love to, if I can. They've gotten pretty strict with visitors since September 11th but since you're a pilot it should be ok. If I ask right away I should be able to get it approved by Tuesday. Why don't you call me when you get into the airport on Tuesday and I'll let you know?"

He paused for a second, then in a quiet voice he said, "I don't mean to freak you out but....I miss you already."

My heart lodged in my throat. When I'd left for work, the next few days with no prospects of seeing him yawned in front of me. Afraid to speak for fear of my feelings showing, I hesitated too long.

"Sorry, I probably shouldn't have said that. I just had such a great time with you and I like being with you. Tuesday just seems far away..." he trailed off as if embarrassed by his admission.

"I'm not freaked out. I feel the same way. I guess I just have to get used to straightforward when all I'm used to is passive aggressive manipulation. I can't wait for Tuesday. I know you need some time with Josh but I would love to have you over for dinner then. Or if it would be easier, the four of us could go out. It's up to you. I don't want to intrude."

"I'd enjoy it but let me talk to Josh. I'm not sure what his emotional state is right now."

"I understand," I assured him.

I asked him for his flight number on Tuesday. I planned to get the pilot to announce a welcome to Josh over the airplane's P.A. system when they landed. I didn't know many nine year old boys who wouldn't be thrilled with that. I'd make a special request to work local when they were due to land.

There were lots more things I wanted to say but with so many people within hearing distance, I didn't want to chance it.

"Well, I'll let you go on your break. I need to go to bed anyway. I have to get up at 4:30 am. This bed I bought from Rhonda isn't that uncomfortable but it sure is lonely."

I groaned out loud. "Don't go there. I still have three more hours to work."

"You must be tired."

"No, not at all, it's the picture I just got in my head that's bothering me," I said with another groan.

"Does it involve me naked, using my tongue to drive you wild?"

"You are evil," I said as I felt the wetness in my panties. "I've got to go."

"Got an audience, huh?" He laughed.

"Mmmhmm," I said as I looked around the tower cab; everyone's attention was focused on my conversation.

He laughed again. "Think of me tonight when you crawl into bed. Good night Cassie," he said in a low sexy growl.

"I don't think there's any doubt about that. Good night," I added softly as I hung up the phone.

Ignoring everyone's expectant looks, I asked the supervisor when I should be back from my break. Even he looked curious about my conversation but I knew he would never ask. I just waited until he gave me a be-back time. Then I smiled and headed for the stairs. Finally, Chuck, who was working clearance delivery couldn't stand it anymore.

"So, Cassie, who was on the phone, anyone I know?" he asked and waggled his eyebrows comically.

"No, you haven't met. It's just a friend of mine," I said with a smile and walked down the stairs, effectively ending further questioning.

I knew I was just putting off the inevitable but I wanted the break to regroup before I answered any questions. By the time I got back upstairs, they were so busy that no one questioned me any further. In fact, I was so busy that I didn't have time to think about anything except moving airplanes until it was time to go home.

I spent a restless night. I woke several times with a feeling something was wrong. The last time I awoke I realized the bed felt empty. I'd been sleeping by myself for over two years and enjoying the hell out of my solitary state, reveling in my ability to stretch out diagonally across the bed if I chose to.

One night with John in my bed and I'd lost the joy of sleeping alone. I wanted to wake up and feel him curled around me, to be able to reach out and run my hand over his muscular chest. I wanted to wake him up in the same amazing way he'd brought me out of dreamland. I wanted more than I was comfortable wanting and it scared the hell out of me.

I'd spent so much time putting my fears and insecurities behind me. John was ten times the man George was. But he was also trying to get his life together. What he said he wanted now was not necessarily what he would want six months from now. Of course, who knew what I would want six months from now, I reminded myself. Before I'd even completed the thought I knew

244

the answer…. John. I would want him six months from now or six years from now. I couldn't imagine not wanting him.

I'd known him less than a week and already I couldn't fathom not having him in my life. Of course I would survive, I chastised myself. I had Sam; I would go on as before. But, a little voice in the back of my head chimed in, the world wouldn't look nearly as shiny and colorful without him in it.

I groaned out loud. I looked at the clock and saw it was six am. John would just be getting to the airport. I groaned again. "Stop it," I said aloud. "You've got a good life, you don't need a man to make you complete." I continued with my pep talk.

Then why did I feel like a jigsaw puzzle with the last piece missing? It was almost a complete picture but that missing piece would make it whole. With George I'd felt as if he'd actively torn the puzzle apart, destroying the picture more and more until I couldn't tell what it was. I'd spent a lot of time picking up the pieces and carefully fitting them back together until I could recognize myself again. Then John came along and he was the last piece I didn't even realize was missing.

With a growl of frustration I threw the covers off. It was obvious I wasn't going to get any more sleep. I might as well get a start on the day. I grumbled to myself about how much trouble a man was as I pulled on some old clothes. I needed physical activity and lots of it. Unfortunately, it was too soon to work out again so I decided there was only one alternative. I was going to clean. I hated cleaning, doing only what was absolutely necessary and nothing more. But I needed something to keep my mind off John and cleaning was it. I grumbled some more about this all being his fault.

By the time I left for work at one o'clock the house was sparkling. I was pleased. I had a clean house. But most importantly, I'd managed to scrub John from my mind for a whole day.

When I got to work, Sunday, it seemed everyone had forgotten about my phone call and I breathed a sigh of relief. No one else was thinking about my mystery man but I couldn't keep my mind off him. The shift at work was uneventful. By the time I got home I was exhausted from all the physical activity of the morning and the lack of sleep the night before.

I walked into the house and found George sitting on the sofa. Since George always brought Sam home and put her in bed on Sunday nights, I wasn't really surprised to see him, but I wasn't thrilled either.

I figured George would take advantage of the fact I was alone to grill me about John. So, I was surprised when he just told me a little about his weekend with Sam and then got up to leave. When he got to the door, he paused as if he wanted to say something. He stood there for a moment and looked at me. Then he said good night and walked out the door.

I was mystified but thankful he hadn't said anything. I just wanted sleep and lots of it. Unfortunately, tonight was a quick turnaround because I had to be up early to take Sam to school and then get myself to work by seven-thirty. I quickly made a lunch for Sam and got all of her school stuff together so we would be able to run out the door in the morning. I was asleep within minutes of turning the light off and slept soundly until the alarm went off the next morning.

At work I was able to get a few minutes to see the manager after my first session on position. She agreed to the tour as long as they followed all of the guidelines for not disturbing controllers who were working traffic. I assured her that I would personally give the tour and there would be no problems.

Around lunch time I was working Ground control when Nationwide 339 came off the runway. I taxied him to his gate and watched him turn north on the taxiway. Then I heard, "Hi

Cassie," on the frequency. The voice was one I already knew by heart.

"Hi John, the tour has been approved."

"Great. I'll see you tomorrow afternoon then."

"See you then," I replied and couldn't keep the grin off my face.

I watched the aircraft all the way to the gate and even used binoculars to see him through the cockpit window. When I realized what I was doing I quickly put them down with a grunt of disgust. I chided myself for juvenile behavior but couldn't seem to keep the smile from beaming across my face. I was just glad that all of the other controllers were busy and weren't watching me act like an ass.

Sam and I had a great evening. We laughed and joked and generally enjoyed each other's company. Sam was usually pretty affectionate when she got home from her father's house. It was almost as if she needed to reestablish the bond with me to prove all was right with the world. I was enjoying our time together so much I read her three stories before I finally turned off the light. I sat in the rocking chair for a few minutes just keeping her company while she went to sleep. I thought she'd fallen asleep when I heard a small tired voice call my name.

"Mommy, can I tell you something?"

"Of course honey, you can always tell me anything."

"I told Daddy that I missed him when I didn't see him but I was glad that you weren't sad anymore."

I hesitated; I didn't want to guide Sam's revelations at all. I wanted her to tell me what she needed to tell me rather than what she thought I wanted to hear. I just said, "Okay," and waited for her to continue.

"Daddy got that mad look on his face and I thought he was mad at me. But then his eyes got tears in them and he said he missed me too."

She sounded troubled and I wanted to go to her but I made myself wait for a moment.

"How did that make you feel?" I asked gently.

"I was a little scared because Daddy doesn't cry. But then I thought that sad things give me tears so they prob'ly give

Daddy tears too. So I gave him a hug and told him I was sorry he was sad," she said with pride in her voice.

"That was a good thing to do for your dad. I know he loves you very much and I'm sure he misses you a lot," I said as I moved over to sit on the edge of the bed and held her hand.

"But Daddy said part of him was sad and part of him was sorry. He said sometimes he had such bad feelings inside that he wasn't very nice to you, Mommy. He said he felt really bad that he made you sad and he was glad you weren't sad anymore too. He told me that him moving to a new house was because he did things wrong and I never did anything wrong."

I was terrified to say the wrong thing and I didn't want her to stop talking before she was finished. I squeezed her hand and realized I couldn't speak without crying anyway. Luckily she wasn't finished.

"I remembered you always tell me if I do something wrong that doesn't make me bad and you still love me no matter what, but I should always try to make it right. So I told Daddy that what he did doesn't make him bad and I always love him but he should try to make it right," Sam said with conviction.

I felt strangled with emotion but managed to ask, "What did Daddy say?"

"He hugged me real hard for a long time. Then he said I was very smart and he was glad he had me around to teach him stuff like that."

Sam giggled at the last part but she looked very pleased and proud of herself.

"Daddy's right honey bun, you are very smart but even more important you're very kind and I am so glad I got you for a daughter." I said as I leaned forward to kiss her. I sat there, running my fingers through her hair until she fell asleep.

Stepping out into the hall, I quietly closed the door before letting the tears flow. I fell onto my bed and sobbed. I cried for the failure of my marriage and all of the pain we'd endured. There'd been so much anger at the end I'd never really grieved. When I stopped crying, I felt a new serenity rather than any feelings of anger or sadness. The tears washed away my hurt like a summer thunderstorm soothes the heat of the day. I truly hoped George was able to find happiness.

More of my insecurity slipped away as George's admission that he had been deliberately unkind to me finally redeemed me. While one part of my brain knew I was being manipulated the other part had always believed George's hurtful words. That niggling doubt gave rise to the little voice that said, "What if he's right?" The voice had been silenced. I still had 'issues' with my father and his abandonment. But those problems didn't seem insurmountable any more.

In the past few days John had relentlessly attacked my reality. He'd held up a mirror to me and insisted I see myself realistically instead of as an extension of someone else's beliefs. I realized, even if things with John didn't work out I would still come away a stronger person.

I put a lot of my concern about the future of our relationship aside. I would stop trying to predict the future and enjoy what we had. With this decision made, I relaxed and was able to anticipate our time together without looking past it. I slept very well.

Tuesday morning was the usual, chaotic, get Sam up and out, get her to school, get to work on time kind of day. But the previous night's revelations gave me the calmness to face it all with serenity and good humor. Sam also seemed as if she'd gotten a big worry off her mind. It made me wonder if she had been feeling any responsibility for either of her parent's sadness.

My serenity deserted me, somewhat, the closer it got to John and Josh's arrival. I'd never thought I would be so worried about meeting a little boy. Josh had enough upheaval in his life. I didn't want to make a mess of things. I wanted him to feel as if he was home.

At about half past noon I was able to convince the supervisor to let me work local. I checked the traffic management computer to see how far out they were and saw that John's flight, Nationwide 249 was about twenty minutes from touchdown.

Nationwide was one of the airlines that let passengers listen to air traffic control over their entertainment headphones. I had no way of knowing if they were actually listening but figured that John would probably have suggested it.

Fifteen minutes later, Nationwide 249 came on frequency reporting a ten mile final. I cleared them to land. Not wanting to distract the pilots, I waited until they were on the ground before I spoke.

"Nationwide 249, I have a favor to ask if you have a moment?"

"Go ahead tower," the pilot responded.

"You have a very special young man on board who is coming to Seattle to live. If it's not too much trouble, I'd appreciate if you could tell Josh Clay, welcome to Seattle from the tower?"

"No problem tower, is he any relation to John?"

"His son, they are both on board. Cross Runway 16 Left and contact Ground and thank you sir," I responded and was glad the pilot knew John. He was more likely to carry out my request.

The phone rang just as I was being relieved on local. The supervisor waved me over as soon as I unplugged my headset. "Your tour is here. You can go down and bring them back up. I won't need you again so you can sign out when you're finished," he said as he handed me the phone.

I told John I'd meet him at the elevator in the terminal since the general public couldn't get up to the FAA offices without an escort. I was surprised at the butterflies in my stomach while I waited for the elevator. I wondered if my nerves were a result of meeting Josh or seeing John again.

When the elevator door opened down in the terminal the first thing I saw was John's smile. His obvious pleasure at seeing me again made my stomach do a little flip-flop. I figured he'd just say hello but he stepped forward and gave me a hug and a kiss. Josh stood off to the side looking uncertain.

John stood with his hand on Josh's shoulder and introduced me. "Josh, this is Cassie. She was working our airplane when we landed."

I held out my hand to Josh. "Hi Josh, it's great to finally meet you. Your dad has told me a lot about you."

Josh was a bit tentative about shaking my hand. He gave me a shy smile and said, "Hi."

I turned to John, "So you were listening to me?"

"Yup, all the way in, we got your message," he said as he turned to smile at Josh.

Josh's smile brightened and he looked animated for the first time. "Yeah, the pilot announced my name to the whole plane. It was really neat," he said in an excited voice.

"I'm glad you liked it. Now, I know you've been on a plane for a while so if you want just a quick look around I'll understand. But if you want the super-duper VIP tour, I'm ready to start any time you are."

Josh's eyes brightened. "I'm not tired. I'll take the VIP tour."

I ushered them into the elevator and slid my id card through the card reader. As I keyed in my password I said, "One VIP tour coming up."

I started in the management offices and introduced them to the managers of the tower and TRACON. When I took them up to the tower, there was a little bit of a departure rush going on. I stood behind each position and described the controller's duties. I showed Josh the radar and all of the other equipment.

John asked just as many questions as Josh. Since John was a pilot I hadn't thought that he would be seeing anything new. Then I remembered that most pilots just knew enough about air traffic control to do their own jobs. A lot of pilots had never even visited a control tower.

By the time I'd described all of the duties and shown them the equipment, the departure rush had died down enough and I was able to introduce them to my co-workers. Chuck, who had been working when John came up to the tower the first time nodded at him and said, "Hello again." He raised his eyebrows at me but didn't say anything. I was sure I'd get grilled later.

All of the controllers were great with Josh and I was glad to see that he'd lost all of his shyness. They even plugged in a handset and let him listen to the frequency for a while. While he was busy listening to airplanes, I called the TRACON and made arrangements to bring them down to the radar room. One of my favorite radar controllers was working and he said he'd be happy to conduct the tour.

When I asked if Josh was ready to see the radar room his eyes got even wider. He looked like today was Christmas and his birthday all rolled into one as he practically trembled with anticipation. As we walked into the room, Randy, our tour guide, came right over to us. He introduced himself and spent a few minutes explaining the setup of the room while he waited for us to get used to the extremely dim lighting.

Then Randy proceeded to take us on one of the most in-depth tours that I'd ever witnessed. I found that I was even learning a thing or two as he described the radar controller's job in detail. He introduced us to several of the controllers and took us to each of the radar scopes. He explained how the airspace was divided up and which controllers were responsible for which areas.

I was impressed with Josh's intelligent, insightful questions. The fact Josh was such an avid listener led Randy to go into even greater detail. I looked at my watch and was surprised to see it had been an hour and a half.

"Well, if you don't want to be a pilot you've sure got the makings of a great controller. You're welcome back anytime as far as I'm concerned," Randy said as he shook Josh's hand.

Josh beamed and I was thrilled that the visit had gone so well. I had a feeling the boy I was seeing now was closer to the real Josh than the shy hesitant one I'd met at the elevator. He had a natural curiosity about the way things worked and he had the patience to sit and listen to the explanation.

We walked back out to the main entrance and I asked him if he'd enjoyed the tour. Josh's smile would have been answer enough but he went on at length about how cool everything was. John looked more relaxed than I'd ever seen him. He was not a jumpy person but seeing him this relaxed made me realize he'd always had a tension about him. His concern for Josh weighed on him.

"You know Josh, when you start school you could talk to the teacher about bringing your class here for a field trip. I know the class should only have about a dozen kids in it. That shouldn't be too large a group and if your teacher gets in touch with me early enough I'm sure I can get all the approvals I need.

Plus, maybe your dad can make arrangements for the class to go on one of Nationwide's jets and I have a friend who works at Spring Aviation who might be able to get you into a flight simulator. I think you'll probably study weather and aerodynamics in science and it could be an all day event to give the kids ideas for a class project of some sort."

Josh's excitement seemed to grow with each thing I said and by the time I stopped talking he was practically bouncing with approval. "That would be awesome. I'll ask the teacher." He practically yelped in excitement. "Dad, do you think you could get us in an airplane?"

"If I talk to the right people, I'm sure I can work something out," he assured Josh then he turned to me. "That's a great idea. You're always thinking. And thanks for that tour, now I'm even more in awe of what you do," he said as he leaned forward and kissed me lightly on the top of my head.

I saw a look of uncertainty cross Josh's face when John kissed me but it vanished quickly and I figured I'd imagined it. I pressed the elevator button and asked if they were going to come over for dinner.

"I was figuring that we'd do make-your-own-pizza night. I make individual crusts and then put out all of the toppings and everyone builds his own ultimate pizza. Sam has made some pretty interesting pizzas," I said with a laugh.

When I mentioned pizza, they were enthusiastic about accepting. We agreed to meet at my house at six to give Josh and Mrs. Sullivan time to get acquainted before he was left alone with her the next day. I had no problem with the late dinner; it gave me plenty of time for preparations.

They arrived right at six. Sam gave John a hug then looked at Josh for a moment. I introduced them and suggested that Sam take Josh to meet the dog. His expression brightened when he heard we had a dog and he happily followed Sam into the living room. A minute later we heard laughter coming from that direction.

I finished pressing the last pizza crust into the pan. I'd made four individual size ones and a larger one that I was going to give John to take home. I figured having some food in the refrigerator was a good idea with a growing boy in the house. Besides, I'd seen how much John could eat.

I washed the dough off my hands and turned to dry them on a towel. Instead I ended up in John's arms. He barely whispered "Hi," before he covered my mouth with his.

I melted into him, winding my arms around his neck. It felt like weeks since I'd seen him and it had only been three days. Knowing the kids would be back soon, I was just convincing myself to let go of him when I realized it was too late.

"Yuck, kissing," Sam said in a loud voice.

John pulled back from me and burst out laughing. I couldn't help laughing too but my laughter died when I looked at Josh's face. He looked upset and even a little bit scared. I could understand he would have trouble getting used to his dad being with a woman other than his mom but I couldn't figure out why that would scare him. John was still smiling and didn't look overly concerned about Josh so I figured it must be all right.

Josh's good mood came back as we created our pizza masterpieces. Sam was a purist after some of her more outrageous combinations had failed, so she used just pepperoni. The rest of us loaded ours with lots of toppings. I tried to use just a little meat and lots of vegetables to cut back on the fat content but John and Josh had no such compunctions. They loaded theirs with pepperoni, sausage, ham, bacon, and hamburger, as well as four or five different vegetable toppings.

The pizzas were a big hit. Sam ate half of hers, which was unheard of as she'd never eaten more than two pieces before. The large pizza came out of the oven half way through dinner. I thought it looked like a professional job and remarked on it. John and Josh gave each other a high five on their expertise.

By a quarter to eight Sam was yawning and John said they had to get going. Mary was going to come over to their house so Josh could sleep in but John had to be out early for his flight. I put all of their pizza in a container and told them not to worry about the dishes. John remarked that it was a shame to leave them since the house was so clean.

"I needed something to occupy my mind Sunday so I cleaned. I cleaned a lot," I said with a look of distaste.

"Really?" John said with a keen look of interest. Then he waggled his eyebrows. "Why did you need to occupy your mind so much? Did you have some thoughts that you were trying to get rid of?"

I felt the heat rise in my face and decided I didn't like this penchant for blushing that had become so commonplace since I'd met John. I scowled at him. "Never you mind."

I ushered them toward the door. Sam gave John a big hug and a kiss and then turned and hugged Josh. Josh looked embarrassed but also somewhat pleased. John gave me a light kiss on the lips and said good night. I looked at Josh but he didn't seem to be upset at the kiss and I was relieved. I told him I'd see him Thursday and patted him on the shoulder as he walked out the door.

Chapter 12

I smiled when I got home Wednesday to find a message from John on my voice mail. He left his new phone number and asked me to call before I went to bed.

"Hi babe," he said in a husky voice.

I was surprised at the greeting. Wondering if he thought I was someone else, I hesitated to respond.

"Cassie, are you there?"

"H-how did you know it was me?" I stammered, feeling foolish for doubting him.

"It wasn't difficult since you're the only one who has this number so far."

I was thrilled that he'd given me his number before anyone else, then embarrassed at my reaction. "Good thing I wasn't a salesman."

"This number is off limits to salesmen."

"Good luck with that."

"Yeah, I know. Listen, I called for two reasons. First, I wanted to confirm I'm going to drop Josh off at about six-thirty. Sorry it's so early."

"Don't worry about it. I know all about having to be at work early."

"Thanks, and second, I forgot to ask if you can come over on Friday. My brother Jacob is driving up with my stuff and I'm having a moving party. I'm bribing people with beer and a barbecue to help me move my stuff in."

"Sure, I'd like that. Is your brother bringing all your stuff?"

"Yup, he's even towing my Shelby up here."

"Great, I bet Mike would come over to help if he can. After seeing the look on his face when you mentioned the Shelby I bet he'd do just about anything to get a look at it."

"Invite him and Trish too. Steve Rayburn is coming over and I think he's bringing a couple of friends. If you know of anyone else just invite them, but let me know tomorrow night if any of them accept so I'll have enough beer and food on hand. Jacob should get here by eleven so you can have people start showing up around then."

"Okay, if I think of anyone else I'll call them."

After a few moments of silence John spoke. "I thought about you all day today. I think I'm going through Cassie withdrawal. If I don't get you naked soon I'll go out of my mind."

I groaned. "Don't go there; I don't have anything else to clean."

"Ah-hah!" John said triumphantly. "I knew that's why you were cleaning. I wish I could come over there."

"I'll just keep telling myself the anticipation will make it even better when we finally get together."

"If it gets any better we'll set the house on fire."

He laughed but a hard edge to his voice said he wasn't feeling humorous. He cleared his throat.

"Is George picking Sam up Friday night? I'd like her to join in the barbecue after school but I just need to make sure we cook early enough to feed her before he picks her up."

"I'm not sure, I'll call him tomorrow."

"Well, I hope he gives you a straight answer. I don't like how he manipulates you."

"Actually, I think things are going to get better."

I checked to make sure Sam wasn't in earshot, and then filled him in about her weekend with her father.

"Good for him, I hope he means it."

"I hope so too. It will be better for him and Sam."

"And you. You know, if you want to invite him over for the barbecue part of our day, Friday, you can. Then he can just take Sam when he leaves."

"That's very generous of you. Let me think about it, okay?"

"It's completely up to you, Cassie. I just thought it would be a good olive branch to speed along a better understanding. I have to admit, I'd rather have you all to myself and if he gets nasty I can't promise I'll keep my mouth shut," he warned.

"Thanks, I'll let you know. Now I've really got to go. Sam just walked in and said she's starving."

"Okay, don't starve your child on my account," he said with a laugh, then added in a husky voice. "I'll see you in the morning. Sweet dreams. I hope I'm in them."

"I'm going to go clean something. Good night."

I could hear his laughter as I hung up the phone.

I slept well and was up brewing the coffee before John arrived. He came through the door with a smile but Josh looked quiet and somewhat sullen. I said hello to him anyway and got a grunt in return. I offered John some coffee but he said he couldn't stay. Rummaging through a drawer, I pulled out a plastic commuter mug and showed it to him.

"Thanks Cassie, it's been a rough morning and I could use the coffee."

Josh's expression darkened at this last comment. He probably wasn't much of a morning person. I knew how that was. As I poured the coffee into the plastic mug, I addressed Josh.

"Josh if you're still tired you can go sleep in the guest room. Sam doesn't have to leave for school for a couple hours so you could get a little more sleep."

He scowled at me. "Are you trying to get rid of me so you can make out with my dad?"

My jaw dropped in surprise. I searched for something to say. John had no problem speaking.

"Josh, Cassie has done nothing but help us since the moment I met her. If it weren't for her you'd be at your grandmother's house. She's even spending her day off taking care of you. You've got about ten seconds to apologize to her or you'll spend the rest of the summer in your room without TV or computer."

Josh looked almost as shocked as me right after he spoke, as if he couldn't believe the words had come out of his own mouth. By halfway through his father's scolding his eyes were filled with tears.

I put a hand on John's arm. "It's okay."

"It most certainly is not okay," John insisted to me then turned back to Josh. "Well...?" he asked with an expectant expression on his face.

The tears escaped Josh's eyes and silently traversed his cheeks. His lower lip trembled as he whispered, "I-I'm s-sorry Cassie."

John gripped his neck with his right hand, kneading the muscles there as he looked at his watch on his other wrist. He groaned in frustration, realizing he had to leave.

"John, don't worry, we'll be fine. I'm sure Josh is sorry and I think once he gets a little more sleep he'll feel better."

John glanced at his watch again and then back and forth between Josh and me. His son's eyes never left the floor.

"Do I have your word you won't give Cassie any trouble or make any other nasty remarks?"

"Yes, I promise Dad," Josh replied in a barely audible voice.

John studied him for a moment longer and then sighed. "I'll see you tonight, we'll talk then."

Then he turned to me. "Are you sure you'll be all right?"

"Really, we'll be fine. You're going to be late. Tell me what time you expect to be back and we'll have dinner waiting for you," I said as I brushed a kiss across his lips and ushered him toward the door.

"I'll probably be here around six if we don't have any delays but don't go to any trouble on my account."

"Fly safely. We'll see you tonight. I'll leave the door unlocked for you, so let yourself in when you get here."

He waved as he drove away, a worried frown still etched upon his face. Closing the door, I turned to face Josh. He stood there, unmoving, staring down at the floor as if he wished to become one with it.

"C'mon Josh, I'll show you where the guest room is and you can get a little more sleep. I'm sure you'll feel better when you're not so tired."

He followed quietly as I lead him down the hall. I folded back the bedspread and told him to take off his shoes. I'd wondered if Josh was upset about his father's relationship with me. His outburst had confirmed it. After his experiences with his mother he was one confused little boy. I understood how it felt when a parent didn't want you. If only I could get him to talk about it.

I tucked him in bed, pulling the bedspread over him. He curled up in a ball on his side, a study of shame and misery. I lightly pushed his hair back from his forehead in a typical mother's caress. Josh froze for a moment, at my touch, but then relaxed. I stroked his hair a couple more times and saw some of the tension ease out of him.

"Try to get some sleep Josh. I'll wake you for breakfast." I said softly as I leaned forward to turn off the lamp.

"C-can you stay with me for a minute," he asked in a trembling voice.

"Sure, just try to sleep. I'll stay right here."

I hesitated, and then continued gently brushing his hair back from his forehead. The touch soothed him and within minutes he was fast asleep. I sat there for a few minutes more. Finally, I went back to the kitchen to plan breakfast.

Sam came into the kitchen about an hour later. Still in her pajamas, she was rubbing the sleep out of her eyes. I picked her up and gave her a hug. I must have squeezed Sam extra hard because she squealed.

"Mommy you're squishing me," she said, making a choking noise.

I laughed and put her down; asking if she wanted waffles or pancakes. Her eyes lit up.

"Waffles, do I have school today?" she asked hopefully.

"Yes." I laughed at her instant scowl. "We're having a special breakfast because Josh is here."

Sam looked around. "Where is he?"

"He's getting a little more sleep in the guest room. He had to get up really early so his dad could get to work on time. No waking him up. I need you to get dressed, quietly please, and then come back down here to help me."

For once Sam didn't argue or dawdle. She went right upstairs. I listened to make sure she wasn't deliberately, 'by mistake', making too much noise. I mixed up the waffle batter and filled the frying pan with bacon.

Sam came back downstairs fully dressed. She'd even brushed her hair. Having Josh around was a good influence on her. I let her pour the batter in the waffle iron and then asked her to set the table. Just as the first waffle came steaming and golden out of the waffle iron, Josh walked through the door looking sheepish. I smiled at him and told him to sit at the table. Sam gave him an exuberant welcome and Josh managed to smile. I split the waffles between the two kids and asked Josh if he could help Sam with the butter and syrup.

"I can do it myself, Mommy," Sam said indignantly.

"I just meant if you needed help, honey."

I split the bacon among the kids and started making eggs for myself. I asked Josh if he wanted eggs too. His mouth was full of waffles and he just shook his head. Josh's plate was empty when the next waffle was done and I offered it to him.

"That's okay, you haven't had any yet," he said quietly while he eyed the waffle covetously.

"I always eat eggs before I eat waffles, so I won't eat as many waffles. I'll get mine from the next batch unless you're full."

I waved the waffles in front of him. "Okay," he said with a genuine grin.

He smothered it with butter and syrup and the rapturous look on his face made me laugh. Under Sam's constant onslaught of questions he relaxed a bit. Rather than resent her pestering, he showed an indulgent protectiveness toward her. He put up with a lot more than most nine year old boys would.

We dropped Sam at her classroom. As soon as Josh was alone with me he withdrew into himself. As we walked back toward the car in silence, I had an idea.

"Josh, since we're here, if you'd like to see your classroom and meet your teacher we could go over there. Then you'll at least know where to go when school starts." He hesitated. "Mrs. Wilson is really nice. I think you'll like her and I figured you could run the idea of the airport trip by her," I offered as extra incentive.

He nodded and we turned back toward the classroom. Mrs. Wilson, his new teacher, came right over with a broad smile and showed him around. All of the kids were involved in a project and barely looked up as we walked by. When the tour was complete, after some prompting, Josh told her about the field trip idea. He was hesitant at first, but the more he talked the more animated he became. By the time he was finished, she looked just as excited as him and turned to tell the class.

"Everyone, can I interrupt you for a moment? This is Josh Clay. He'll be in our class when the school year starts."

She went on to explain the field trip idea. The kids crowded around us, all talking at once. They peppered Josh with questions. Mrs. Wilson let them talk for a few minutes and then called a halt, telling them they would all have plenty of time to ask questions when Josh started school. Reluctantly, the kids went back to work, but they were still buzzing with excitement. Mrs. Wilson decided October would be best for the trip because they would be studying weather and wind patterns. I told her I'd start working on it right away.

As we walked back to the car Josh was happy and excited. I told him I would have to leave him at the day care at the gym while I worked out and he didn't seem to mind. He'd brought a book with him. There was a new girl at the day care but she was friendly enough. When I left, Josh was happily ensconced in reading.

I cut back on my exercises so Josh wouldn't have to wait too long. After taking a quick shower I headed back over to collect him. He was still in the same spot, completely immersed in his story.

"Josh, your Mom's here," the day care worker called out before I had a chance to say anything.

His head snapped up and he glanced my way with an expression conveying hope and wariness at the same time. When he saw me waiting, he scowled for a moment and then his face became devoid of all expression.

"She's not my Mom," he said as he stood and gathered his things. He followed me silently out to the car.

All the way back home he stared out the window. I wanted to get him to open up but wasn't sure how to do it. When I opened the door to the house Keesha came bounding up to greet us. Josh smiled for the first time since we'd been at the school. Making a quick decision, I told Josh to put his stuff on the counter and get back in the car. He shrugged and walked back out the door. I grabbed a leash and my other dog paraphernalia and loaded Keesha in the back of the car.

Glancing in the rear view mirror as I drove, I watched Josh spend almost the entire trip petting the dog's head and scratching her ears. Every once in a while Keesha slurped his hand and he smiled. We pulled into the lot of the local dog park and she started whining low in her throat. Josh petted her head soothingly.

"What's the matter Keesha?"

"Don't worry, she's just excited. She knows this is where we always come for play time," I explained.

I let Keesha out of the back, snapped on her leash and then handed it to Josh. He looked surprised but intrigued, taking it from me as if he wasn't sure what to do with it.

"Okay, Josh, let me clue you in about Keesha. She is well trained and will respond to your commands but she usually takes a few minutes to settle down at the beginning of a walk. Don't let her pull on you. You need to establish you're the boss right away and she'll do a good job. Tell her to heel. She should walk right beside your leg. If she starts to walk ahead, give a light tug on the leash and firmly tell her to heel again. There's a place further down where we can let her off the leash and play ball, okay?"

Josh nodded solemnly. I grabbed my backpack and locked up the car. Josh gently but firmly told her to heel and we set off down the trail. Keesha was on her best behavior and he didn't have to correct her at all. I figured it was a testament to how much they had already bonded.

We walked in silence for a few minutes. Then I started pointing out the various sights and explaining where the different paths led. Josh didn't say a lot but he looked like he was enjoying himself.

After fifteen minutes of walking we got to the off-leash area. Keesha's tail started wagging in anticipation long before we arrived. As we passed through the gate I told Josh he could let Keesha go. He took the leash off but she just sat there trembling. He looked at me as if to ask what she was waiting for. In answer to his unspoken question, I opened the backpack, got out a tennis ball and handed it to him.

"If she wasn't your best buddy before, she soon will be," I said with a laugh.

Keesha stood up as soon as she saw the ball. Josh drew his arm back and threw it as hard as he could. She took off after it, tail wagging, barking in glee. No matter how many times we threw the ball, she went after it. After about a half an hour I could see she was getting tired. Knowing the dog wouldn't stop until we did, I told Josh we should take a break.

I handed Josh a small bowl and a bottle of water and told him to give the dog some water. Keesha came running over and licked Josh's hands while he poured. He was having trouble getting water in the bowl because he was laughing so hard at the affectionate licking. When it was finally full Keesha transferred her licks from him to the water bowl.

I handed another water bottle to Josh so he could have a drink, and then sat on a nearby log to rest. After Keesha drank her fill she flopped down near the rock Josh was sitting on and, with a sigh of contentment, proceeded to take a nap.

"I've always liked this place because it is one of the few places I remember having my Dad all to myself," I said and waited to see if Josh would respond.

After a few minutes he took the bait. "Do you still come here with your Dad?"

"No, I haven't seen my Dad in years. He and my Mom got divorced when I was a child and my Dad moved across the country. We stayed in touch for a while but then we just…..stopped," I said and was amazed how much it still hurt.

"Why did you stop?" Josh asked and I could tell he was more than a little interested in my response.

"Well….there are lots of answers to your question. I guess the real reason is because I wanted to see if he wanted to be with me." I paused and gazed out toward the forest, reliving those days in my mind. "A few years after my parents were divorced I realized I was always the one who got in touch with him. He was always friendly and interested in what I was doing whenever I called him but I realized he never called me. So, on my thirteenth birthday, I waited for him to call. He never did. I just kept waiting and years went by. Finally, I had to admit he didn't want to talk to me." I shrugged but it was a struggle to appear unaffected.

"My Mom doesn't want me either." Josh said softly and the devastation he felt as a result of his mother's rejection was right there on his face. I wanted to cry. I wanted to yell at this woman who would throw away the gift of such a wonderful child's love. But I sat there quietly and waited to see if he would continue.

"She just wants to go out and have fun. I just get in her way, she said." There was a lot of sadness and a little edge of anger in his voice. "It's a good thing my Dad wants me or I'd be in trouble. He'd rather be with me than anyone else." I could see the uncertainty in his eyes. The fear was there as much as he tried to hide it and, suddenly, I knew what prompted his outburst that morning.

I got up and walked over and squatted down in front of him.

"Josh I'm going to tell you some things and it's really important you listen to me with both ears, okay?" I asked and waited for him to look at me.

Josh stared at the ground for a moment and then looked at me and nodded.

"Have you ever gotten a toy that was broken from the moment you got it and never worked right?" I asked.

Josh looked surprised and a little confused but nodded again.

"No matter what you did, that toy never worked the same as the others or the way it was supposed to because it was broken, right?"

"Yeah."

"Well, I'm afraid my Dad and your Mom are like that broken toy. No matter how good you are, how many wonderful things you do, how much you try to get your Mom to act like the Mom you want and deserve, it won't happen. It won't happen because she's a little bit broken inside and she doesn't know how to act any other way. I don't know why and I don't know any way to fix her. But the most important thing for you to understand is it's her that's broken, not you. You are an amazing person. You are kind and you are smart and you are funny, but you could be the most amazing, best child, there ever was and it won't matter. It won't matter because there is something broken in her and you didn't break it, you can't fix it and it's not your fault," I said earnestly, never breaking eye contact.

Josh's eyes were filled with tears and his lower lip was trembling by the time I finished speaking. I sat down next to him and pulled him into my arms. Josh sat there stiffly for a moment and then he just dissolved. His face crumpled and he sagged against me and sobbed as if his heart was breaking and I thought it just might be. I ran my fingers through his hair as I had that morning, letting him sob out all of the pain and anguish he had been holding in for so long.

When his sobs had decreased to sniffles I handed him the water bottle. He drank deeply and sat up a bit but didn't move away from me, so I decided to broach the second subject. This one was a bit trickier, but I didn't know if I'd ever have this opportunity again.

"Okay, I have one more thing to tell you. It's just as important as the first thing but I don't think it will hurt as much," I said and waited until he nodded.

"Your father is nothing like your mother. He is not broken in anyway and no matter what you do, he will still love you. You are the most important person in the world to him and no matter who he meets or who he becomes friends with that will never change....ever," I repeated for emphasis.

"Do you know what your father told me when we decided we really liked each other?" Josh shook his head.

"He told me he really liked me and he wanted to spend time with me but he couldn't make any promises about the future because you are his first priority. He hates the way your mother has made you feel and he told me the most important thing in his life is making you happy." I stopped talking for a moment to let this sink in, and then continued.

"I like your father a lot. I like spending time with him. But, no matter what happens between us, I could never take your place and I would never want to. Just as no matter how much I care about your father, he could never take Sam's place. Do you understand?"

Josh sat for a moment and looked at me as if he was searching for proof I was telling the truth. "I understand," he said and then studied me for a moment longer. "I'm glad you're friends with my father."

"Thanks, Josh. I hope we can be friends too," I said with a smile and a squeeze.

I stood up and looked at Keesha who was lounging on her back with her paws in the air. I laughed and Josh laughed with me.

"Come on; let's get this lazybones moving."

As soon as we spoke her name, Keesha leapt up as if she was the one who'd been waiting for us. We let her run around and check everything out as we walked through the rest of the off-leash area. Josh didn't talk very much but I knew he needed time to process what we'd talked about so I wasn't worried.

An hour and a half later we put a very tired Keesha back in the car. We dropped her off at the house and decided to go to a newly released Disney movie. I knew Sam would want to go but thought it was important to spend the time alone with Josh. We liked the movie so much we decided we'd like to go again with Sam and John.

Josh suggested a leg of lamb for dinner because it was one of his Dad's favorites. We finished shopping in record time because he, unlike Sam, didn't stop every five seconds and ask me to buy something. When we got back to the house he didn't wait to be asked, he just grabbed groceries and lugged them inside. I gave him instructions on how to prepare the lamb and let him do it.

After the lamb was in the oven we went to get Sam. She grinned from ear to ear when I told her she was expected to make the biscuits. The rest of the dinner preparations were accomplished with a great deal of laughter. We used cookie cutters to cut the biscuits into various designs. The designs got less recognizable as the bakers got sillier. The kitchen was warm and smelled of lamb. We were laughing so hard I had tears streaming down my face.

This was the scene John walked into. He looked tired and more than a little apprehensive. I realized he must have worried about our morning altercation all day. Josh yelled, "Dad" and Sam yelled "John", at the same time and both ran over and flung themselves into his arms. John hugged them both tightly to him, looking relieved as he laughed at their onslaught.

"Hey, hey, watch out, I'm so weak with hunger I might fall over," he joked. "Something sure does smell delicious."

"We made lamb for you," Josh said enthusiastically.

"And biscuits," Sam chimed in.

"And asparagus and rice," Josh added.

I put the biscuits in the oven, set the timer and then poured glasses of wine for John and myself. As I came around the counter and handed it to him, he thanked me but took both glasses and put them on the counter before pulling me into his arms.

"C'mon Sam, I think we should go wash up for dinner," Josh said as he led Sam out of the room.

"But dinner's not ready yet," Sam said with a look of confusion as she followed.

"It's almost ready and you really don't want to be in the kitchen anymore," he said with a shake of his head. Then he dropped his voice to a stage whisper and said, "I think there's gonna be kissing."

As Sam followed him up the stairs all we could hear was "Eeeeeew."

We laughed but John stopped abruptly as he looked down at me. He placed his palm against my cheek and said, "How did you do it?"

"We just talked. He was afraid I was going to take you away from him and the thought of losing you as well as his mother petrified him. I just told him no matter what happens between us, he would always be the most important person in your life and I wouldn't want it any other way. We talked about other stuff too but I'm still waiting for the kissing part," I said with my hands on my hips.

I didn't get a chance to say anything else. I was in his arms with my mouth sealed to his in an instant. Within moments we were both breathing hard. John was the first to pull back but he didn't let me go. He wrapped his arms around me and rested his cheek on top of my head.

"God, the effect you have on me. I can't wait to get you alone," he said in a husky voice.

I knew we only had a couple of minutes until the kids came back downstairs, so, with one last squeeze, I stepped away from him and handed him his glass.

He gave me a wry smile and took a sip of wine. The buzzer went off on the oven. I was tempted to grab onto him again so I was glad to have something to do with my hands. I removed the golden biscuits from the oven, before wrapping them in a cloth and putting them in a serving basket. I turned the knife block toward him and handed him a fork.

"You get to carve."

He flexed his biceps and said, "Ah yes, my manly duties."

I laughed again and lightly smacked him on the arm. "No, it's just the only thing left to do and my least favorite task."

He affected a crestfallen look and said, "Ouch, talk about bursting my manly bubble."

I patted him on the butt and smiled slyly. "Don't worry; I still have need of some of your manly parts."

Heat flared in his eyes and he leaned right up to me and in a breathy whisper said, "Just for that, I'm gonna make you beg for my manly parts."

I wasn't dissuaded. I leaned into him and whispered, "John, all you have to do is look at me and I feel like begging."

He sucked in a breath and set me away from him. "Woman, don't distract me when I have a knife in my hand. I might slice off something vital."

The kids came downstairs with a lot of noise and talking, almost as if they were trying to warn us of their approach. I caught John's eye and we laughed. Dinner was a lively event. There was loud praise for the dinner, which we all took credit for in some way or another. Even John said the lamb wouldn't have tasted quite so good if he hadn't cut it superbly. This resulted in a lot of hooting and hollering from the rest of us.

Everybody pitched in to help clean up after dinner which actually led to more of a mess as soap suds flew through the air. When I announced it was bath time then bed time for Sam, she grumbled a little but gave John and Josh hugs good-bye without too much prompting. I told John Mike and Trish would help with his move and I hadn't heard back from George yet. Then I realized I'd never checked voice mail. I quickly checked and was surprised when George not only responded but said he'd like to come to the barbecue. I was even more surprised when he asked if he could bring a friend.

"He can show up any time after five and I don't have a problem with him bringing someone unless you have a problem with that,"

"No, not at all, I'm kinda hoping it's a date."

Josh gave me a big hug good-bye and John caught my eye and smiled, then pulled me into his arms for his own quick hug. He dropped a light kiss on my lips.

"I'll see you tomorrow, right? After you drop Sam off?"

"I'll be there; do I need to bring anything?"

"Just your delectable self," he answered with a leer.

I laughed, "I can't wait to meet your brother, is he anything like you?"

"He's older and prettier, but you're already taken by his younger, smarter brother," he said with a growl.

"Yes, I am quite taken with him," I said with a soft smile.

John's eyes darkened at my response and he dropped one more kiss on my lips before heading toward the door.

Chapter 13

Friday dawned bright and sunny and I hoped it would stay that way. It was much nicer to unload a moving truck in good weather. Sam wanted to help with the moving. I convinced her she was lucky, though, because she didn't have to do any of the work, but she still got to go to the barbecue. Satisfied, she helped pack the bag for her weekend at her father's with a minimum of fuss.

I arrived at John's house just after nine. Josh answered my knock and greeted me enthusiastically.

"Dad's in the kitchen. He's working on the food for the barbecue."

John leaned forward, keeping his messy hands well out of the way and kissed my nose. I laughed and said, "You missed."

"Nah, I just thought your nose might be getting jealous of all the attention your lips were getting."

I asked what I could do to help and he put me to work wrapping corn on the cob in foil for barbecuing. He had steak and chicken marinating and he was in the midst of forming hamburger patties.

"How many people are coming?" I asked in bemusement as I looked at all of the food.

"At least ten, Steve said he would bring a few of his friends, so I'm not sure of the exact number. Do you think there's enough food?"

I laughed. "I don't think you'll run out." I opened the refrigerator and saw he had at least thirty hot dogs and more hamburger meat. He also had potato salad, Cole slaw, and baked beans. I hoped Steve brought a lot of friends.

All of the preparations were done within an hour. Josh went up to his room to read until people started arriving. John had just gone into the kitchen to call his brother when Steve Rayburn showed up with two of his pilot pals. From the good natured ribbing going on between the three men, I could tell they were all single and spent a lot of time out carousing. All three were attractive and intelligent and I figured the women of Seattle were in trouble.

The three men flirted with me and I teasingly rebuffed them. John came back and put an arm around me as he stuck his hand out and introduced himself. By the look of surprise on Steve's face, I got the impression John hadn't told him of the change in our relationship.

I was surprised; they spent a lot of time together. I wondered if John had felt uncomfortable about our relationship or if he hadn't felt strongly enough about it to mention it to Steve. Then I chided myself, he was making it quite obvious now we were a couple. Still, I couldn't completely silence the small voice in my head saying he hadn't wanted anyone to know. I reminded myself I had no hold on him and should just enjoy the time we had.

Mike and Trish showed up next. I gave each of them a big hug. John shook their hands and thanked them for coming. He put his arm around me again as we stood there and talked. Trish raised her eyebrows at John's possessive stance and I felt myself blushing. A couple minutes later when Trish asked me to show her where the bathroom was, I knew I was in for the third degree.

I showed her the bathroom and turned to walk away but Trish had other ideas. She grabbed my arm and pulled me into the bathroom with her. Closing and locking the door, she turned, planted her hands on her hips and said, "Okay, dish!"

I was still blushing but I laughed at the look on her face. "Well, I told you I was attracted to him," I said in defense.

"So, obviously the attraction is mutual. What's going on?"

"We're just two adults enjoying each other's company. No promises. That's all," I said, trying to shrug it off.

Trish was having none of it. "I know you Cassie. You don't do casual affairs. No matter what you tell yourself, you know your heart will be involved."

"I'm fine. He's really amazing and I'm having a great time," I insisted.

"I just don't want to see you get hurt, sweetie. I was there after George, remember. I don't ever want to see you in so much pain again," she said with a worried expression on her face.

"Well, there's some new news on the George front also." I told her about Sam's revelations. "Actually, he's coming today and, get this, he's bringing someone," I finished with a waggle of my eyebrows.

Trish commented on George's change of heart and I was glad she'd accepted the change in subject. I hoped by the time it came up again I would have a better idea of where my relationship with John was heading.

I left so she could actually use the restroom for what it was intended. I walked back outside in time to see the moving truck pull up. The much talked about Shelby was attached to a trailer being towed behind the truck. The car was obviously a work in progress, but every male in attendance instantly gravitated toward it as if pulled by an invisible tractor beam.

A man who was obviously related to John jumped down out of the truck cab and came back to the car. "Typical," he said dryly, "I knew my brother was more interested in seeing his car than me."

"My car never threw up all over me," John bantered back but grabbed his brother in a big bear hug.

Jacob groaned. "You're never going to let me live that down are you?" he asked as he hugged John back.

"I've gotten such great mileage out of it," John said with a twinkle in his eye.

He turned and looked around at the small crowd as if looking for someone. Spotting me, he gestured for me to come forward and said, "Come here, sweetheart, even though I know I'm going to regret this, I'd like to introduce you to my brother."

I blushed slightly at the endearment but came forward with a smile. I held my hand out as John introduced us. Jacob shook my hand and held onto it for longer than necessary. I didn't try to remove it, just studied him as he was studying me.

Jacob was about an inch shorter than John and, though he was well built he wasn't quite as broad as John. He had curly dark hair and pale blue eyes. He was very handsome, what most women would consider a hunk, but I still thought John was the more intriguing of the two.

Suddenly, he grinned at me and pulled me into a hug. "So you're the reason why John has been in such a good mood lately," he said as he released me.

I laughed at his outrageous behavior. I figured he got away with a lot. He had a mischievous look about him most women found hard to resist.

"Well, I don't know about that."

As soon as Jacob released me John pulled me against him and scowled at his brother. Jacob laughed louder. "Don't worry bro' I'm not poaching." Then he added seriously. "I'm just glad you're over W cubed."

I looked at John questioningly. He looked down at Josh who was standing there next to him and hesitated. Josh smiled at his dad.

"It's all right Dad, I know what it means." He turned to me. "It's what my uncle Jacob calls my Mom. It stands for wicked witch of the west. They think I don't know," he said with a mischievous grin. Then he turned back to John and his smile faded. "It's okay Dad, you don't have to pretend with me. Like Cassie told me, Mom's broken. I didn't break her and I can't fix her so there's nothing I can do. I don't feel bad about it anymore," he said with a shrug.

By the look on John's face, I could tell this was the first he'd heard of my analogy. I stiffened a bit waiting for his response. I had overstepped my bounds, and I wasn't sure if he'd be angry. John didn't let go of me but pulled Josh against his other side and then dropped a kiss on each of our heads.

"She's a pretty smart lady, huh?" he said to Josh.

I relaxed at his words. Apparently, he wasn't upset and I was glad. I hadn't meant to intrude, but I knew exactly how Josh felt and I couldn't ignore his pain.

"By the way, there is some news on the W cubed front," Jacob said, cutting into my musings.

John arched an eyebrow at Jacob, waiting for him to continue.

"Seems there's trouble in paradise, through the grapevine I heard Sharon came home early from the islands. I think they broke up. And if I was a betting man, I'd place money on the fact that she'll be up here within the month," Jacob said with a grimace.

"That bridge was incinerated a while ago," John replied. "I don't think I'll be hearing from her."

Jacob rolled his eyes. "Don't bet on it." He paused and looked as if he were going to say more but then just clasped his hands together. "So, introduce me to the rest of these people, and then let's get going. The sooner we unload, the sooner we eat," he said as he rubbed his belly.

The rest of the introductions were made quickly. John oversaw the removal of the Shelby from the trailer and its reposition to the driveway. John needn't have worried. Mike hovered like a hen over her prize chick. In fact all of the men treated the car as if it were made of glass. Mike looked apoplectic when he learned John was only going to protect the car with a car cover.

"It's just temporary. I haven't had time to find a place to store it yet," John said soothingly.

"I've got an extra bay behind my store. I'll come over tomorrow and tow it over there."

"How much per month?"

"Very reasonable, you let me work on her with you and we'll call it even," Mike said, still unable to take his eyes off the car. When John hesitated, I though Mike was going to break down and beg. "I'll never touch her unless you're there and you call all the shots," Mike assured him. John finally agreed and he and Mike shook on it.

Once we got the truck open the real work began. We numbered the upstairs rooms one, two, and three. As each item was carried inside, John told us which room to put it in. When everything was out of the truck we took a lunch break.

John cooked hot dogs and hamburgers, saving the steak and chicken for dinner. He also served chips and Cole slaw. After seeing some of the huge appetites at lunch, I began to understand why he was worried he wouldn't have enough food.

When I finished lunch I asked him if he wanted me to take a ride down to the warehouse store to get some more food for dinner just in case. He laughed.

"You thought I was crazy for worrying, huh?"

"Well, I had no idea how much these guys eat. Of course, they had so much for lunch they probably won't be as hungry at dinner."

All of the men hooted with laughter. Jacob answered for them. "Cassie, in about three hours I'm gonna be hungry. In five I'm gonna be starving. If it's any longer, I'll start gnawing on anything handy," he warned.

"Okay, okay," I laughed as I turned back to John. "Should I just get more steak and chicken or more of everything?"

"Everything," all of the men said at once. Trish and I looked at each other and shook our heads in unison.

I grabbed my purse and headed out to the store. By the time I returned, the living room was in order and everyone was upstairs working on the bedrooms and the office. I called up to John asking if there was any more marinade. John told me where

Flight to Forever

it was located and I set about marinating the new steak and chicken.

I finished preparing the food and started unpacking the kitchen supplies and washing them. When John came downstairs a while later I had stacks of clean dishes, glasses and silverware all ready to be put away.

"Watcha doin'?" he asked as he wrapped his arms around me from behind.

I was always taken aback by the instantaneous response I had to his touch. Just his hands sliding around my hips made my nipples harden and a shiver race through her body. John saw my reaction and took advantage. He was standing behind me and his large body blocked me from the view of anyone who walked through the door.

He slid his hands up my belly and rubbed his thumbs over my nipples while he lightly ran his tongue around my ear. I felt as if my knees were going to give out. I leaned back against him and arched my back, thrusting my breasts against his hands. I felt warmth and wetness between my thighs. I pressed my bottom back against him and wiggled it back and forth. I could feel him getting hard.

"If we were alone, I'd rip your pants down and bend you over the sink and bury myself inside you," John breathed against my ear.

The combination of his words and the warmth of his breath against my neck and ear made me sag against him. My breath was coming out in gasps. He supported me with one hand and slid the other down over my belly and between my thighs. He lightly rubbed back and forth, causing the seam of my jeans to press between the lips of my vulva and caress me where I was the most sensitive.

Just as my legs started to tremble I heard someone coming down the stairs. John heard it too because he slid his hand back up to my waist and just held me against him, giving me time to get control of myself. A few minutes later I heard Jacob's voice from the doorway.

"Geez, get a room you two. Oh, yeah it's your house isn't it?" He added before John could respond.

I couldn't help but laugh and, although it sounded breathless to my ears it helped me come back down to Earth. John gave me one last squeeze and then stepped back.

"Was there something in particular you wanted?" John asked Jacob with a scowl.

"We need direction. We waited as long as we could. Then they elected me to come break up your tryst," he said with a look of suffering on his face.

"You'd better go help them but before you go, give me a general idea of where you want stuff so I can start putting things away," I said.

Jacob gave a melodramatic sigh and headed back up the stairs, grinning as he went. John shook his head at his brother then turned back to me.

"I trust your judgment. When I was at your house you had all of your kitchen stuff in basically the same place I would have put it," he said with a shrug.

"Okay, you asked for it. Why don't you send Trish down here with me? I don't think so many men should be inflicted on her at one time," I said with a teasing look.

"I'm going to make you pay for that remark, woman."

"I hope so," I responded with a throaty growl.

John groaned and headed back out the door. I burst out laughing when I saw him talking to the front of his jeans saying, "Down boy, behave. You'll get your chance."

Trish joined me a few minutes later and we spent a good part of the afternoon getting the kitchen organized. When we were finished we went in search of the men and found them outside oooohing and aaaahing over John's Shelby.

"We should have known you'd be out here." I said with a laugh before turning to Trish. "I have a feeling we have some competition for their affection."

"No kidding," she agreed with a laugh.

John and Mike had the good grace to look abashed and came over to us immediately. I laughed again. "We're just kidding guys. But I don't want to hear anything when we spend hours at the fabric store around Halloween getting makings for costumes." I said as I shook a finger at them.

"Never!" they both said and then held up their hands and added, "Scouts honor," with serious expressions.

This sent Trish and I into peals of laughter. The four other men were shaking their heads and making snorts of disgust. Josh was smiling as he watched the exchange until Jacob covered

Josh's eyes mumbling something about John setting a bad example of manhood. I rolled my eyes and John changed the subject by asking if we were finished in the kitchen. I took his hand and pulled him inside to show him where we'd put everything.

After the kitchen tour, John took Trish and me around the rest of the house to show us the completed product. I liked it; it was cozy and looked like a home. When we came back downstairs, John started the grill and began cooking the meat over low heat. I went to the school to pick up Sam, arriving back at John's house just as George drove up.

I took a deep breath before I got out of the car, hoping I hadn't made a mistake inviting him. Sam ran to him and gave him a big hug. I waited for a moment to give them time alone to say hello, then walked over to greet George.

Two women got out of the car and I knew both of them. My good friend, Jasmine, got out of the back seat and a woman who worked with George, named Elaine, got out of the front seat. Now I was really confused.

George spoke first. "Hi Cassie, I stopped by the house to feed Keesha. I figured you would be busy most of the day. Jasmine was just pulling out of the driveway. She stopped by to say hi so I dragged her along. I didn't think you'd mind," he said nonchalantly but I knew him well enough to know he was nervous and trying to put a good face on it.

"No, not at all, it's great to see you Jasmine." I turned and gave her a hug.

"And you remember Elaine, right?" he continued as I stepped back from the hug.

"Of course, Elaine it's good to see you. It's been a long time." She stood there clenching her hands together, looking uncomfortable. At my words she relaxed.

"It's good to see you too, Cassie. I hope I'm not intruding," she said shyly.

"Not at all, the more the merrier," I said with a laugh. "You won't believe how much food there is."

Her hands unclenched and she gave me a tentative smile. I realized she was worried about how I would react to her relationship with George. The looks she kept darting at him were very telling, they bordered on adoration. I hoped it worked out because complete devotion from a woman was exactly what he needed.

George took Elaine's hand and followed me to the back yard. Jasmine walked along beside me and we chatted about what we'd been doing recently. When we got to the back yard, I introduced the new arrivals to everyone. While I'd been out, someone had set out all of the food. It sure looked like a feast and the smells coming from the barbecue made my mouth water. John took a moment away from the grill to shake George's hand and say hello to Elaine and Jasmine. Mary Sullivan walked into the yard just as John was taking the meat off the grill.

"Mary, I'm glad you could make it," John said with a smile.

"How could I stay away from all of these luscious smells?" she responded as she sniffed appreciatively. "If a couple of you strapping males come with me I have a large portable table and chairs we can set up so everyone has a place to sit," Mary said, ushering the men ahead of her into her side of the duplex.

Steve flirted shamelessly with Mary and she was giggling like a girl by the time the table and chairs were set up in the back yard. Everyone served themselves and found a place to sit. Steve insisted on sitting next to Mary and even held her chair for her.

"You've definitely got Irish in you, young man," she said with a laugh as she sat down.

He just grinned at her and then dug into his food. Once everyone started eating there was silence except for groans of enjoyment. Mary remarked on the taste of the chicken.

"What's in the marinade?" she asked me.

I shrugged and pointed at John. "You'll have to ask him. This is all his."

"You've been holding out on me John. I didn't know you could cook. What's in this?" she asked as she took another bite of the steak.

John just looked mysterious and said, "It's an old family recipe."

"You devil," Mary said with a laugh. "Well we'll just have to trade recipes. You let me know which one you want in return."

John looked pleased at the prospect and I marveled at the many facets of his personality.

"Be sure to save room for dessert," Mary said halfway through the meal.

John groaned. "I'm afraid I forgot to make a dessert. I knew I forgot something."

Mary's eyes twinkled. "I didn't forget.

The people at the table who had tasted Mary's baking all grinned in anticipation. Steve told her he'd heard her cinnamon rolls were legendary.

"You are shameless Steve," Mary said as she patted his hand with a smile.

I'd been glancing at Jasmine when Steve made his latest comment and was surprised to see her roll her eyes. It looked as if she wasn't as taken with Steve as Mary was. Then I remembered she'd survived a bad relationship with a pilot and here she was surrounded by four of them. In fact, I could remember several disparaging remarks about pilots and infidelity she'd made. I worried about it for a minute but on further observation it looked as if Jasmine was having a good time despite the company. The more I watched, the more I realized it was only Steve who rubbed her the wrong way. I stored the thought away to ask her about at a later time and gave myself up to the sheer enjoyment of the food.

When most people were finished, Mary enlisted the aid of Steve and Mike and, once again, disappeared into her kitchen. A few minutes later she followed as the two men carried out a huge sheet cake. It was elaborately decorated. Written on the top was, 'Congratulations on your new home'. Everyone admired it. "Where did you get that cake?" It's amazing." George said.

"I made it," Mary said simply. When George gaped at her in astonishment she added, "I put two of my kids through college by decorating cakes."

No one wanted to cut into it because it was such a work of art. Then Mary told us it was chocolate chip-carrot cake with a cheesecake filling. Jacob jumped up and said, "Give me the knife!"

Everyone laughed but no one argued when he cut into the cake. Then, once again, silence reigned except for groans of pleasure and the sound of forks scraping against plates.

Jacob finally pushed his plate away and turned to Mary. "Will you marry me?"

"Hey, not so fast mister," Steve said.

Mary shushed both of them and, with a twinkle in her eye, said it was late and she was going to head back over to her house. "That's the beauty of being the oldest one in the group. I don't feel guilty about not helping with the cleanup," she added with a smile. She allowed both Jacob and Steve to escort her twenty feet to her door and then told them to behave themselves.

George announced he really needed to get Sam to bed as she yawned for the third time in as many minutes. Elaine offered to help before they left but I told her not to worry about it. Jasmine asked if she could catch a ride back to her car with them. Sam gave John and Josh hugs and then cuddled against George as he carried her to the car. I walked along with them and took the opportunity to pull Jasmine aside and ask about her reaction to Steve.

"Typical pilot," she responded with a snort of disgust. "He thinks he's God's gift to women and I bet he has one in every city he flies to. I'm sure he thinks fidelity only belongs in the motto of the FBI."

"Hey, he's not a bad guy. And John's a pilot, too, you know," I said with a small smile, trying to make light of her remarks.

"John seems like a good guy but I'd still be careful if I were you. Steve is too good looking for his own good. I wouldn't trust him for a minute," Jasmine said definitively.

I decided now was probably not a good time to point out she, herself, was super model beautiful. It was like the pot and the kettle business but I remembered how devastated she'd been by the pilot who couldn't keep his pants zipped. I figured she had a right to her prejudices, considering how much she'd paid for them.

I hugged a sleepy Sam and told her to have a good weekend. Sam mumbled a good night and proceeded to fall asleep in her car seat before the car doors were shut. George and Elaine thanked me again for the invitation. I waved to them as they drove away and went back to help clean.

The remaining guests pitched in and fifteen minutes later everything was cleaned up and all of the leftovers were put away. One by one, the rest of the guests left, thanking John for the great meal. They'd all enjoyed the feast so much they'd almost forgotten how hard they'd had to work for their food.

On his way out the door Steve casually asked me about Jasmine. I mentioned he already had a strike against him; briefly explaining about Jasmine's painful past relationship which turned her off pilots. Steve shrugged good-naturedly and said, "You can't win 'em all." But I got the impression he was more intrigued by her than he was willing to let on. He reminded me he still wanted to talk to me about places to live and then he allowed himself to be ushered out by his buddies. Mike and Trish walked out the door right behind them.

Finally, it was just John, Jacob, Josh and me left. Before John could say anything Jacob spoke.

"Hey, I was hoping for some one on one time with my favorite nephew. I was going to keep him up late watching scary movies and stuff like that. Any chance you can make yourself scarce so you don't cramp our style?" Jacob asked as if John would be doing him the favor by going away with me.

John looked at Josh and saw he was practically holding his breath in anticipation. "Is it okay with you if I go out for a while?"

"Sure Dad, if you want some time to yourself that's fine. Jacob and I will be okay." Josh said with an ultra casual air, belied by the fact he was practically bouncing.

John turned to me. "Will you take pity on me?" he asked plaintively.

I had to stifle a laugh. "I guess I can put up with you for a while longer," I said with a long suffering sigh.

"Now don't come home too early and ruin our wild and crazy night." Jacob warned him as he showed us to the door.

Once the door was closed we burst out laughing. "I take back every nasty thing I ever said about my brother," John said.

"But what will we do for all that time?" I asked.

"I'm sure something will come up." John replied dryly as he opened his car door. "Race you to your house."

Chapter 14

I wanted to race all the way to my house. All day I'd thought about being alone with him...forget that, all week was more like it. This was an unexpected gift and I didn't want to waste any of it. I exceeded the speed limit on the way home but John beat me there anyway.

My hands were shaking as I tried to fit the key in the lock. It didn't help that John was standing right behind me and I could feel the heat of his body. He took the key from me, unlocked the door, pulled me inside, tossed the key on the table and had me in his arms before the door closed.

My mouth opened in welcome as soon as our lips touched. His tongue thrust past my teeth and mated with mine. I pressed my hips into his and felt his hard length. I wanted him more than I'd ever wanted anything else in my life.

He pulled away from me, sucking in air, and yanked my shirt over my head. Seconds later he had my bra off, flinging it aside, before cupping my breasts in his hands. With a look of reverence on his face, he kissed each one before gently sucking a nipple into his mouth. I moaned and arched my back. He suckled harder and lightly rasped his teeth across the turgid peak. I grabbed the back of his head and held his mouth against my flesh.

I tried to remove his shirt, groaning in frustration because my hands didn't seem to be capable of following my brain's commands. John stepped back, ripped his shirt off and pulled me against him, once again plundering my mouth. His light sprinkling of chest hair teased my nipples, keeping them erect and tingling.

I went to work on his belt buckle. My hands were trembling and not very cooperative, but eventually, I managed to get his belt open. I unsnapped his jeans and carefully unzipped his pants. I slid my hand past the elastic waistband of his boxers and felt rather than heard him moan deep in his throat as my hand closed around him. I ran my thumb over the head of his cock, smearing the fluid that leaked out of him around and around.

John growled and stepped back. He quickly undid my jeans and yanked them down my legs, kneeling down to pull them all the way off. While he was on his knees in front of me he wrapped his arms around my thighs and pressed his face against the thin wisp of cotton covering my mound, inhaling with a groan.

"I'm all sweaty from today," I said with embarrassment.

John locked eyes with me and slowly peeled my underwear down my legs and then tossed them on top of my discarded pants. He pressed his face back between my thighs.

"You smell like heaven," he said as he coaxed my legs apart.

John pressed his fingers inside me and groaned again as his fingers easily slid into my warmth. He stood up, pulled a condom out of his jeans pocket, and handed it to me.

"You do the honors, my hands are busy," he said huskily.

John pulled one of my legs up and wrapped it around his thigh so he would have better access for his marauding fingers. He slid them in and out of me while rasping his thumb over my swollen clit. My hands were trembling so hard I was having trouble getting the condom on him. He wasn't complaining though, because my fumbling hands were making him even harder. When I got the condom on I sagged back against the wall.

319

"Grab my shoulders Cassie. I need to be inside you and I can't wait any longer."

I grabbed his shoulders as he slid his fingers out of me and grabbed my other thigh. He pulled my legs wide, lifted me up against the wall and thrust inside of me in one stroke. I fell off the edge of the Earth with a shriek. He shook his head as if trying to fight off his own orgasm. He stayed imbedded inside me for a moment, just enjoying the wet warmth contracting around him.

"Wrap your legs around me, honey," he whispered in my ear. "I don't think I have much control here. I'll try not to be too rough," he continued in a husky voice.

"Don't hold back," I panted. "I want to feel all of you hard and fast. You won't hurt me. Just do it, please."

Any last bit of control he had snapped at my words. He pulled out and thrust into me, increasing in tempo until his hips were moving like a jackhammer. I pulled back just a bit and tilted my hips, creating constant friction against my clit. I could feel another orgasm building; the warm pins and needles started in my toes and worked upward.

John's head was thrown back and he was gritting his teeth. The tendons were standing out in his neck in his effort at control. My orgasm began and I could hear cries coming out of my throat, although, it was almost as if they were coming from someone else. There was a hazy ring around my vision as I felt the contractions go on and on. John thrust one last time, impaling me and shouting out as he erupted.

He collapsed against me crushing me against the wall, but I wasn't complaining. A few minutes later when he had recovered sufficiently, he stood up and let me down onto my own two feet. My knees buckled at first and he held on to me until I could stand upright.

I looked at him and grinned. His pants had only made it as far as his knees and otherwise he was naked. He reached down to his pants and I forestalled him. "Don't bother to pull them up. Just take them off and we can go take a shower," I said with a grin. "I haven't seen you naked all week and I'm going to keep you naked as long as I can," I added as my eyes drank in the sight of his muscular body.

He didn't argue; just pulled his pants off, grabbed up the rest of our clothes and followed me. I had him throw our clothes in the washer although I didn't turn it on. I was planning a nice steamy shower and didn't want the washer to interfere.

Both of us enjoyed the shower, letting the hot water ease muscles that were sore from the long day of moving. We explored each other's bodies but our movements were unhurried rather than the frantic desperation of earlier. When we finally got out of the shower, I wrapped a towel around myself and ran down to start the washer.

I came back up to the bedroom to find him lounging against the headboard of the bed with a towel wrapped around his hips. I just stopped and stared for a moment. He looked so at home, so right, sitting in my bed that it made my heart ache. Finally, I realized I was staring. I felt myself blush a little and looked away. I crawled onto the bed next to him, still not meeting his eyes. He reached out and tilted my chin toward him until I looked at him.

"What's going through that amazing mind of yours?"

His voice was soft but his eyes were demanding. They held mine and wouldn't let me look away, daring me to speak my mind. They saw a part of me that no one had ever seen before.

"I-I was thinking how much I like seeing you in my bed," I said shyly and then blushed more furiously and dropped my gaze.

His soft "Hey", brought my gaze back up to his and the tenderness in his eyes took my breath away.

"If it's even a quarter as much as I like being here then I'm a happy man," he said gently as he caressed my jaw line with his thumb.

My heart ached. I knew then that I loved this man. He had taken a part of me forever. He had used passion and sincerity to make me believe in myself, breaking down all my barriers and making me love again. It was exhilarating and terrifying at the same time.

I was afraid he would see the love in my eyes so I turned my face toward his hand and pressed a kiss into his palm. He pulled me toward him and wrapped me in his arms. He pressed a kiss into my hair and held me for a moment without saying anything.

Gently, he laid me back into the pillows and tenderly kissed my eyelids and nose. He continued on to my neck with a soft caress of his lips and feather light swipes of his tongue. Gone was the urgency of our earlier coupling. He stood for a moment and removed my towel and his gaze consumed me. He dropped his own towel next to mine and gave his full attention to making love to me.

. . . . .

John

I felt as if my feelings for Cassie were going to burst forth like a flower forcing itself through the cold spring ground. I wasn't sure if she was ready for any declarations on my part. I was afraid if I spoke of love at this point she would think I loved casually. She would never believe the depth of my feelings after such a short time. So, I decided to show her with my body.

I kissed her tenderly on the lips, gently easing my tongue into her mouth and languidly stroking against hers in an unhurried mating. I lightly nibbled on her lower lip and sucked it into my mouth. I trailed soft, wet kisses over to her ear and nuzzled the sensitive spot where her neck and ear joined. I felt her shudder in reaction and her nipples hardened against my chest. I was tempted to go right to her breasts with my mouth but I wanted to worship every inch of her and didn't want her passion to escalate too quickly.

I worked my way down her arms, stopping to lave my tongue around the sensitive inside of her elbow. I loved each of her fingers individually and then lightly sank my teeth into the skin at the base of her thumb. I could feel her restless movements as she silently urged me to pick up the tempo, but I resisted any urge to hurry. This was about love, not about sex and I wanted every part of her body to know how I felt.

I worked my way back up to her shoulders after I'd given lots of attention to her other arm. I kissed down the center of her chest between her breasts. I could feel her trying to turn her body and bring her breast into contact with my mouth. Again, I resisted her efforts. Slowly, I began kissing and licking and lightly biting my way from the edge of her breast inward in a spiral. When I closed my mouth over her nipple she arched upward and a broken cry came out of her throat.

I gave lots of loving attention to her nipple and then began the same slow inward spiral on her other breast. By the time my mouth left her second nipple and began a downward trend again I could hear the harshness of her breathing. Whenever I hit a particularly sensitive area, her breathing hitched and she moaned my name.

I ran my tongue into her navel and felt her belly quiver. I nipped her skin lightly on her lower belly all along the edge of the silky hair that covered my ultimate destination. She was twisting and writhing. I started the same slow travel down her leg. When her breathing hitched, I stopped and gave that area extra attention, especially the inside of her knee and the arch of her foot.

When I'd completed my tour of her first leg and reached the juncture of her thighs I heard her suck in a breath and hold it. I paused for a moment, letting the need build inside her, watching her unconsciously rotating her hips. I could see the moisture of her arousal glistening on the downy curls of hair that sat before me like a tempting present waiting to be opened. Her musky scent almost did me in but I continued on down her other leg.

Her breath came out in an explosive moan. She called my name again in a pleading tone. I continued my languorous trail. I knew that she knew where I was going to end up and the anticipation was driving her arousal to a fever pitch. When I began to nibble on her foot she was able to get her other leg away. She raised her knee and let her leg drop to the side. The sight of her, all pink and wet and glistening drove me wild. It took all of my concentration to keep from skipping the rest of the body tour and going right home. For, her feminine core that she displayed so enticingly to me, I now considered home.

When my wandering tongue and lips eventually reached the juncture of her thighs she was sobbing out her need. I pressed her other leg wide and raised her hips to slide a pillow under them. I wrapped my arms around her thighs and pulled them wider still. My hands draped across her belly and I used my fingers to pull her lips open.

I lightly kissed all around her center, with a light, teasing pressure. Her fingers wound through my hair and tried to pull my face deeper. She wanted hard contact but I wasn't ready to give it to her yet. I lightly flicked my tongue across the wet swollen skin and she cried out. I pressed my tongue inside her and felt her muscles clamp around it. As I'd done with her breasts I worked from the outer edges inward. Several times I got right to the center and worked my way back out again.

I knew her clit was so sensitized that when I touched it she would explode. Finally, I could hold off no longer. I was as greedy for her orgasm as she was. I closed my lips around her clit and sucked gently and pressed my tongue back and forth across the center. She erupted in a shriek that sounded almost like pain. She was arching her hips, pressing herself hard against my mouth, the muscles in her legs straining as she cried out over and over. I kept working her with my tongue, trying to draw her orgasm out as long as possible. Shudders racked her body in time to the contractions I could feel pulsing against my lips.

As her contractions began to diminish I pulled away and quickly rolled on a condom. I lay between her thighs but didn't enter her. I cradled her head between my hands and kissed away the tears streaming down her face. She was looking at me, but her eyes were still out of focus.

I waited until I saw awareness return, and then locking gazes with her, I slowly slid into her. She sucked in a breath and her eyes darkened as my hard length stretched her. I kept a lock on my emotions because her uninhibited reactions always made me crazy. But now, feeling her warm wetness close around me almost undid me. I closed my eyes, trying to regain control, wanting this to last, wanting to make her come again.

I took a deep breath and opened my eyes to watch her response to my invasion. I slowly withdrew, feeling her walls cling to me, fighting me all the way. Then I thrust forward again watching her eyes widen and her breathing quicken. As I increased the tempo of my thrusts her reactions all ran together in a blur. Just as what I was experiencing coalesced into a never ending feeling of warm wetness grasping, clutching, and sucking my hard length until I could feel my balls tightening. I wanted to make it last, but I could feel my body giving into the primal demand to spill my seed. The demand began to overcome any intent my brain had.

Her eyes had gotten hazy but I could see she was watching my reactions. I could tell she was getting close again by the way she was gasping and frantically thrusting her hips up to meet mine. She arched her neck and my name escaped her lips in a guttural groan. She tilted her head back down and her gaze bore into mine.

I wish…..you weren't wearing……a condom," she gasped. Her words so closely echoed my thoughts I felt my control slip even more. I growled and thrust harder but she wasn't finished.

"I want to feel it……when you fill me up. I want to know…..that you're leaving part of yourself…….inside me," she panted out the words and as their meaning sank in I lost all control. I threw my head back and my mouth opened wide in a silent yell. The cords in my neck tightened as I arched further back and thrust into her with a shout, and then again, feeling the compulsive need to empty myself completely into her. I heard her cry out as she let go. Her contractions milked me and I almost cried out again at how good it felt. I shuddered as my release seemed to go on and on until finally my muscles gave out and I collapsed into her arms.

In the back of my mind I knew I was heavy on her but I couldn't seem to make my muscles work to move. She still had her legs wrapped tightly around my hips, holding me embedded deep inside her. As I felt feeling return to my legs I began to move but she protested.

"No, please, not yet, I don't want it to be over yet," she whispered and kept her legs locked around me.

Since I could think of nowhere else I'd rather be than buried deep inside her, I stayed where I was. I raised my chest up and braced myself on my elbows to take some weight off her. My eyes took it all in, her flushed face, the light sheen of sweat on her skin, the soft unfocused look in her eyes. My heart swelled as I realized I had done this, I had made her look this way.

She released her hold on me and I rolled off her, pulling her into my arms. We lay cuddled together without speaking for the longest time. It was as if we both knew there were no words to describe what we'd experienced.

When we'd recovered, I propped my head on my hand and smiled down at her. I traced her eyebrows and her nose with a finger. When I did the same to her lips she kissed my fingertip.

She stretched, looking like a lazy cat all curled up on a rug in front of a fire. I couldn't believe the sight of her stretching made my loins tighten. I shook my head in amazement. She smiled at me.

"What's the matter?"

"I'm just....well I'm completely done in. But just now.....when you stretched like that....I wanted you again," I said with a helpless shrug. "I have a feeling that I'd want you even if I was told it would kill me."

She smiled at me tenderly. "I know what you mean. I never knew it could be like this and I can't seem to get enough. Even when you're inside me I still feel like I need to get closer," she said with a mystified expression.

I kissed her gently on the lips and then on each eyelid. "But," she said, "I know that eventually you'll have to leave and unless you want a really uncomfortable drive home, I'd better go put our clothes in the dryer."

She sat up and pressed a kiss into my hair before she stood. My eyes followed the sway of her ass all the way across the room. In the doorway she turned and looked over her shoulder and caught me watching her. She deliberately swished her bottom back and forth a few times. I glanced up at her face and smiled a lecherous smile.

She laughed in disbelief as I saw her nipples tighten again. "Do you want a glass of wine?"

"Okay, that would be nice."

When she walked back in with the wine I was leaning against the headboard with my hands laced behind my head. I sat up so I could take the glass from her. We sat there naked, side by side, drinking and talking. Then she laughed at something I said and accidentally spilled wine on herself.

"Let me get that for you," I said as I leaned forward and licked the spilled wine off her.

Soon we were deliberately spilling wine on each other. A short time after that I was

reaching for a condom. A while later she was collapsed sideways across the bed trying to recover once again. I was laying the opposite way on the bed, also trying to catch my breath.

Eventually, I stood up and grabbed her by the ankle. "Come on woman, time for a shower," I said with a groan.

We, once again, used most of the hot water getting clean and relaxing sore muscles. When we'd dried off she ran downstairs to get my clothes out of the dryer. She put on a robe and walked me downstairs when I was dressed.

"I wish I could stay."

She smiled up at me. "I wish you could stay too, but Josh needs you. I appreciate his giving me some time with you. I don't want to be greedy."

"Josh does need me but I kind of like it when you're greedy about time with me," I said as I rubbed my hands up and down her back.

I looked at my watch and with a sigh, gave her one last kiss. "Josh's school starts a week from Monday and I think we'll be off at least one day together. So we should be able to get some time alone at least once a week," I said with a rueful smile.

"I'd like that," she answered but couldn't seem to help the sad look at the thought of so much time spent apart. Then her eyes brightened.

"Before I forget, Josh and I saw the new Disney movie and we wanted to go again with you and Sam. So think about that, okay?"

"Sounds good, I'll call you," I said and waved as I got into the car.

Chapter 15

Cassie

When I closed the front door Friday night, the week stretched long in my mind. But, as it turned out, I didn't have to wait long at all to see John. He called mid-morning on Saturday and asked me to join him and Jacob and Josh for lunch before I left for work.

We went to a local restaurant where the food was good and the service was friendly. I heard lots of stories about John and Jacob's childhood. They, along with their sister Joanne, were quite the terrors as children. Or, so it seemed, if the stories they told were anything to go by.

Josh had obviously heard the stories many times because he added his own information even though, what they were talking about, had occurred years before he was born. I commented about everyone's name starting with the letter J and that brought on a whole new spate of stories.

I was surprised when I looked at my watch and saw it was almost two. I had to go home and change before work so I told them I should probably leave soon. John and Josh went off to the bathroom and told me to wait until they got back so they could say good-bye. That left Jacob and me alone and after a moment I realized he was studying me quietly.

"I'm glad you and John are together. You're good for him," he said after a minute or two.

"We're just enjoying each other's company." I shrugged.

He gave me a look of disbelief. "From the look on my brother's face when he looks at you I'd say it's a bit more than that."

"Well, we're a couple, but we agreed, no promises."

Jacob studied me again for a moment. "W cubed did a real number on him. I've seen him with other women since then but not very often. And he never looked at them the way he looks at you. Despite the way my brother and I act around each other, I love him and I don't want to see him get destroyed again. So, if you only want a casual fling, you'd better let him know before he's in too deep. Although, from what I've seen, it may already be too late," he said with a worried shake of his head.

I put my hand on Jacob's arm. "Jacob, he's the one who said he couldn't make any promises. He's trying to get some

336

stability back into Josh's life and I respect that. I would never deliberately hurt either of them."

He laughed lightly. "I'm willing to bet that he reconsidered his 'no promises' statement almost as soon as he said it. But you're both adults, you can work out your own issues. I'll just feel better knowing that you care about him a little," he said and studied my reaction.

I could feel myself blushing and I couldn't meet his eyes. "I do care about John….and Josh," I added, as if to insinuate my feelings for both were similar.

Jacob smiled at me knowingly. "Ah….I see … well, I won't worry then."

I was afraid Jacob had seen all too well. I thought he might have seen right through my feeble attempt to keep my feelings for John a secret and from the smile on his face I was pretty sure I was right. My feelings for John were new and special to me and I couldn't help but react when he broached the subject. I hoped I wouldn't be so transparent to John. I wouldn't want him to feel uncomfortable or even worse, feel pity for me.

I could tell by the look on Jacob's face that John and Josh must be heading back toward us. I drank a sip of water and concentrated on getting my feelings back under control. When they walked up and asked if I was ready to go I felt more in control and I smiled at them and nodded.

"Yes, I need to stop at home before I go to work so I'd better get going."

When we got out to the parking lot I said good-bye to Jacob. He was going back home and I didn't know when I'd see him again. I gave him a hug and he hugged me right back. He hugged me for a little longer than necessary and, finally, John interrupted.

"Okay, Jacob you can let her go now," he scowled.

Jacob let me go and laughed at his brother. "You are so easy."

I was pleasantly surprised when Josh stepped up and hugged me too. "Dad and I talked about the movie. Do you think we could go Thursday when Sam gets out of school?" He looked hopeful.

"Sure, that will work. I'll look forward to it and I know Sam will be excited when I tell her," I said and gave him a squeeze before I let him go.

Then John stepped up and folded me into his arms and dropped a kiss on the top of my head. "Thanks for inviting me. I was feeling a little lonely all by myself," I said against his chest. Then I pulled back and looked at him with a mischievous twinkle in my eye. "Besides, now I have all sorts of blackmail material if you ever get out of line."

"Oh, really?" He arched an eyebrow. "Well, I'm in trouble then because getting out of line with you seems to be a matter of course," he said and the carnal glint in his eye made me blush again.

I smacked him on the arm. "Don't start," I said warningly but I couldn't help smiling.

I walked toward my car and then paused and turned back for a moment. "Josh, I'll talk to my friend at Spring Aviation this weekend and I'll speak to my manager at the tower on Monday. We'll try to come up with a couple different dates that might work in October. Then your father can see if any of those dates will work for him. I'm going to try for a Thursday or Friday since those are my days off and your Dad is off on those days also, okay?"

"Great Cassie! Thanks," he said and bounced with glee all the way to the car.

With one last wave I headed for home. As I changed for work I looked around my room. I had redecorated after the divorce and up until recently I'd always seen it as a haven. I usually felt comfortable and safe here. But now I pictured John here. I could see him on the bed, standing next to the bed, in the bathroom. Everywhere I looked reminded me of John. When he wasn't there the room just felt empty rather than cozy.

I sighed and went down to feed Keesha. Then, with the dog happily gulping up her food, I grabbed my keys and headed into work.

Saturdays were usually pretty quiet and I dreaded all of the down time. Luckily, the crew I was working with was in rare form and the night flew by. I did manage to get a hold of my friend Tim who worked at Spring Aviation. He told me he'd speak to the necessary people and get back to me.

When I got home that night I was glad that I'd managed to keep my mind off John for most of the evening. I checked my voice mail and there was one message. I listened to the message and my heart clenched.

"Hi babe, I'm just going to bed and I'm thinking about you. I miss you. I wish I could curl up with you tonight. Dream about me. Good night." His low husky tones sent a shiver of longing right through me. I couldn't bring myself to delete the message and saved it. I laughed at my own sentimentality but knew I'd want to replay it.

When I went to bed that night I brought Keesha into my room. I never let the dog sleep in my room and even the dog seemed confused by the change. I told myself it was because I felt bad about not spending much time with Keesha lately. Deep down inside, though, I knew it was loneliness that prompted the change.

Sunday night when I got home from work George was, once again, sitting on the couch waiting for me. For the first time in a long time I didn't tense up when I saw him and my smile was genuine as I said, "Hi George how was your weekend?"

"We had a great time. Elaine and Sam got along well too so that made it easier."

"How long have you been seeing each other?" A week ago I never would have asked the question because I would have expected a sarcastic or nasty reply but George truly seemed to have changed.

"Just a couple of weeks, I talked to her a lot after the divorce but I didn't really pay attention to her. It's only recently I realized she's pretty special," he said with a self-conscious shrug. "I appreciate the invitation on Friday. Elaine was a little nervous but you were really nice to her and I appreciate that also," he said and I knew it had taken a lot of courage for him to say it.

"I don't wish you any ill will George, I never have. I just wanted to stop hurting. I'm happy for you if you've found what you want with Elaine. I mean that sincerely."

"I wish I could say I've always been that noble," he said with a look of chagrin. "But I'd like to put that all behind us. I know we may never be friends again but…..I want you to know that I'm trying to do the right thing and…..I'm sorry for any pain I caused you," he said haltingly and the sincerity of his words was evident.

"I'm sorry too George. I know I caused you pain also. But I think most of our problems were caused by miscommunications. So, let's make a pact that from here on out, if one of us says something that bothers the other, we'll talk about it. We'll assume positive intent, okay?" I said and stuck out my hand to shake on it.

He smiled and shook my hand. "Well, I think you're being way more gracious than I deserve, but I'm not going to argue. Okay, deal. From now on I'll try to make sure what I heard is really what you said," he said with a laugh.

He walked toward the door and I felt more hopeful about the future than I'd felt in a long time. At the door he turned and looked at me for a moment as if he wanted to say something else. I waited to see what he'd say.

"John is a nice guy. You two seem good together. Sam sure likes him. She talked about him so much that it made me a little jealous," he said ruefully.

If I'd needed proof that George had changed, that statement was certainly proof. George would never have admitted to vulnerability before, especially to me.

"He could never replace you George. She adores you. You're her father. I know that and so does he. We would never try to change that."

"Thanks," he said simply. Then he turned and walked out the door.

I went up to bed with a skip in my step. Even though I had to be in to work early in the morning I didn't feel tired. I changed for bed and crawled under the covers. I was just reaching for the phone to check my messages when it rang. I checked the clock and saw it was almost eleven. I answered the phone, curious as to who would be calling me at this time. There was a brief pause before the person spoke.

"Hi, Cassie, I didn't wake you did I?" John said in a concerned tone.

"Hi, no I just crawled into bed but I'm worried I won't be able to sleep anyway."

"I thought you worked later and I was going to leave you another message but I'm glad to actually talk to you."

"I got off at ten. Thanks for the message yesterday. It made my night."

"I wanted my voice to be the last thing you heard before you went to bed. I figured it increased my chances of being in your dreams," he said with a laugh.

"It worked." I remembered the hot dreams I'd had the night before.

"Good."

We talked for a few minutes about our days. When he heard I had to be in early he told me he'd better let me go.

"Wait, there's something I want to tell you." I forestalled him. I knew I had to tell someone about my discussion with George or I'd go over it in my head all night. He listened intently while I told him about our conversation.

"That's great, now you won't be hurt anymore and I won't have to hurt him," he said with satisfaction. Then he added, "Unfortunately, Sharon and I will never get to that point so I'll just have to stay as far away from her as possible."

"I'm sorry," I said, wishing he could experience the same feeling of relief I was feeling.

"It's okay. Listen, you'd better get to sleep. Let me know about Thursday for the movie, okay?"

"I'm sure it'll be fine but I'll talk to Sam about it tomorrow."

"Okay. Josh told me to say Hi to you. Get some sleep and call me tomorrow about the movie."

"Tell Josh, Hi for me too. I.....miss you."

"Me too. Good night."

"Good night," I said in a strangled voice. I'd almost said I love you. At the last second I realized what I'd been about to say and changed it to I miss you. I chastised myself. I would have to watch myself. Every time I spoke to John, the feelings welled up and I had an incredible urge to tell him how I felt. I shook my head and resolved to be more careful.

Monday I spoke to my manager and started the process for getting approval for the class tour. Security had been really tightened since September 11, 2001 and there was a lot of red tape to cut through. By the end of our discussion, though, I was confident that I'd be able to get approval eventually.

My friend Tim called back and told me he'd gotten preliminary approval. Once we came up with some firm dates he was also confident he'd get final approval. He also suggested a paper airplane contest for the class project. He told me of other places that held the contests and they were very popular. The entrants got very sophisticated with their designs.

I was thrilled with the way the plans were coming together. I thought the paper airplane contest was a great idea and got on the web to research it. Tim was right, there were several places that held paper airplane contests and a few of them gave ideas for how to design a contest of our own.

When I talked to Josh he was just as excited. He told me his Dad had talked to the chief pilot and he thought they'd be able to work it out. We talked for a few more minutes, batting around ideas for the class project. Josh promised he would talk to his teacher on the first day of school the following Monday.

John got on the phone and we talked a little more about the project. He told me how much he and Josh had bonded and how much they'd learned about each other just since Friday. John was on vacation for the next week and a half. He and Josh had been spending all of their time together. John was happy and relieved because he said that Josh was, once again, the happy enthusiastic child he remembered.

We decided to get together for lunch and then a workout on Thursday. Josh said he'd read more about aerodynamics while he was waiting for us to finish our workout. Then we'd get Sam and go to the movie. When I crawled under the covers alone again, I comforted myself with the idea that there were only two more days until I'd see John again.

Sam seemed just as excited about seeing John and Josh again as I was. Each of the next three mornings, Sam asked how long it was until we went to the movie with Josh. By Thursday morning she was bouncing in her excitement and I wondered if she would get any schoolwork done during the day.

John and I had a good workout. With him to spot me I was willing to push myself a little harder. Even Travis remarked that I'd made some gains in the amount of weight I was lifting. He also looked back and forth between John and me, and then gave me a little waggle of the eyebrows. I knew he was teasing me about my relationship with John, but I just smiled at him.

Our lunch went well also. Josh spent the entire lunch telling us all of the things he'd learned about aerodynamics and different paper airplane competitions around the country. He told us about a contest at Georgia Tech for middle school and college entrants. He also told us about a children's book publisher that sponsored paper airplane contests at schools around the country.

"We could make this a yearly event. Maybe schools could compete against each other," he said excitedly.

"Spring Aviation might even be interested in sponsoring a contest," I suggested.

"Yeah, that would be great."

We talked about the possibilities for a contest for the rest of lunch. When we were finished I asked if they wanted to come with me to take Keesha for a walk before we picked up Sam.

Josh looked at his father. John said it was a great idea and he needed to work off lunch anyway.

We went to the same off-leash area we'd gone to before. With all three of us throwing the ball for Keesha she got plenty of exercise. When she'd exhausted herself we gave her water and let her rest before taking her home.

For the first time since she had started school, Sam was waiting with all of her school paraphernalia and her coat when I arrived to pick her up. She grabbed my hand and headed right out the door. When I suggested we stop at Josh's class so he could tell his teacher about their progress in planning the field trip, I thought Sam was going to explode with impatience. But when I explained the movie didn't start for another hour anyway, Sam was happy to go to the big kids' class.

Mrs. Wilson was just as excited as Josh about the possibilities for an airplane contest. She figured they would be teaching physics and weather at the same time. She told us to find the date that worked best for us and she would plan her class schedule around it. She decided she'd plan the contest for a little while after the field trip so the kids would have a chance to apply what they'd learned.

Sam loved the movie. Josh enjoyed it the second time just as much as the first. Sam and Josh talked about funny scenes during the entire car ride to dinner and then halfway through dinner. I figured she would know the movie by heart eventually once we got the video and Sam watched it every day for a month.

John seemed to enjoy the movie too. He was quiet for a while during dinner but I figured he was just tired from an active week. Josh, Sam and I were having a lively conversation anyway and when I told them the local county fair had started that weekend both of them got excited.

"Can we go Dad?"

"I want to go too," Sam immediately chimed in.

John looked at Josh in confusion, as if he hadn't been paying attention.

"The fair, Dad, it just started. Can we go tomorrow with Cassie and Sam?"

"Sam, you're going to your father's house tomorrow." I told her and was glad George wasn't there to see the disappointed look on Sam's face.

John took it all in and then addressed me. "I don't want to create any problems and I don't want to overstep my bounds but I have a suggestion."

"Sure, I'm all ears."

"Well it's completely up to you but now might be a good time to test out your new understanding with George. I mean he might want an adult night out with Elaine on a weekend and Sam could go there Saturday morning instead. Then we could all go to the fair tomorrow night." He ended with a shrug.

I felt both kids' eyes on me as I considered it. "I guess it's worth a try," I said, and then turned to Sam. "But don't count on it yet. Your Dad may already have plans. I'll go call him." I added when I saw Sam was wriggling in her seat in anticipation.

I called George and put the request to him. I was surprised when he jumped on the chance.

"That would be great. Elaine and I never go out alone on weekends. How about if I come over and get her Saturday morning?"

"Whenever you want to come is fine just as long as you get her before I have to leave for work at three."

351

"Great, thanks a lot Cassie," he said and I could tell he was sincere.

"No problem, actually it will be great for Sam to be able to go to the fair with another child so she'll have someone to go on the rides with her. It works out for everyone. So, I'll see you on Saturday."

"Okay, Saturday it is. Have a good time at the fair," he said and hung up.

I slowly hung up the phone. This new relationship with George was great, if a little disconcerting. I kept waiting for old resentments to crop up. But I also realized this might have been the problem with our marriage all along. Maybe we were never meant to be anything more than friends. Maybe trying to make our friendship into something more than it was meant to be was what had created all of the dissension and bad feelings. With a shrug I decided to just go with it and hope our new relationship continued. It was healthier for everyone concerned.

As I walked back to the table I gave Sam the thumbs up. Sam shouted with glee. I couldn't help laughing even though several other diners turned around to stare at Sam. I shushed her but I couldn't stop smiling. I was looking forward to tomorrow night almost as much as Sam, although I figured it was probably for a different reason.

Friday was one of those Seattle days that made me glad I lived there. It was sunny and mild and Mt. Rainier was so clear it felt like I could reach out and touch it. The fair was packed with people but we still had a great time.

I managed to resist most of the food but finally gave in and had an elephant ear. "There are just some things you have to eat at the fair and for me this is it," I said as I took a big bite of the sugary fried dough.

"For me it's caramel apples," John said as he guided me toward a vendor that sold them.

Josh chose a sno-cone and Sam chose cotton candy. Then we sat at an empty table and watched the crowds go by while each of us enjoyed his or her individual treat. Then it was on to the petting zoo and the animal exhibits. Once we'd had a chance to digest our food it was on to the rides. Sam was thrilled to have someone to go on the rides with. She took advantage of it by going on her favorites several times.

I ran into Mike and Trish. They said they'd watch the kids for a little while so John and I could go on a couple rides children weren't allowed on. John seemed delighted to find out I was a daredevil and we spent our time alone going on the scariest rides.

We were both happy and exhilarated when we reclaimed the kids. Trish had noticed that John and I were holding hands wherever we went. She raised an eyebrow at me as if in question, but I just smiled at her and waved good-bye. I was enjoying myself immensely and didn't want any discussions about the future to impinge on it.

We stayed late and John carried Sam back to the car. She fell asleep on his shoulder and didn't wake up even when he strapped her in the car seat. Josh fell asleep in the car on the way back to my house. We let him sleep while John carried Sam up to her bedroom and put her in bed. Then he took advantage of the few minutes we had alone to remind me of what I was missing.

I was clinging to him, breathing hard when he pulled back and said he'd better go. I groaned in frustration.

"I'll call you when I get Josh to bed, okay?" he asked with a little waggle of his eyebrows.

"At this point I'll even take phone sex." I sighed as he walked out the door.

"Hey, beggars can't be choosers," he said jauntily over his shoulder.

"I'm not complaining. Phone sex with you is still better than full contact sex with anyone else."

He stopped mid-stride and turned back to me. He strode back and pulled me into his arms and kissed me until I was breathless again. "Thanks for the extra incentive," he growled in my ear and then turned and walked back to his car.

Chapter 16

School started on Monday and John and I fell into a routine. We spent our days off together and we even, eventually, made it out of bed. We worked out and, generally, just spent time getting to know each other. Often, the four of us had dinner together on Thursdays and I had dinner with John and Josh on Fridays when Sam went over to her father's house.

Josh really blossomed once school started. Because he had already been introduced to the kids in the class when he visited during the summer, he didn't feel the same awkwardness that most kids do at a new school. He also had the advantage of being the one to suggest the field trip to the airport and all of the kids were excited about that.

Mrs. Wilson had dubbed the field trip the "Day of Flight". I'd received authorization from my manager and John had been able to work out the logistics with Nationwide. We were just waiting on final approval from Spring Aviation. The "Day of Flight" was scheduled for Friday, October 15th. We planned to have the follow-up paper airplane contest four weeks later on November 12th.

Mrs. Wilson was going to start teaching about weather and wind currents the first week in October. Then the children would have some understanding of what keeps aircraft aloft before they went to Spring Aviation. At Spring Aviation they would learn about aircraft design and get a chance to fly an aircraft in the simulator.

After lunch they'd go to Nationwide where the children would get a chance to go into a real airplane. They would look at the different flight surfaces on the aircraft and the equipment in the cockpit. John would lead that part of the tour and Steve had agreed to help out.

Then they'd go up to the Tower and I would take over the tour. I'd explain about weather observing and wind shear and other effects that weather had on flight. I'd also explain a little about air traffic control and the effects of hazards like wake turbulence.

The children would be responsible for taking notes and asking as many questions as they needed answered. They were expected to take the knowledge they learned from the field trip and use it to design their own paper airplane. The paper airplane competition would be judged in four categories; time aloft, distance flown, most original design, and best overall. We hadn't decided where to hold the contest yet but we weren't very worried about that. We were more worried about whether we would get final approval from Spring Aviation.

Finally, on September 29th, I got a call from Tim when I was on my last break during my shift. "Cassie, I have good news," he said when I answered the phone.

"You got the approval?"

"Even better than that, we're going to show the kids the wind tunnel, explain the manufacturing process and let them try the simulator."

"That's great Tim, thanks a lot."

"But I have even better news." I could hear the grin in his voice.

"What could be better than that?"

"Spring Aviation would like to sponsor the paper airplane competition. They will provide the space and the judges. They'll also provide prizes in the form of education savings bonds. If it goes well there is talk of making this an annual event," he said and I could tell he was thrilled with the response he'd gotten from the company.

"That's amazing Tim; Mrs. Wilson is going to bounce off walls when I tell her. How'd you do it?"

"Well, all I did was make the suggestion and explain how it could benefit our image. Also, I said it couldn't hurt to have our finger on the pulse of the future. Today's fifth grader could be tomorrow's aircraft designer. The reason it took so long to get back to you is it went right up to top management. I just hope things go well this year. There will be a lot of eyes watching this," he warned.

We spoke for a few more minutes, discussing logistics for the visit to Spring Aviation. He told me he'd taken the day off October 15th so he could take part in all the activities. I was amazed but thrilled at the great response I'd gotten from everyone about the "Day of Flight" idea.

When I hung up the phone in the break room I did a little jig of delight. The other controllers asked what was up. I explained the phone call and they were excited for me. Several, who were parents, remarked that they thought their kids would love something like that. I told them to cross their fingers that everything went well because it might become an annual event.

I couldn't wait to tell John and Josh. Normally, I would have to head right to the school to take Sam to gymnastics but

Sam's coach had cancelled the class for today. I decided to swing by John's house to tell him in person. John was as excited about the whole project as I, and had asked me a few times, recently, if I'd heard from Spring Aviation. I knew he'd want to know right away. He'd had an early flight this morning, but I figured if he wasn't home already he would be shortly. I hurried to my car and headed south.

. . . . .

John

When I heard the knock on the front door I was hoping it might be Cassie. In fact, I counted on it being Cassie so I was shocked when I opened the door and found my ex-wife Sharon standing there. I just stood there for a minute staring at her. She was as beautiful as ever but I'd seen the real Sharon and so her beauty was tarnished to me.

"Well, aren't you going to invite me in?" She fluttered her lashes.

That little flutter used to make me do all sorts of stupid things but I'd gotten over it. "Well, that depends Sharon, what are you doing here?" I really didn't give a damn if I sounded ungracious or not.

"Is that any way to speak to the woman who bore your child?" She put her hands on her hips.

"And that's pretty much the last time you had anything to do with him so I don't think that's a good subject to bring up if you want something from me." I said matter-of-factly.

"You're right; I have been a bad mother. But I want to change that. Please, John, just give me one more chance," she said with what looked like sincere regret on her face.

I was hesitant to trust her. She'd had many changes of heart throughout our marriage but they'd only lasted until she'd gotten what she wanted.

With a sigh, I decided I would give her the benefit of the doubt for Josh's sake. Despite his new understanding of his mother's shortcomings, I knew, deep down inside Josh hoped his mother would change. For his sake I hoped she would too, but thought it unlikely.

I ushered Sharon inside and closed the door. I brought her into the kitchen and asked if she wanted coffee. She said she would like that and sat at the small kitchen table overlooking the back yard.

"This is a nice place," she said.

Just that statement alone made me wonder if she really had changed. She would never have chosen this apartment; it was way too middle class for her tastes. I was intrigued but wary.

When I'd made the coffee and served both of us I sat down across from her and said, "Okay, Sharon, what's the reason for the visit?"

Sharon looked at the floor for a minute and she really did look troubled and somewhat nervous.

"Well, Ryan and I broke up," she said hesitantly. "It was a really horrible scene and he said some really awful things. So, anyway, I came home early and I spent a lot of time by myself just thinking about everything. I realized a lot of what he said was probably true. I guess I realized I had a good thing and I blew it. I know I was selfish and I know I wasn't a good mother to Josh but I'd like to make up for that. I'd like to try again," she ended in an almost pleading voice.

I was shocked anew. I'd always hoped Sharon would come to her senses about Josh but I'd never expected it to happen. I still wasn't sure if I quite believed it but if there was a chance I would take it in order to give Josh what he'd always wanted.

"I hope you're sincere Sharon. But, I've got to tell you, if you really want a relationship with Josh you're going to have to work at it. He's been badly hurt and it will take a lot for him to trust you again," I said as bluntly as possible.

She looked at the floor. "I know it will be work but I'd like to give it a try….and not just with Josh." She looked back up at me as she finished the sentence.

"What do you mean?" I asked. I had a feeling I knew what she was getting at but I wanted her to spell it out.

"I-I mean, I want another chance with you too," she said with an earnest look.

I was already shaking my head before all of the words were out of her mouth. "Sharon, it's over between us. Maybe, some day we could be friends, but that's it."

Sharon shot out of her chair and started pacing back and forth. She looked really devastated and I was taken aback. I'd been certain she didn't have any feelings for me. In fact I'd begun to wonder if she ever had.

"John, we were good together once. We could be again," she said with a pleading note in her voice as she stopped in front of me.

"Sharon, all we ever really had was a decent sex life. You and I never wanted the same things. You can't build a life together based on good sex."

There were a lot of reasons why I would never want to be with her again but I figured I'd appeal to her common sense.

"Maybe I want different things now. We could learn about each other again. Sex isn't a bad place to start," she said as she moved closer to me.

"Sorry Sharon, I'm not interested."

She rarely took no for an answer and she didn't this time either. She was always convinced she knew better. She stood there for a moment, staring at me with her hands on her hips.

"I know you still want me," she said almost petulantly.

She sat on my lap, wrapped her arms around my neck and kissed me. My first inclination was to stand up and dump her off my lap but I decided the best way to deal with Sharon was to show her I wasn't interested rather than tell her. So, I sat there and let her kiss me. She tried everything that used to make me crazy and I didn't respond.

In fact, I was thrilled when I realized I felt nothing at all. I had no desire for her and I wished she would give up and go away. I couldn't help comparing her kiss to Cassie's and found they weren't even close. Cassie aroused me just by looking at me and her kisses were genuine and passionate. Sharon's were passionless and calculated to get the response she wanted. Finally, with a sound of frustration, she stood up and stalked away from me.

"At least you used to be good in the sack," she said in a venomous tone.

"Ah.....now here's the real Sharon; so, what's this really all about?" Then, before she could answer, suddenly, I knew.

"It's about money isn't it? When Ryan dumped you, you lost your gravy train and you were hoping you could hop on board mine for a while until you could find another one, weren't you? You don't have any interest in Josh at all, do you?" I said and was surprised I could still be shocked by her callousness.

"I finally got rid of the little brat. Why would I want to saddle myself with him again?" she said with a laugh.

I heard a little gasp and turned to see Josh standing in the doorway of the dining room. I wanted to cry. For the first time in my life I could honestly say I wanted to hit a woman. I walked over to Josh and put an arm around his shoulder. Josh was pale but he didn't look hurt as much as angry and I was glad about that.

"Sharon, you need to leave. Please, don't ever come back again. If you do I'll get a restraining order against you. I'm pretty sure I can convince a judge you are a danger to my son," I said and the coldness in my eyes made her realize I meant every word.

She shrugged her shoulders as if she could care less but I could see her hands were shaking. As she turned to leave the room Josh spoke.

"You know, Sharon, I used to think you were so beautiful, like a fairy princess. But Uncle Jacob is right; you are just like an old witch. It doesn't matter what you look like on the outside when you're ugly on the inside," Josh said, and the calm almost analytical way in which he said it made it all the more powerful.

She hesitated for a moment and then, once again, affected an uncaring attitude.

"Well, actually, this is better anyway," she said as she walked toward the front door. "I could never live here. It's so low rent."

She opened the door, gave me one last look and then slammed the door on her way out.

Josh and I looked at each other and burst out laughing. It had been such a feeble attempt at a put down that it was humorous. I looked at Josh after a few minutes and said, "I wonder how she knew our rent was so low?"

Josh laughed even harder. I knew then he was going to be all right.

A couple of minutes later the doorbell rang. I wondered if Sharon would dare to come back. When I opened the door, though, it was Mary Sullivan.

"Hi, Mary, what's up?"

"I wanted to thank you for the great job you did fixing that leak in the roof. I know I'll have to bite the bullet and replace the roof eventually but it's nice to put it off a bit longer."

"No problem. I'm glad I could help. Do you want to come in for some coffee?"

"No thanks, I've got something in the oven. Did Cassie find you?" she asked as she turned to walk back to her side of the duplex.

"Cassie? When was she here?"

"About ten minutes ago. She drove in, walked around back and then took off a minute later. She sure was in a hurry." Mary added as she opened her door.

Suddenly I couldn't breathe. There was only one reason I could think of why Cassie hadn't knocked on the door. Mary must have noticed how pale I'd gotten because she asked if I was all right. I mumbled something, said good bye and headed for the phone to call Cassie.

. . . . .

Cassie

I wondered if this was what it felt like to be bi-polar. I'd gone from the highest of highs to the lowest of lows in minutes. I lay curled in the fetal position on my bed. I'd known it was going to be bad when John finally walked away but the reality of the situation was so much worse than I'd anticipated. I felt adrift in a yawning pit of blackness.

369

I'd walked around the corner of John's house and stopped. I saw the woman talking to him and was awed by her; she was stunningly beautiful. She was one of those people you couldn't help staring at and the fact that she was standing in front of John with, what could only be described as a predatory look on her face, didn't even register at first.

Then the woman sat on his lap and kissed him. He sat there. He didn't protest. He didn't push her away. He just let her kiss him. I was halfway back to my car before I even realized I'd turned away. I kept seeing the beautiful woman kissing John.

I saw the future without him in it and it was very dark. I'd driven home on auto-pilot. Later I couldn't even remember the trip. I'd called George and told him I wasn't feeling well and asked if he could get Sam. He agreed right away and I had the momentary satisfaction of knowing at least one thing in my life was going okay.

I didn't undress. I didn't eat. I'd stayed curled in a ball on my bed since I'd hung up the phone with George. The phone rang several times but I ignored it. Talking to John was out of the question. My pride was all I had left and I knew if I saw him I'd probably start sobbing.

George had told me he'd keep Sam over night and take her to school in the morning. So, I was free to sink into the pit of blackness. I knew I'd have to go down and feed Keesha eventually but I decided the dog would be okay for a little while.

I felt a little hysterical laugh bubbling up in my throat. Had I really started to think a guy like John would want me? Well, he had wanted me. Nobody could fake the amazing sparks we struck off each other. But, I'd always known he would tire of me. I just hadn't expected it to be so soon.

I knew I could never compete with that ethereal creature I'd seen in his lap. Even those beautiful feminine arms she had wrapped around John's neck made me feel inadequate. I hoped, for Josh's sake, the woman was kind as well as beautiful. Hell, I even hoped it for John's sake as well.

I was surprised I wasn't angry. All I felt was a sense of inevitability. I figured the anger would come later. I just had to stay away from John as long as possible. Hopefully, I would get myself under control and then I'd act as if there was nothing wrong.

Maybe, eventually, we could even be friends. More hysterical laughter bubbled up out of my throat. *Friends, yeah, that could happen.* I laughed and laughed and suddenly I was sobbing. I sobbed as if someone was wrenching my very soul out of me. I sobbed until I was exhausted, then I slept.

Later, I crawled out of bed to go feed the dog. That duty completed, I went right back to my sanctuary and shut out the world. A little while later I heard knocking on the door and looked out to see John's car in the driveway. The thought that he was so close and yet so out of reach made me give in to the wrenching sobs again. Eventually, he left.

I spent the night crying myself to exhaustion and then sleeping. In the morning, when I went to the bathroom, I caught a glimpse of myself in the mirror and grimaced. God, no wonder John had dumped me. I looked like a hag. I thought about taking a shower but decided to go back to bed.

I must have fallen back to sleep because I awoke a while later. I couldn't figure out what had awakened me. I figured it was a noise of some kind. Then I heard another noise and turned around. John was standing in the doorway. He looked just as haggard as me and my first reaction was one of concern. Then I steeled myself and rolled back over.

"Go away John," I said dully.

"Give me a chance to explain, Cassie. It's not what you think. I know that sounds like a cliché, but it's true."

"Don't worry John, I'm not mad. You told me you couldn't make any promises. I just want you to leave me alone," I said with a sigh.

He didn't speak for a moment but he didn't leave either. Instead, he walked into the room and around the bed to stand in front of me.

"Why aren't you mad, Cassie?"

It was the last thing I expected him to ask and I reacted in confusion, "W-what?"

"Why aren't you mad? If you saw what I think you saw then you think I cheated on you. Why aren't you mad? You should be angry at me, furious even. So why aren't you?"

"I knew you'd get tired of me eventually. I mean I knew you didn't want anything permanent. I didn't expect you to move on so soon but she is very beautiful so I can understand the attraction..." I trailed off.

"Funny, Josh told her she was ugly," John said, but there was no humor in his smile.

"W-why would Josh do that? Josh met her already?"

"Josh said that because it's true and he's known her since the day he was born," he answered but didn't continue.

I stared at him for a second as my mind made the connections. "That was Sharon, your ex-wife?" I asked but I already knew the answer. "I hope for Josh's sake you're not thinking of getting back together?"

"For Josh's sake, huh, not for your sake?" he asked but I could tell it was a rhetorical question.

He sighed and ran his hands back and forth through his hair. "Here's the short version, Cassie. Sharon showed up on my doorstep yesterday, about fifteen minutes before you got there, as a matter of fact. She told me she'd broken up with her boyfriend and she'd done a lot of soul searching and realized she'd been a bad mother and wanted to try again. She meant she wanted to try everything again, including me. I told her it would be great if she wanted to finally have a relationship with Josh but I wasn't interested. She tried to convince me using the one thing that was always good in our relationship.

I knew she would never listen to me but if she discovered I had no interest in her any more it might sink in. So I let her kiss me. I felt nothing. She didn't like that at all. The real Sharon came out then. Turns out, she was hoping to get me to pay her bills until she could find another sugar daddy. It was actually a good experience because I realized I have no feelings for her any more except maybe a healthy dread, kind of like what you'd feel for a poisonous bug.

The only unfortunate parts of the whole incident were that you saw her kiss me and Josh overheard some of the nasty stuff she had to say about him. In the long run, I think it was good for him, but I hated to see him hurt. He did a good job of putting her in her place before she left and I don't think she'll be back again."

He stopped talking and paced back and forth a moment.

"I love you Cassie, but I'm not sure it's enough," he finally said.

"Y-you love me?" I asked in disbelief.

"I've loved you for a while. But I knew you had a lot of issues to work out with George and your father so I didn't want to push it." He paused again, and then continued.

"When I say I'm not sure it's enough, I mean for you. I know I love you enough but I'm not sure if you'll ever believe it.

You and George are working out your differences but the scars your dad left are still there. You were angry at the thought Sharon might hurt Josh again but you weren't angry at the thought she might take me away from you. You still think you aren't deserving or something like that and I don't know if I can handle that.

I want you more than I've ever wanted anyone. I think we can be happy together. I want that happiness. I think I deserve it and I'm willing to fight for it. But you have to want it just as badly. I'll never convince you that you deserve it. You'll have to come to that realization yourself."

He stopped talking again for a few minutes and paced, then came to a halt in front of me.

"I want you in my bed but I'm not going to give you an excuse. I'm not going to let you tell yourself I only want you for sex. I want you in my life but not because of anything other than the fact you are a wonderful, beautiful, sexy, caring woman and I love you. But you need to believe me when I say that. You need to believe it in here," he said and tapped on my chest above my heart.

"So, I'm going to give you time. I don't want a life without you but I don't want half a life with you either. I've already had half a life for too long and I'm not willing to settle. You have to believe you deserve this. It's special and it needs to be cherished, not second-guessed. I'd like the four of us to still get together on Thursday nights because I don't want to worry the children until we've made a decision about our future. But, I'll give you some space the rest of the time, okay?" he asked, but again, it was a rhetorical question.

He bent over and kissed me on the top of the head. "I do love you Cassie. Try believing in me and yourself." He turned and walked toward the door.

"Oh yeah, could you give George back his key. Don't be mad at him. I was so upset when he showed up at school with Sam I nearly went crazy. When I told him what had happened he gave me the key. He really does want what's best for you. He thinks it's me. I hope you decide he's right," he said and tossed the key onto the bed. Then he was gone.

Chapter 17

After another hour in bed just mulling over what he'd said, with a sigh of disgust, I forced myself to get in the shower. Even though I'd have to wash again after my workout I was hoping the needle sharp spray would get me motivated.

When I walked into the gym Travis waved to me and looked around as if looking for John. When he didn't see him he gave me an enquiring look. I just smiled and went into the locker room.

I forced my way through my workout. I'd gotten so used to having John around to spot me, and without him, I wasn't able to lift as much weight. That was only part of the problem, though, mainly I just missed him and he'd only been gone an hour.

He said he loved me, wanted a life with me. I was happy, I was dumbfounded, and I still didn't believe it. He was right, I couldn't believe someone wanted me as much as he said he wanted me. I'd never had that problem with George. What was the difference? And then, as if someone had whispered the answer in my ear, I knew. I loved John much more than I'd ever loved George. I'd always cared about George but he was never

379

my grand passion. Forget grand passion, he wasn't my passion at all. I didn't know what true passion was until I met John. George was never really more than a friend in my mind, I finally admitted to myself. I'd thought it would be enough. It wasn't.

I'd chosen George because he was safe. If he left, I wasn't in danger of feeling the agonizing pain I'd felt with my father's abandonment. With John I'd already felt a prelude of what it would be like to lose him permanently. It was agony. I was afraid to risk feeling that much pain. Then it hit me, I didn't have a choice any more. I already loved John. Losing him now or a year from now would hurt just as much.

With a start I realized Travis was standing beside me talking to me. I'd been lost in thought, sitting on the bench press, staring off into space.

"I'm sorry Travis, I was daydreaming. What did you say?"

"I asked if you're okay. You've been sitting there for five minutes."

"I'm fine; I've just got something on my mind. What's up with you?" I asked and tried to look natural.

"I've been drafted."

380

"Drafted? There's no draft anymore," and I'm sure my face showed the confusion I was feeling.

"I've been drafted by the guys to find out if you're still seeing John or if the field's wide open."

"What do you mean, if the field's wide open?"

Travis just looked at me for a moment and then rolled his eyes. "As soon as you walked in here without John at least a dozen guys asked if you broke up because they all want to ask you out."

"They want to go out with me?"

"Geez, Cassie, I figured John had clued you in. Lots of guys want to go out with you. You just always have a hands-off attitude so they never bothered. They've all gotten courage from John, though, and so now they want to know if the field's open?"

"Which guys?" I asked out of curiosity.

Travis rolled his eyes again and named half a dozen men I'd known for over a year at the gym. With each name my jaw dropped a little further until I felt like a fish nailed to a plaque with its mouth hanging open. He'd named some extremely attractive guys.

He laughed. "Cassie, you are so clueless it is humorous."

"Why me?"

"Why not you, Cassie? You're pretty, kind, smart, you have a great body and you ooze sexuality. What's not to like?"

His tone of voice was so matter of fact I believed him. Well, I believed he believed it but I was beginning to wonder if maybe he knew what he was talking about.

"So, what's the answer? Enquiring minds want to know?"

"We didn't break up."

I must have looked as troubled as I felt because he just stood there for a minute and then said, "What's going on, Cassie?"

My eyes filled with tears and he took my arm and said, "Step into my office." He pulled me into one of the salesmen's offices, pushed me into a chair, sat on the edge of the desk facing me, crossed his arms over his chest and said, "Tell Travis your troubles."

I spilled my guts. I told him about George and Sharon and my father. I told him about Sharon's visit and the kiss and

John's subsequent declaration and his intention to give me space. Throughout my monologue Travis just leaned against the desk and listened. He asked a few clarifying questions, but other than that, I did all the talking.

After I finished, he hopped up onto the desk and dangled his legs off the edge.

"I could have told you he loves you. No man looks at a woman the way he looks at you unless he's in love. When you're both in the gym he's always aware of where you are even when you're not with him. And when another guy talks to you the testosterone comes off him in waves."

Travis hesitated for a moment as if gauging my reaction. "From the misery you're in I'd say it's a pretty good guess you love him too."

"I love him more than I've ever loved anyone. But he's right, I have to trust him or it's not fair to him."

"I don't think it's a matter of trusting him is it? Really, it's a matter of believing in yourself. If he has to spend all his time convincing you he really does love you, how much will he get out of the relationship? You've got such confidence in everything else; you have to figure out how to have it where it counts."

"Oh, I should be able to figure that out in a week, no problem," I replied sarcastically.

"Well you have more incentive than ever before. Do you really want to lose him?" he asked with a sympathetic smile.

"Good point."

"You're a smart lady. You'll figure it out. I think you should skip the rest of your workout, though. You're distracted and you might get hurt. I'll go tell the guys the bad news."

For a moment I thought he was going to tell them what we'd discussed. It must have shown on my face because he laughed.

"I meant I would tell them you aren't available. Geez, you really do have a confidence problem." He shook his head as he walked out of the office.

I decided to take Keesha for a walk. Just because I was depressed didn't mean the dog should suffer. I took the ball and threw it in the off-leash area for over an hour. Then I took her on a long walk. Walking always helped me think. Half way through it, I decided to call my mother when I got home. It was time I worked out some issues anyway and what better place to start than with my mom. I turned around and headed back to the car.

My mom answered the phone on the second ring and sounded excited to hear from me. We talked for a few minutes about family happenings. When I brought up the subject of my father I could tell right away she wasn't comfortable with the topic. She kept changing the subject and after the third or fourth time I told her I had to go and hung up in frustration.

I paced around the kitchen for a few minutes, trying to figure out what to do next. I was so tired of Mom's constant refusal to discuss the subject. Suddenly, I wasn't willing to take no for an answer anymore. I dialed again.

"Mom, I know you don't want to talk about this but it's important. I've been seeing this great guy and....I love him and he says he loves me. But I'm so afraid he's going to leave me it's ruining our relationship. I need to know why Dad left. But even more importantly, why haven't we heard from him? Did he really care so little for his kids that he could just forget us?"

She must have heard the desperation in my voice. "I'm sorry Cassie. I know I should have talked to you about this a long time ago. But you never asked about him and I figured you'd made your peace with it."

She paused, took a deep breath and then continued. "Truthfully, I hoped you'd made your peace with it because I didn't want to talk about it. That wasn't very fair to you."

"Mom, just tell me what happened," I pleaded.

"Your father is a very smart man. He had so much hope for the world; he always wanted to fix society's ills, but he could never fix his own. His parents were cold and unemotional. He needed to feel needed so he set out to help everyone, to right every wrong he could. But he ignored the people closest to him. We argued about it all the time. I told him to stop trying to save the world and start with his own little corner of it. But I think he was too scared, I think he expected rejection from you kids because that's what he always got from his parents. You kids were so important to him and rejection from you would have devastated him. So, to protect himself, he distanced himself from you. Ironic, isn't it, that none of you speak to him now, kind of a self-fulfilling prophecy," my mother said with a bitter laugh.

"Cassie, don't turn into your father. Don't be so afraid of failure that you quit before you even try. You were never a cause of any of his problems. You worked so hard at being the perfect kid. It wouldn't have mattered. It was his problem and nothing you could do could solve it," she said earnestly.

"Thanks Mom, I appreciate you talking about this. I know it's a painful subject."

"We should have talked long ago. I'm sorry we didn't. I'm responsible if you've been blaming yourself all these years. Your father was a lot of things; he was absolutely brilliant in so many ways. But he never should have been a father. He wasn't built for it."

"Thanks Mom, I'll let you know what happens, okay."

"You do that, Cassie. I know you'll do fine. You've always been a wonderful person and I'm very proud of you. It's too bad your dad couldn't be more like you."

"I've gotta go Mom. I'll call again soon."

When I hung up I sat in the chair and stared at the wall, mulling over my mother's revelations. I certainly didn't want to become my father. I knew my relationship with my daughter was strong and nothing like the one I'd had with my father. There were no emotional barriers there.

Thinking of Sam made me look at the clock and I realized I needed to go pick her up. All in all, dinner at John's house should be an interesting time. I was a little nervous about how he was going to act but knew I shouldn't be. He was a caring person. He wouldn't make me feel uncomfortable. With a sigh, I got up and grabbed my car keys.

Dinner was delicious. John was polite, friendly and charming but he never touched me. Gone was the constant contact that made me feel cherished. Nothing could have illustrated better what life would be like without him in it. By midway through the meal I ached to have him squeeze my hand or put his arm around me.

Right after I'd finished my food, I realized I'd never told them about Tim's news from Spring Aviation. I'd gotten so upset about the incident with Sharon it had completely slipped my mind. I dropped my fork with a clatter and everyone looked up.

"I can't believe I forgot to tell you. It's the reason I came over yesterday." My smile faltered a little as I thought about the results of my impromptu visit.

"What Cassie?" Josh broke the silence.

My excitement returned as I told them about Tim's phone call. Josh was ecstatic. He ran around the table and hugged me. John reached over and, for the first time that night, squeezed my hand. I felt such an immense sense of relief I was staggered. But, when he released my hand, he went back to his polite and friendly demeanor.

Josh had looked back and forth between his father and me several times during dinner. I could tell he was a little confused and concerned about the change in us. When we were leaving, John hugged Sam but just waved at me. Josh ran over and hugged me fiercely before I walked out the door.

The next week was a very lonely one. I realized the lyrics to the old song were painfully true. You don't realize what you've got until it's gone. I saw John a few times at the school when we were both dropping off the kids. He was always friendly and asked how things were going but he didn't mention our relationship. He didn't ask if I was any closer to making a decision about our future.

I worked out by myself several times. By the third time, men were beginning to hang around me again. I felt a little uncomfortable at first because my new knowledge of their intentions toward me changed the dynamics of our relationships.

But, eventually, I fell back into my previous buddy persona and relaxed a little.

As the week wore on I found I was fielding questions at work about whether or not I was feeling okay. Several of my co-workers noticed my state of distraction. I didn't have the same interest in working heavy traffic. I actually avoided it a few times in favor of working the flight data position, which raised a few eyebrows.

By Thursday evening dinner I was frustrated and unhappy. I knew I wanted John and Josh in my life. Having tasted the wonders of being loved by John, this alternate relationship was a pale comparison. I wanted him to love me. *Damnit, I deserve it!* I thought to myself as I put the finishing touches to dinner.

I was a little surprised at my resolve, surprised and pleased. The talk with my Mom had helped as did Travis' revelations. Apparently, my reality was far removed from the way others saw me. I felt I was making progress and it cheered me up.

When John and Josh arrived, I hugged them both, ignoring the fact that John froze when I put my arms around him. I spent a good part of dinner discussing the plans for the "Day of

Flight." I'd had several discussions with Josh's teacher about all the logistics of the field trip. I told them what Mrs. Wilson and I had discussed and what plans we'd made.

Josh seemed to be less uncertain tonight. He didn't look as worried as last Thursday. He actually had a look of determination about him I found intriguing.

Sam was the same as ever. She was invariably cheerful. The only thing that upset her was she wanted to be a part of the field trip. She was suffering from a bad case of envy. I considered whether or not to keep her out of her class and let her come the following Friday.

Dinner ended and everyone helped clean up. When John said it was time to go, Josh walked over to him and quietly conferred for a moment. I saw John look at Josh questioningly. Whatever Josh said in response seemed to satisfy his father because John shrugged in acquiescence.

Josh came over to me and said, "I need to talk to you alone for a minute. It's important."

I looked over at John, but he just shrugged and shook his head. I followed Josh down the hall to the guest room. He closed the door and asked me to sit on the bed.

When I was seated, Josh walked right up to me and put his hands on either side of my face. The gesture reminded me of Sam when she was trying to get my undivided attention and it made me smile.

"I'm going to tell you some things and it's really important that you listen with both ears, okay?" Josh asked and, when I nodded he continued.

"I'm sorry but your Dad is broken. He doesn't know how to be a Dad and he doesn't see how great you are. No matter what you do, he'll never see how great you are because he's broken. It's not your fault he's broken because you didn't make him and you can't fix him, okay?"

My eyes filled with tears and I nodded again. "I have something else to tell you. Are you ready?" he asked and his eye contact never wavered.

"Your Dad is nothing like my Dad. My Dad is not broken at all. He loves you a lot and he's not going to change his mind. I've been pretty rotten sometimes and he still loves me. He's not going to stop loving you and take off because he's not broken, okay?"

I wrapped my arms around him and hugged him tightly while tears streamed down my face.

"I guess I shouldn't give advice unless I'm willing to take it myself, huh?" I said when I sat back.

Josh grinned at me. "That's right."

I stood up and took his hand and walked toward the door. "Your father is probably dying of curiosity by now."

I put my hand on the door and he stopped me. "Cassie....I-I love you too," he said and it was the first time he'd seemed uncertain since he'd walked into the room.

"I love you too, Josh. You are wise beyond your years. How did you know what was wrong, anyway?"

"My Dad told me just a little because I was upset after dinner last week. I saw how you were acting and it scared me. When he told me what was going on with you it sounded like how I felt so...."

"So, you decided it was time I took my own advice," I finished for him. He nodded and grinned again.

"Don't worry Josh. I love your Dad too. I'll work it out with him, okay?"

"Okay. Oh, I told my Dad that I wanted to talk to you about a girl if he asks what we talked about," Josh said with a conspiratorial look.

I put my arm around him and opened the door. "So....is there a girl?" I asked and waggled my eyebrows at him. Josh blushed. "I'll tell you later."

We walked back out to the kitchen where John and Sam were telling really bad knock-knock jokes. When we walked into the room, he raised an eyebrow in inquiry, but I just smiled at him. I leaned forward and brushed a quick kiss across his lips.

"Josh is all set. So what are you doing tomorrow?" I asked conversationally as we walked toward the door.

"I promised Mary I'd do some work around the house, why?"

"Oh, I just wondered. Drive carefully, I'll see you later," I said and waved as we walked out to the car.

After I'd put Sam to bed I went downstairs and made a fire in the fireplace. I sat in my favorite rocking chair next to the fire, pulled an old quilt across my knees and began to rock. It was time to make a decision. I rocked and stared into the fire as I thought about all of the conversations I'd had with people in the past week.

My mother told me my father was afraid to risk rejection from the people most important to him, so he distanced himself from them. Which was a backward way of saying my brothers and I wielded such power over his own view of his self worth he was afraid to show his love for fear it would be thrown back at him. How completely different John was; he had stood there with no guarantees about how I felt about him and he'd declared his love openly. He'd walked right out onto the most fragile part of the limb and put his trust in me. He had such faith in me he'd laid himself bare. He'd taken all of the chances and all he asked was that I believe in myself enough to trust his love.

I froze in mid-rock. I'd been just like my father. Was that the legacy I wanted? I'd left John hanging there, vulnerable. I had to show him I was willing to take a chance. I had to lay myself bare and chance rejection to prove I was willing to fight for what we had. I only needed to figure out a way to do it.

I started rocking again. I rocked until the fire was just embers. When I stood up and walked toward the stairs, my decision was made. Tomorrow I would fight for what I wanted and keep fighting until I got it.

Chapter 18

John

Friday morning I set out to replace the banister on the stairs. It'd been rickety for a while and Mary asked me to fix it. I'd been measuring and cutting wood since dropping Josh off at school. I was starting to work up a sweat, but was glad for the distraction. I had to do something to keep my mind off Cassie.

I'd felt tortured for the last week, wanting to reach for Cassie hundreds of times. I did such a good job of pulling back that Josh noticed and got worried. I told him I loved Cassie and wanted her in our lives. Josh wholeheartedly agreed with that. I explained my reservations. I told him Cassie and I had to come into the relationship whole if we were going to have a chance at a future. I didn't want to put Josh through another painful break-up.

Josh quietly listened to my reasons and made some very adult observations. He told me not to worry. He seemed to have resolved his concerns because he was no longer looking worried or upset. Last night he even went off to ask Cassie about a girl so he must be feeling secure.

I wished I could say the same. I was feeling anything but secure. In fact I couldn't remember a time when I'd felt this vulnerable. I was right on the verge of going to Cassie and begging her to take me any way she wanted. I didn't think I could take one more day of pretending coolness when inside I was like a volcano about to erupt.

I'd been so crazy yesterday I'd gone over to Mike's to work on the Shelby and ended up not doing any work at all. I'd made a couple of glaring errors almost immediately and Mike finally stopped me and asked what was wrong. I found myself pouring out the whole story to him. He was surprisingly easy to talk to. Mike told me he knew Cassie and was pretty sure she'd work everything out. He promised me if Cassie didn't get it together then he'd go over and give her a little taste of her own medicine. I remembered the story Mike told me about Cassie getting in his face. I had to smile at the thought of Mike laying down the law.

With a curse of frustration I tossed the wood I'd been marking on the floor. I'd marked it incorrectly again. I stripped off my shirt, hoping if I cooled off it would also settle my brain. I ran my fingers through my hair again. Well at least I'd noticed the mistake before I cut the wood. I picked the wood back up and began to re-measure it. The doorbell rang.

I yanked the door open, ready to chase away any salesmen who would dare bother me. I was so frustrated I'd take great pleasure in a little intimidation. Cassie was standing there. When she saw me she hesitated, almost as if she was afraid to see me, then her face hardened. My heart clenched. *'Oh God, she's going to dump me'* Pictures of life without Cassie flashed through my head and I shuddered.

"H-hi John, can I come in? I need to talk to you," she said, starting out tentatively but finishing in a firm voice.

"Hi, sure come on in. Be careful about the debris all over the place. I'm replacing the banister," I said and was proud of my calm demeanor although I had to clench my fists to keep from reaching for her.

She stepped inside and looked around. I looked my fill, drinking her in while her attentions were elsewhere. God, she looked good. She was wearing heels and nylons but that's all I could see of her outfit because she was wearing a coat. A full length coat, as a matter of fact, which I thought was strange because it wasn't cold out. I shrugged it off knowing I was overheated anyway. She must be going out somewhere because she was wearing make-up and she smelled delicious. I could smell perfume but also something sweeter, something edible but I couldn't quite place it.

I had to stop looking at her or I'd attack her. I turned back to start measuring again, vowing not to cut it until after she'd left. I'd probably have to re-measure it anyway, but I had to do something to occupy my mind and hands.

"So, what did you want to talk to me about?"

I was quite proud of the nonchalance with which I said it. I was glad she couldn't see my hands shaking. I couldn't look at her. I didn't want to see the pity in her eyes when she said she was sorry, she never meant to hurt me, etcetera, and etcetera.

"Well, I've been thinking about what you said. I've talked to some people and I've done a lot of soul searching."

I chanced a glance up at her and saw her standing with her back to me, staring out the window. I gazed at her hungrily for a moment then forced myself to go back to work.

"I came to the realization that you were right. It would never be enough for you to always have to be convincing me that you really loved me. I mean, you laid yourself bare for me, without any guarantees that I would love you in return. To put yourself out there like that is an amazing leap of faith and it's not fair to you."

I couldn't look at her. I could tell by the sound of her voice that she'd moved closer to me. My heart was shattering; I couldn't let her see my devastation. All I'd have left was my pride. I clenched the wood in my hand and closed my eyes. In a slightly detached way I wondered how she would deal the killing blow.

"So, I decided in order to be fair, I'd have to take the same risks. I'd have to lay myself bare to you also. I needed to make a leap of faith," she said and her voice quavered at the end.

I opened my eyes and stared at the wall. What was she saying? This didn't sound like she was blowing me off. I was afraid to turn around, afraid to have my burgeoning hope dashed.

"So....I'm walking out to the edge of the limb to join you. I sure hope it will support both of us," she said with a little laugh. Her voice was just above a whisper and sounded strained.

I took a deep breath and slowly turned around. I was sure the sight of her would be seared into my brain until the day I died. She was standing there in her heels and thigh high stockings and nothing else, except there was something on her chest just above her left breast. It looked like writing; damned if it didn't say my name. It was just above her heart. The look in her eyes was what dreams were made of.

"I love you John, so much I ache with it. I believe in you. I believe in us. I'm fighting for us as hard as I can fight. I already marked my heart as yours. Is there anything else you'd like to claim?" she asked in a husky voice and handed a tube to me.

The label on the tube read 'Edible Body Paint'. The flavor was caramel apple. That was what I'd smelled. I was so overwhelmed by emotion I didn't know what to say. I just stared at her and took it all in. I drank in the vision of her like a man who had been dying of thirst.

"You're not going to cut the limb out from under me are you?" she asked in a nervous voice that cracked with emotion.

With a start, I realized I'd left her hanging there. I hadn't said anything and I could tell she was starting to worry. In one stride I was in front of her. I reached up and tenderly cupped her face with his hand.

"Never, but if it ever breaks I'll be there to catch you," I promised.

Cassie's eyes filled with tears. I kissed her tenderly and then lifted her into my arms. I carried her upstairs and placed her on my bed. Again I just stared at her for the longest time.

Rather than shrinking from my view, Cassie seemed to revel in it. I watched her nipples harden at my gaze. I loved the stockings but I wanted to kiss every inch of her. I rolled the stockings down her legs, caressing as I went. I grabbed the tube of body paint and, starting at her heart, I dribbled it all over her until she was covered from head to toe and the tube was empty. Then, starting at her feet, I licked every bit off her. By the time I finished she was panting and her thighs were trembling as I pressed them open. I lightly bit the inside of her thigh.

Cassie jumped in reaction. I looked up at her and was once again awed and grateful for the love that fairly blazed in her eyes.

"Now that I've claimed all of you, do you mind if I spend a little time getting that caramel apple taste out of my mouth with my favorite taste in the world?" Cassie's answer was to widen her legs further. She reached down and ran her fingers into my hair and pulled me toward her.

"I don't mind at all but it's my turn next," she said with a carnal promise in her eyes.

Her voice ended in a moan as I thrust my tongue into her. Minutes later she tripped over the edge into an explosive orgasm.

I continued until she was screaming again and again, not letting up until she was weak and trembling.

Finally, she pulled me up to her. I lay with my erection pressed against her throbbing flesh. She looked at me with such love it squeezed my heart.

"Cassie, I want to feel you around me when I come. I'll get a condom if you want....I don't want to push you into anything you don't want so it's your call," I said as I fought to keep from pressing into her.

She pushed me hard and I rolled off her. Before I had a chance to say anything she straddled me. She raised herself up, grasped me tightly in her hand and guided me to her entrance. She pressed down just a little until just the head of my cock was inside her.

"John, I really don't think I can get pregnant. But I would love nothing better than to feel your baby growing inside of me," she said in a hoarse whisper.

As she spoke she pressed down until her pubic hair tangled with mine and I was buried all the way inside her. She leaned back a little and went even deeper. I groaned at the pleasure she created then gasped as she reached around and cradled my balls in her hand. She rocked back and forth and lightly caressed me.

"You have what I want John. Give me what I want," she demanded as she rose up and plunged back down.

Her words drove me. I grabbed her hips and moved her body in time to my thrusts. The sight of her with her head thrown back in ecstasy and her breasts bouncing was one I'd never forget. I was close and wanted her to share this with me. I pressed my thumbs between us and stroked her as I thrust harder. I could feel her legs clenching against my thighs as her cries got louder.

"I'm going to come now, Cassie," I said with a growl.

"Fill me……give me…..what I …want," she demanded in a breathless voice that ended in a shriek as her contractions began.

I impaled her with one last thrust and shot my seed deep inside her. Tremors wracked my body. I gasped out my love and pulled her down on top of me, clasping her against my chest in a tight embrace.

When I could move again I cradled her face in my hands.

"Tell me again."

"I love you John," she said firmly as she gazed into my eyes. All of her feelings were right there for me to see.

"Thank God, I thought you came here to tell me you didn't want to see me again. I was getting ready to get down on my knees and beg."

"You've been so cool all week that I was sure I was too late. I was afraid that….that I had you….this, us…..in my grasp and I let it go. But I wasn't going to let you go without a fight. Do you know why?" she asked as she sat up.

"Why?"

"Because I realized…..since I met you, you've held a mirror up to me and forced me to really look at myself. You made me look at the good things in myself. I saw myself through your eyes and I liked what I saw a lot better.

Then I realized my father had never done that for me. I called my mother and she told me my father was so afraid of being rejected he never wanted to try at all. And I didn't want to be like that. I also finally realized that if my father left because of his own problems, then it really had nothing to do with me at all.

Suddenly, I saw I was basing all of my beliefs on an assumption I made when I was a child.

I'm not saying I've figured everything out, because it took a long time to build up, it will probably take a little longer to tear down. I may need you to remind me every once in a while if I start falling back into old habits. But I've got the best incentive in the world. I've got this gorgeous, sexy, wonderful man and he wants me.....me! And for the first time I feel like I deserve it. I'd do a lot to keep feeling that way. Besides, I've seen the alternative this week and it almost killed me. So you're in for it, buddy. I'm not letting go."

The sheer joy on her face made my heart turn over. It also turned me on. But, then again, everything about her turned me on. I was still inside her and I saw her eyes widen as she felt me getting hard again.

"Confidence is so sexy," I said with a wink. Cassie laughed in delight. But then I began to move and the laugh turned into a moan.

Chapter 19

Cassie

October in Seattle was usually cloudy and rainy. So, when the 15th dawned a beautiful, sunny day I hoped it was a good omen. We were meeting at John's place for breakfast then, off to Spring Aviation.

In the last week I learned closing the door on my fears opened my heart to more love than I'd ever known. We spent every moment we could together. When John got home late from work, I picked Josh up and fed him dinner.

I spent yesterday afternoon making love to him during our weekly Thursday rendezvous, but I was already anxious to see him again. It didn't seem possible, but I thought each time we made love was better than the last.

We didn't talk about the future and, for once, I really didn't care. John showed me his love in different ways every day. I figured the future would take care of itself.

When we walked through the door, he twirled Sam around and planted a resounding kiss on her cheek before he pulled me into his arms. Instead of shuddering at our constant displays of affection, Sam just smiled and rolled her eyes.

While John was loading my plate with heavenly smelling food, Josh was tilting a Mickey Mouse shaped pancake onto Sam's. Sam shrieked in delight when she saw it and Josh glowed with pride.

We were meeting the class at the Spring Aviation plant in Renton for a quick class on how aircraft flew and how they were manufactured. Mrs. Wilson told the class to pay particular attention to this part of the field trip because it was where they would learn how to make a successful paper airplane.

We arrived about fifteen minutes ahead of the rest of the class. I was glad to see my friend Tim waiting in the parking lot. He brought us inside and got us visitor badges. By the time we had our badges other people in the class started arriving.

Mrs. Wilson told me, usually, she had to beg, borrow or steal parents to drive and act as chaperones for field trips. This time she turned parents away.

The Spring Aviation plant was fascinating. Children and parents alike asked question after question. The engineers rose to the challenge, appearing particularly pleased they were in the limelight. At the wind tunnel the kids got to see aerodynamics in action. Plumes of smoke showed the air currents that created lift to make an airplane fly. But the flight simulator was what seemed to awe the children into silence. John got the virtual aircraft airborne and then each child was given a chance to try their hands at the controls. I think a few pilots were born that day.

Some Spring Aviation executives stopped by the simulator to meet everyone. They were impressed with the kids' enthusiasm and I crossed my fingers that the day would engender many more field trips.

We managed to keep a pretty tight schedule and arrived at a local pizza joint for lunch only 20 minutes late. As the staff scurried around to feed everyone I got the impression they were glad for the extra time to prepare. The kids discussed what they learned without any prompting from adults which, I figured, was a testament to the success of the trip. Josh was beside himself with excitement. Even Sam was having a great time. I overheard her ask John if he would teach her to fly.

"You should be proud. This is a huge success," John whispered in my ear.

I turned to look at him and saw the love and pride shining in his eyes. I brushed a quick kiss across his lips. "Thanks, I am proud. You should be too; you had a lot to do with this."

After a quick trip through the Nationwide dispatch center we went out onto the ramp of their hangar and walked around the Boeing 737 parked there. John pointed out the flaps we'd seen in action in the wind tunnel. When we went inside the aircraft they had some of the hatches open so the kids could see the wires connecting the instruments in the cockpit to the different flight systems.

Steve Rayburn met us outside the cockpit door. Each child sat in the pilot's seat while John and Steve explained the different instruments to them. Even though Josh's class was a small one, if John was the only one doing the talking it would take a long time to get them all through. Steve volunteered to come in on his day off and help so we could get two students through at a time.

By the time we finished with the aircraft tours it was two-thirty. We warned the parents the trip might run a little long because we had so much to see. We didn't want to be late, though, so we decided to cut our visit to the radar room short and concentrate on the tower.

We only spent about fifteen minutes in the TRACON but the large dark room filled with radar screens made an impression on the children and the parents. I saw a lot of wide-eyed looks as we came out of the TRACON and headed up to the tower. I took over the tour when we got upstairs. I stopped them all one floor below the tower cab and reminded them how important it was to stay as quiet as possible upstairs and not interfere with the controllers who were working. In order to keep the distractions to a minimum we split the group into three smaller groups and brought them up one at a time. Josh said he'd go in the last group and I was proud of him for putting the other kids first, especially since the excitement was written on his face.

The Manager allowed me to use the extra unused radio frequency. John and Steve stayed in the Nationwide aircraft so each child would get a chance to talk to them on the radio. I showed them some of the tower equipment while we waited until just after the mid-afternoon rush. When there was very little activity on the airfield we gave each child a chance to say something over the spare frequency to John and Steve. I only heard Steve's voice on the radio but figured John was busy with some other task.

It took about forty-five minutes to get to the last group of students. Josh was grinning when he came up the stairs holding Sam's hand and I was so glad he was enjoying it. By the third group I'd distilled my tour down to the pertinent information without a lot of hesitation to decide what to say next. I was just finishing up my spiel and about to put the first child on the radio to talk to Nationwide when I noticed Grace standing over by the Supervisor's desk. I was pretty sure it was her day off. She just smiled when I gave her an enquiring look so I shrugged and put the next child on the radio.

Once again, Josh said he'd go last. I marveled at his patience because he was obviously impatient to get his chance. After all of his work to make this whole day work out, I figured he probably should have gone first, but I didn't argue when he urged everyone to go ahead of him. Finally, Sam got up to the mike and called Nationwide. This time John answered and I was glad he'd gotten finished with whatever he was doing in time to talk to her. I smiled when Sam said, "Cleared to land."

Josh took the mike in his hand and called Nationwide over the radio. Once again, John answered and asked for a landing clearance. Josh told him, "Cleared to land", while his eyes sparkled. I had a great time, but was glad it was finally over. I started to turn away from the radio when I heard a crackle of static and then John's voice calling the tower.

"Seattle Tower, Nationwide 225."

I smiled and wondered what he was doing, especially since he was using the same call sign as the fateful night I'd opted to check the runway rather than clear him for takeoff.

"Nationwide 225, Seattle Tower," I responded.

"Tower, I need to declare an emergency."

He was on the ground at the hangar, what possible emergency could he have? My training kicked in and I answered as I would have under normal circumstances.

"State the nature of your emergency, Nationwide 225."

I noticed everyone in the tower cab was watching, but they didn't look particularly concerned. In fact, most of them were grinning. Grace walked over and I just looked at her, mystified.

"Well a couple of months ago you saved my life as well as the lives of everyone on my aircraft. I'm afraid to say it, but I need you to save me again," he said. I could hear the tenderness of his tone right over the airwaves.

I wasn't sure how to respond. Everyone was watching and Josh was practically bouncing out of his shoes.

"What do you need, Nationwide 225?"

"Well, I'm out here in the dark all by myself, just trying to get home. The problem is, it's only home if you're there. You're the only beacon I see and I need you to guide me home to you. Give me a clearance, clear me to land. Bring me home safely. Marry me Cassie," he said in a husky voice.

Even over the radio his tone brought tears to my eyes. I looked up and realized, for the first time since I'd worked there, there was complete silence in the tower cab. Everyone was waiting for my response. No one was even calling on the radio. I glanced down and saw someone had fiddled with my radio while I wasn't looking and my conversation with John was going out over all the frequencies.

I looked over at Josh and he was pulling something out of his pocket. I saw a black velvet box and then Josh was holding the open box up to me and I was looking at the most beautiful diamond ring I'd ever seen. Sam looked so proud and I figured she'd been in on the secret too. All of these observations took less than thirty seconds, but I realized the whole airport was holding its breath, waiting for my response. The only sound was footsteps coming up the stairs.

"Nationwide 225, cleared to land today and every day for the rest of my life," I said as John's head appeared at the top of the stairs, a portable radio in his hands. "Yes, John, I'll marry you."

I was pretty sure Josh's whoop of glee went out over the air before I let go of the mike button. Within moments the airwaves were filled with the voices of pilots calling and offering congratulations. Everyone in the tower cab cheered. John walked up to me, took the ring out of the box Josh was holding and slid it on my finger.

"I'm home," he whispered in my ear right before he kissed me. Mrs. Wilson guided all the kids down the stairs except for Josh and Sam. John took Sam's hand and I took Josh's as we followed the rest of the class. We walked down the stairs with my coworkers yelling out congratulations. By the time we met up with the rest of the class, Mrs. Wilson had filled everyone in on what had just occurred. They all crowded around us to offer congratulations.

Grace came over and gave me a hug. "Congratulations, Cassie. You know it was so amazing you ever noticed that F.O.D. I just knew it was some sort of karma. So, I pushed Steve and John to go meet you. I was kind of hoping Steve would finally find the right woman; he's such a great guy. It looks like you were the right woman but just for a different guy. I was right, it was fate."

"Why do I get the feeling you had something to do with John's proposal going out over the airwaves?"

"Guilty as charged," Grace said but she didn't look as if she felt the least bit guilty. "Don't worry; I'll keep the big bad wolf away from you when the regional office hears about this. Everyone on the airport is so thrilled with what happened today I don't think they'd dare deal with the bad press by doing anything to you. Besides, you didn't know anything about it and I'll back you up." Grace assured me, giving me another hug before stepping back to let others offer their congratulations.

Finally, someone turned to Josh and asked, "How do you feel about this?"

It got quiet and I was worried Josh would be nervous about being put on the spot. I needn't have worried. If it was possible, Josh's grin got even wider. "Great, my Dad's happy and I finally get to have a real Mom," he said as he hugged me.

I was afraid I'd cry when Josh spoke but I was saved by Sam who said, "Yeah and I get to have a brother and make fortune cookies whenever I want."

Everyone was confused by Sam's statement but the four of us. We burst out laughing. John looked at me as he responded to Sam. "That's right, Sam, I'll help you make fortune cookies whenever you want as long as I get to make some for Mommy."

"I'm so lucky," I said with a smile reserved for John alone.

Epilogue

The paper airplane contest took place on November 12th at Spring Aviation's Museum of Flight. It was a huge success and the executives were already talking about the following year's contest. The regular visitors to the museum were just at enthusiastic about the contest as the people actually participating. John, Mrs. Wilson, and I answered a lot of questions from parents of kids at other schools who wanted to know how to get one of these contests going in their kids' schools.

Several of the Spring Aviation engineers put on a demonstration of their own paper airplanes after the contest was over. I could tell they were really enjoying themselves and hoped they would continue to participate in the following years.

Josh didn't win best overall but he won most original design. I saw some of the engineers looking at Josh's plane with interest. He might have a future in aviation but it might not be following in his father's or my footsteps.

Josh wasn't upset about not winning best overall. In fact, he'd gotten so much attention about his part in putting the contest together; he would've been embarrassed to win the big prize. He said his Dad's marriage proposal over the air already made him famous.

Steve came to help. I put him in charge of marking distances flown by each paper airplane. I also drafted Jasmine and put her to work with Steve. I watched the sparks fly. Jasmine could affect a haughty air when she wanted to and she was in full regal mode while working with Steve. He responded by being a smart ass.

John remarked to me that we'd better keep Steve and Jasmine separated from now on. But I saw each of the combatants watching the other when they thought no one was looking. I sensed an attraction between the two they were both trying to fight. So, I just answered John with a non-committal "Hmmm." Steve asked Mary Sullivan if he could rent her apartment once John moved out. I thought it would be interesting to see what happened when Steve and Jasmine both lived in Federal Way.

George had picked Sam up before dinner and Mrs. Sullivan was going to watch Josh. I'd asked John over for a special dinner. I had news I wanted to share with him privately before telling anyone else. Only Trish suspected what was going on, but I hadn't confirmed it yet.

I'd been feeling tired and queasy a lot the last couple of weeks. I hadn't realized the ramifications until I mentioned my symptoms to Trish, who immediately burst out laughing and suggested a pregnancy test. As soon as Trish said it, I knew what the test would show. I was surprised I hadn't put it together before. The test I'd taken this morning only confirmed what I already knew.

I was finishing dinner preparations when John came through the door. I felt such love when I looked at him I worried my heart would burst out of my chest. He came over and wrapped me in his arms and kissed the top of my head, rocking me back and forth for a minute.

"Looks like you did it again, I heard the Spring Aviation people talking about making the airplane contest an annual event. They're planning on having classes come through the plant all through September and October and then having the event in November again. They're going to open it to ten schools next year and see how it goes," he said with pride in his voice.

"We did it. You worked just as hard on this as I did, man of mine," I said, wrapping my arms around his neck and kissing him.

John groaned as I thrust my tongue into his mouth. He pulled me tightly against him and returned the favor. Several minutes later he broke away, gasping for breath. "Will dinner be ruined if we don't eat for about an hour?"

"No, I just need to turn the oven off. I'm not really hungry…..for food."

John scooped me up in his arms. He reached down and turned off the oven, as he carried me up to the bedroom.

A while later we were sprawled naked on the bed trying to recover enough to go eat dinner. When my breathing returned to normal I crawled up and lay across John's chest, breathing a sigh of contentment. I propped my chin on my hand and just looked at him, trying to decide how best to broach the subject. John's hands caressed my back and he smiled back at me tenderly.

Finally, I said, "I think we need to set a wedding date."

He raised an eyebrow. "You're not feeling insecure are you?" There was humor in his eyes. "If you're feeling insecure after our explosive lovemaking, then I'm really losing my touch."

"No, believe me, you're not losing your touch and I'm not feeling insecure. I'm just being practical. I already bought my dress so we either need to have the wedding in the next month or so… or after next July." I said matter-of-factly as I continued to run my fingers across his chest.

"Okay, now I'm really confused. What does having your dress have to do with when we have the wedding?"

"Well my dress is only going to fit for about the next month or so and then it won't fit again until after July," I said with a shrug of my shoulders.

I thought I was doing a pretty good job of keeping my cool but inside I was so excited I could barely keep still. I smiled at him as I watched his frown of confusion slowly change to one of shocked understanding. He sat up so suddenly I fell sideways, and then he immediately grabbed me.

"Are you okay? I didn't hurt you did I?" he asked with concern.

"I'm fine. I fell about two inches onto a bed. I think I'll survive."

He just stared at me for a moment as if he wasn't sure what to say. "D-did I understand? Are you…..are we…..going to have a baby?" he asked in a whisper.

The smile on my face told him even before I nodded. He placed his hand on my belly and the awe mingling with joy on his face brought tears to my eyes. He leaned forward and kissed my belly gently.

He looked at me and saw my tears. "Are you all right with this? You didn't expect it to happen. You don't mind, do you?"

"I'm so happy I feel like I'm going to explode. To carry a part of you inside me is the greatest gift in the world," I said in a voice that trembled with emotion.

"Cassie, my love, you are the greatest gift in the world. A December wedding works for me. I'd marry you tomorrow if that's what you wanted," he said as he rested his head gently on my belly.

I ran my fingers through his hair. This strong, wonderful man loved me with all his heart. I marveled at how quickly life could change. I still didn't know what wonderful thing I'd done to deserve him, but I was through questioning it. I planned to spend the rest of my life enjoying it.

www.ingramcontent.com/pod-product-compliance
Lightning Source LLC
Chambersburg PA
CBHW070349260626
47161CB00001B/76